GATES OF PARADISE

William Blake, the famous poet, engraver
and illustrator spent three years in the small
rural village of Felpham in Sussex, until in
1803 he was charged with sedition for being
too vocal in his response to a soldier he
found trespassing in his garden. Soon after
the trial he returned to London with his
wife Catherine. Half a century later,
Alexander Gilchrist arrives, intending to
compile a biography of 'the mad poet'.
Beginning his research at the Fox Inn, he
soon encounters hostility when the trial is
mentioned ... what do the locals have to
hide?

GATES OF PARADISE

GATES OF PARADISE

by

Beryl Kingston

Magna Large Print Books
Long Preston, North Yorkshire,
BD23 4ND, England.

British Library Cataloguing in Publication Data.

Kingston, Beryl
  Gates of Paradise.

  A catalogue record of this book is
  available from the British Library

  ISBN   0-7505-2578-9
  ISBN   978-0-7505-2578-7

First published in Great Britain in 2006 by Allison & Busby Ltd.

Copyright © 2006 by Beryl Kingston

Cover illustration © Old Tin Dog by arrangement with
Allison & Busby Ltd.

The moral right of the author has been asserted

Published in Large Print 2006 by arrangement with
Allison & Busby Ltd.

Magna Large Print is an imprint of Library Magna Books Ltd.

Printed and bound in Great Britain by
T.J. (International) Ltd., Cornwall, PL28 8RW

Acknowledgements

My heartfelt thanks to the following for their assistance in the writing of this book.
Heather Howell of Blake's Cottage, Felpham.
Peter and Nina Jones of Robson's Cottage, Lavant.
The staff of the Public Records Office, in particular Ron Iden, Chichester.
Joan McKillop, Custodian of the Cowper and Newton Museum, Olney.
Eileen Page and Peggy Horwood, who lived in the old Fox Inn as children.
Dr Keri Davies, Historian of the Blake Society.

Dedication

I dedicate this book to my dear, dear Roy, who lived with me lovingly for fifty-three years, eleven months and six days; who filled my life with laughter and talk, good food, good sense and magical music; who provided me with accurate research for all my books and finished work on this one six weeks before he died. You are achingly missed, my darling.

'Mutual Forgiveness of each Vice,
Such are the Gates of Paradise.'

'The Gates of Paradise'
William Blake (1757-1827)

Chapter One

The Fox Inn, Felpham. April 16th 1852

My dearest Annie,
   I do believe I have stumbled upon a mystery concerning our William Blake. At the moment it is merely a suspicion, or perhaps it would be more honest of me to say a hope, since, as you know my dearest, my intention is to discover as many truths as I can about this unfairly neglected man, it being insupportable to me that such a blazing genius should have been given so little attention and so little public acclaim during his lifetime. It may well be that there are truths that have been kept secret and if that is the case I shall do all I can to reveal them, you may depend upon it. To write an honest biography demands no less.
   But to begin at the beginning. I arrived here in Felpham in good time and good order, and found it a very pretty place, quiet and rustic and sparsely populated. I can quite understand why Blake called it 'Sweet Felpham' and said 'all Heaven' was here. I have taken a room at the local inn, which is called 'The Fox', not after the animal, as you might imagine, but after a coastguard cutter, a representation of which is

13

painted on the inn sign. It is an old thatched building with a well in the garden and a pump by the back door and uncomfortably old-fashioned, with all manner of unexpected nooks and crannies, uneven floors and a topsy-turvy staircase, which is not at all easy to negotiate by candlelight, as I discovered when I came stumbling up to my room, not five minutes since, after a supper of lamb chops and boiled potatoes washed down with plenty of excellent porter. Ah, you will say, he blames the state of the stairs for his lack of balance instead of the strength of the porter, and you may well be right. However, more to my purpose, and regardless of the strength of the porter, the inn is perfectly placed, for it stands opposite the very cottage where Blake lived for the three years of his stay here, and that is something which is not only opportune but also inspiring, for it is the first of his erstwhile dwellings that is entirely unchanged since the days when he was in occupation. The present tenant is a coastguardsman and not unfriendly. I have arranged to visit him tomorrow afternoon. So you see my dearest, I have wasted no time but have come straight to the heart of things.

I spent this afternoon exploring the village, which is small but compact and consists of three winding tracks, which meander past farmhouses and thatched flint cottages until they reach the church. There are two windmills at the southernmost point of the village, close to the sea, and a row of unassuming houses at the northern end, which have been converted into shops. I found a butcher's and a baker's but no candlestick maker's, and there are also stables, a saddler's, two smithies and a large dairy, which claims to sell milk cream, butter and eggs 'fresh daily'. We will return in the summer perhaps and bring baby with us. I think you would like it here.

The landlord is a bluff but affable man and, mindful of the comfort of his guests, offered that he was willing to answer any questions I might ask. He told me that The Fox had changed hands several times since Blake was here, which is hardly surprising, and volunteered that the landlord in 1800 was a man called George Grinder, who, besides being the owner of Blake's cottage, also owned a hotel in the nearby hamlet of Bognor, and a plot of land in the village which is called Grinder's Mead to this day, and was, moreover, one of the witnesses at Blake's trial. That news encouraged me, so I asked him what else he knew about the trial but, to my disappointment, he said he had no knowledge of it at all and nor, I'm sorry to say, did any of the locals who came in to wet their whistles whilst I was eating my supper. The younger ones had no idea that a poet called Blake had ever lived amongst them and those who were old enough to remember him were – or so it seemed to me - peculiarly reticent. One or two recalled that there had once been two poets living in the village, a 'celebrated' one, called William Hayley, who had lived at Turret House, and a 'mad' one, who had *lived in the cottage, but other than that their faces and memories were blank. However, just as I was beginning to grow weary of negative answers, one of their number – a farmer called Harry Boniface – told me he could remember the day after Blake arrived and gave me a very clear description of him. It accorded so well with Linnell's portrait that I wrote it down as near word for word as I could.*

'I recall his first morning here as if it were yesterday. Bright and clear it was, with a strong tide running and the air smelling of sea-salt. Me and Father was off to plough the lower cornfield while the weather held, and as we passed the cottage I said to Father, "Father," I said, "the gate's open." That was odd, do you see, for I couldn't remember seeing it open before. I was only a little feller at the time. Well, no sooner was the words out of my mouth than out he came, our mad poet himself, with his wife following after, all pink in the cheeks and smelling of yeast on account of she'd been kneading the bread. We had a good fair view of them both. Middling sort of man he was, not over tall but stocky and sturdy looking, with bulging eyes like a hare and a bulging forehead to match. Always wore a wide-awake hat and a blue cloth coat and light brown breeches, with a clean white stock round his neck. He says "Good morning" all warm and friendly-like as if we'd been neighbours for years. So of course we said good morning back and he gave us a smile. Nice smile he had, with a trick of looking straight at you, all bright and sharp like a bird. Then off he goes along the path through the field with his wife walking alongside, holding her hat against the breeze.'

I was much encouraged by this, as you can imagine, and ventured to ask him what he remembered of the trial. But then — and I swear to you I was not imagining things — there was such a change in the atmosphere it was as if a chill wind had blown into the room and frozen the words on his lips. He said he had no memory of it at all and then he looked round at all the men in the room and said he doubted whether I would find anyone else who could remember it either 'after all this time', and at that there were so many meaning glances and so much nodding agreement that I got the strongest impression that they were warning one another to keep quiet. Have I stumbled upon a secret, do you think? Was there something extraordinary about this trial that the villagers want to keep hidden? Or was this simply evidence of a bucolic mistrust of strangers? I shall pursue it further, you may depend upon it. Meantime, I shall write up such notes as are needful and betake me to my slumbers.

It is nearly midnight and my candle runs low.

Take great care of yourself my darling. I will write to you on every occasion.

This from your loving husband,
Alexander.

P.S. I wish I could discover where Mr Grinder is now, if he is still alive. I am sure he would have a tale to tell. A.G.

18th September 1800

Mr George Grinder, the landlord of The Fox Inn, had been waiting for his new tenants to arrive for more than two hours and he was beginning to weary of it. It was well past eleven o'clock and the regulars were long gone. He'd stoked up the fire in the bar so that he was plenty warm enough, but the candles were burning low and candles don't come cheap, not even when they're made of tallow. The potboys dozed in the shadows, Reuben Jones, the village gossip, slept in 'his' chair with his chin sunk onto his chest, and Mr Grinder and Will Smith the ostler sat on the settles on either side of the fire, with their feet in the hearth, pipes in their mouths and beer mugs on the table before them, occasionally grunting to one another that time was getting on but otherwise absorbed in their own weary thoughts. It had been a long wait.

'I'll give 'em another half hour,' Mr

Grinder decided, removing the pipe from his mouth and pointing at the clock with it, 'an' if they 'aven't come by then, I'm for my bed. There's no sense sitting up half the night or we shall be like dead things come the morning. They could ha' stopped along the way and we none the wiser.'

But Will was stirring, sitting up, looking towards the window, his sharp face alert. Wheels were crunching in the street outside and he could hear a pair of horses blowing. The tenants had arrived. Within seconds the lantern had been lit, Reuben and the potboys had woken and all five of them were out in the cold of midnight, breathing in the rousing air as they trudged towards the cottage, ready to give a hand with the unloading.

Mr Grinder's new tenant sprang down from the post chaise as they approached. He looked as spry and lively as if he'd just woken up in the morning. You would never have guessed he'd just travelled nine and sixty miles through difficult country. The chaise had come to a halt beside the wicket gate and the horses were blowing hard, so Will went to their heads to attend to them. But Mr Grinder strode on to greet his tenants.

'Mr Blake, sir,' he said. 'I'm glad to see you arrived at last. We were beginning to despair of you. You had a bad journey I fear.'

'No, no,' Mr Blake said cheerfully, handing his wife from the chaise. ''Twas pleasant enough. No grumbling. It took rather longer than we anticipated but 'twas all cheerfulness and good humour. My wife, sir. This is our landlord, Catherine my dear. And my sister, who is another Catherine. Catherine, Mr Grinder.'

'We've had a fire a-burning for you since nine o'clock,' Mr Grinder told them. 'Will here's been keeping it in. There's logs aplenty in the garden. You'll see the store. Your flour's in the larder, ma'am, an' you can get yeast from the brew house in the morning if you just comes across the road.'

'You are kindness itself, sir,' Mr Blake said, giving a little bow.

Mr Grinder took the compliment as earned. 'Let's have this gate open, then,' he said, lifting the latch, 'an' we can get your boxes inside. 'Tis too cold a night to be standing about. If you'll be so good as to hold the lantern Mrs Blake, ma'am, so's we can see the way.'

There was rather a lot of luggage, sixteen boxes in all – the potboys counted them – and most so heavy it took four men to lift them and there were times when even Reuben had to lend a hand, even though he had a bandage on his foot as proof that overmuch labour was beyond him. But eventually all the boxes were struggled into the cottage, and the two women lit candles and stoked up the fire with fresh logs. Then there was only some sort of wooden contraption left to manhandle. It was wrapped in sacking and Mr Blake said to have particular care of it because it was his printing press and he couldn't work without it. And at last the job was done, the chaise gone and the four removal men could trudge back to the beery fug of The Fox.

'What on earth d'he have in all them boxes?' Will wanted to know, as he damped down the fire. 'They weigh'd a ton. My ol' back's fair creased in two.'

'Copper plates, so he said,' Mr Grinder told him. 'Being he's an engraver, I s'ppose. Leastways that's what he's come down to do, according to Mr Hosier. Engraving.'

'Just so long as he don't go a-changin' his mind and send fer us to carry 'em all out again,' Will said grimacing. 'Oi've had enough a' luggin' ol' boxes about to last me a lifetime.'

'He won't go back, yet awhile,' Mr Grinder said. 'Leastways not for three years, that I *do* know, being as that's the lease he's took on the cottage an' he's paid good money for it.'

'Aye, so Oi've heard,' Reuben said, looking sly. 'Twenty pounds a year, so Hiram was a-tellin' me.' His face was so blown about by constant exposure to wind and weather that his features were all over sideways, one eye lower than the other and his nose squashed

21

like a snout in a trough, and a sly expression made him look more grotesque than usual.

'Well, yes,' Mr Grinder admitted, 'that *was* about the size of it.'

'Bit steep, wouldn't 'ee say,' Reuben teased. 'Rents was a quarter a' that, last year.'

'Last year was last year,' Mr Grinder said. 'There are several cottages hereabouts that might have been let for four or five pounds last year but now they're being furbished up and whitewashed, with a little furniture and stair carpets put into them and they'll make twenty easy. If Londoners are prepared to pay, let 'em, that's what I say.'

'Them's my sentiments an' all,' Reuben said. 'We don't want strangers in our village. 'Tent healthy. Let 'em go back to Lunnon where they come from.'

'Except for this one, eh?' Mr Grinder said and he winked at the potboys. 'You two young fellers can rest easy. You won't be shifting no more boxes for a year or two yet.'

'Amen to that,' the potboys said, and the younger one added, 'Will there be anything else Mr Grinder, sir?'

'No, no,' Mr Grinder said. 'You cut off.' Then he noticed that the boy was holding a crumpled paper in his hand. 'What you got there?'

''Twas up against the garden wall when we come out,' the boy said. 'There's some printin' on it. Look.' And he handed it to the landlord.

It took a while for Mr Grinder to decipher it. He could read well enough most of the time but that was when the paper was smooth and the print clear. This was so smudged and crumpled it required consideration. 'Well, well, well,' he said, when he'd made sense of it. 'Here's a thing.' And as his audience was standing about the dampened fire, agog to be enlightened, he read it aloud. '*Starved fellow creatures, Come Tomorrow Night with proper weapons in St George's fields, where You will meet friends to defend Your Rights Never mind the blood thirsty Soldiers We shall put them to flight, The Cause is honourable & ought to be prosecuted as such Rouse to glory ye slumbering Britons*. My stars. I hope this ent the sort of thing our Mr Blake's thinking a' printing or he *will* be in trouble. That's too radical for the likes of us.'

'We ought to show it to our Johnnie,' Will said, gazing at the crumpled paper with some awe. 'Tha's what. He'd know what to do about it.'

'You may do as you please,' the potboy said. 'Oi'm for my bed. Tha's been a long night.'

'Tomorrow,' Mr Grinder decided. 'We'll show him when he comes in tomorrow. But we don't none of us say nothing to no one, mind. We don't want it getting back to Mr

23

Hayley. There's no point courting disaster.'

Not that their celebrated neighbour would have taken much notice of anything that was said, for at that particular moment William Hayley Esquire was in floods of tears.

The library in his fine new house in Felpham was an elegant room, thirty feet long, furnished in perfectly matched mahogany, and built in the latest style with high curtained windows to let in the light and give a prospect of the sea. The walls were lined with bookcases, glass-fronted to keep out the dust, and his books were displayed in order of size and importance, Latin writers given prominence to the left of the fireplace and Greeks to the right, as behoved their even more impressive status, for it pleased him to be seen and known as a man fluent in both languages. He had designed the room himself and had spared no expense to achieve the effect he wanted. Not a single item had been omitted nor a single detail overlooked. There was a new mahogany table in the centre of the room rising richly from the blues and reds of a Turkey carpet and set about with four elegant matching chairs. The walls were a fashionable sage green, the doors, windows and fireplace fashionably gilded, the fire well tended. There was a canterbury to hold his newspapers and journals, a Pembroke table for cards and two giltwood pier glasses to reflect the light. It only needed a set of portrait heads above the bookcases – which Mr Blake could start producing as soon as he was settled in – and then it would be complete. It was a room for comfort and display and erudition.

But there was no comfort in it that evening. The celebrated poet sat before the fire in one of his elegant chairs with his handkerchief to his eyes and wept like a child. 'Two of the best and dearest gone in a single year,' he mourned. 'First my dearest Cowper taken so cruelly, and then my own dear darling cripple, my dearest Thomas Alphonso – may his darling name be blessed – my one and only darling son, the apple of my eye, nineteen years old and gone in May of all months – Oh, it is too cruel! – gone in May in the first flush of his exemplary youth. And I know you will say 'tis September now but I miss him more keenly than I can express. His loss is insupportable. I cannot bear it.' He looked the very picture of grief, his dark eyes wet and soulful, his long aristocratic nose dripping with distress, that tender mouth as soft and pink as a girl's.

'Try not to grieve so, Mr Hayley, my dear,' his housekeeper said soothingly, mothering him as she so often did. 'You will undermine your constitution.' She knew that was what he required her to say because he liked to be reminded that his constitution was precious and needed care, but if she had given her honest opinion she would have told him she had a great deal more sympathy for the poor child than she had for his father. Poor dear brave Thomas, with that awful twisted spine that pained him so much, he'd not had much of a life of it. Fathered on a young housemaid – and a poor silly creature *she'd* been – and then raised as though he were a motherless child and with far too much expected of him. She could have wept for him in earnest, but this was not the time or the place. 'It's past midnight,' she reminded her master. 'Would you not be better to get some rest?' The warming pan had been in his bed for over an hour now and if he didn't retire soon she would have to set it with hot coals all over again.

'And there's another thing,' Mr Hayley cried, dabbing his soulful eyes, 'here's Mr Blake come and me not there to greet him. What will he think of me? It is most remiss. Most remiss.'

'He'll understand, I'm certain sure,' the housekeeper said, 'for I'm told he's a Christian soul.'

'The best,' his patron cried, 'and excellent company. Think how highly our dear Thomas regarded him. Our poor dear Thomas.'

'Well, there you are then.'

'I must set him to work at once,' William

decided, recovering into thoughts of philanthropic action, 'and find others to offer him commissions. There is no time to lose if I am to establish him. I think I shall teach him to paint in miniature. That would be a great help to him. I see no reason why he should not make as good a living here as in London, if he engraves and teaches drawing to the right families and is prepared to make neat drawings of appropriate size. Of course, if he places any dependence on painting large pictures – for which, according to Mr Flaxman, he is not qualified, either by habit or study – he will be miserably deceived. Oh, most miserably. But he is a man of good sense and will be advised, I'm sure. Flaxman speaks well of him.'

The housekeeper was encouraged by his shift to cheerfulness. Maybe she wouldn't have to re-heat the warming pan after all. 'Well, there you are then,' she said again, standing back so that he could rise from his chair. 'You just think what a lot you've got to look forward to now he's come here. Always look forward, Mr Hayley, sir, that's my advice. No point in looking back. That only brings grief. Now you try and get a good night's sleep and then we'll send young Johnnie to Chichester in the morning to get your papers and everything will look quite different by dinner time. You see if I'm not right.'

Chapter Two

April 17th 1852, Felpham

My dearest Annie,
I have just returned from my visit to Blake's cottage, which was every bit as illuminating as I hoped it would be. It is a simple dwelling, thatched, as are all the cottages hereabouts, the thatch set high on the southern wall, where the windows give out to a fine prospect of the sea, but sloping low on the northern side to keep out wind and weather. There are three rooms on each floor, leading into one another in the cottage style, three bedrooms above and a kitchen and two other rooms below, with a spiral staircase hidden behind a cupboard door in the kitchen and a proper staircase rising steeply between the other two rooms. The door and windows on the ground floor are protected by canopies of thatch, which makes the rooms rather dark but the inside walls are cleanly whitewashed and there are stout brick chimneys to carry away the smoke from the fires and to accommodate the kitchen stove. The coastguardsman was hospitable and answered all my questions patiently, although like so many of the young men hereabouts he had no personal knowledge of his famous predecessor. But he

28

showed me round the house and the garden, demonstrated the purity of the well water, preened when I praised his vegetable plot, and confessed that the place could be damp in bad weather and could give you the rheumatics something chronic if you don't watch out, which I daresay your poet feller found out.'

I took him across to the inn later to treat him to a pint of porter by way of thanks for his kindness and naturally we fell a-talking. He told me my friendly farmer had a brother who must have known 'a fair deal about Mr Blake, on account of he worked up at Turret House and the two poets was very thick together, as I daresay you knows.' *I asked him where I could find this brother, assuming he still lives in the village, but he couldn't tell me. All he knew was that he was a young man at the time and must have known a fair deal. A visit to Mr Boniface's farm is indicated I think for if there is something to be discovered from this brother, I must discover it, must I not.*

Write to me soon, my dearest. I grow anxious if I do not hear from you.

This from your loving husband.

Alexander.

September 1800

Johnnie Boniface was a handsome lad, not quite eighteen but already tall and muscular

29

with the strong arms and sturdy legs of his ploughman father and the wide brow, thick fair hair and gentle grey eyes of his mother Annie. Not that he paid much attention to his appearance. Even when he passed one of Mr Hayley's great hall mirrors on his way into the house with the vegetables, he did little more than take a peek at himself to see that his neck-cloth was neat and his waist-coat buttoned, in case the housekeeper was there to see him and rebuke him for untidiness. Although she was more like to scold if he brought mud into the place. Very particular about mud was Mrs Beke. You had to leave your boots at the door and enter in your stockinged feet.

This morning she was in too good a humour for scolding. 'You're to take the cart to Chichester,' she told him, 'and get the papers for Mr Hayley. There's a list of things I need from the haberdasher's and one or two other errands, which I've written down for you, but you're to be sure to buy the papers first. Betsy will go with you to choose the threads for I wouldn't expect you to do that. Look sharp now. Mr Hosier wants you in the garden by midday to pick the last of the plums.'

She was talking to the air, for once he'd heard that he was to have company Johnnie Boniface was lost to everything else she said. His heart leapt in his chest like a caged bird. He was going to Chichester with Betsy Haynes. Betsy Haynes, the prettiest girl in the village who could take her pick from any unmarried man who looked her way, as most of them did. He'd been looking her way on every possible occasion ever since she first came to work at Turret House and now he was going to drive her into Chichester. He couldn't believe his luck.

Then what a cramming of money and instructions into his pocket, what a rush to the pump, what a combing of unruly hair, what a scrubbing of earth-stained face, what a fidgeting wait by the pony's head before she came tripping out of the kitchen, neat in her brown cotton skirt and her blue and white day-gown, with the prettiest white cap on her dark curls and the most becoming straw bonnet set over the cap, blue eyes the colour of forget-me-nots, pink cheeks as round and tender as a peach, sweet Betsy Haynes, soft and breathless in the translucent bloom of sixteen summers.

'What luck!' she said, as he handed her in to the cart. 'I'm so glad it was you.'

The bird threw itself against the cage of his ribs fluttering wildly, but he took his seat beside her and tried to be nonchalant. 'Are you?' he said, picking up the reins and clucking to the pony. 'Why's that then?'

'I got a purchase to make,' she said mysteriously.

'Who for?'

She gave him the full benefit of those bold blue eyes. Oh, she was such a flirt but she flirted so prettily. 'That *would* be tellin'.'

The pony plodded them towards the church, where it turned, following the curve of the road without need of reminder. Johnnie pretended to be guiding it but his senses were in such a state of delicious alert it was all he could do to sit still. If the cart were to jolt a little he could put his arm round her waist to steady her. Imagine that. And when they were out into open country, where there were no eyes to see them, he might even try to kiss her. Imagine *that*. Meantime he must try to make conversation.

'Shall I see it when 'tis purchased?' he said. 'Or is it to be hid away?'

She pretended to consider the question, glancing at him sideways and dazzling him with her eyes. What long soft eyelashes she had, as thick and dark as her hair, and eyebrows that curved like the flight of a seagull's wings. Oh, Betsy, Betsy. You beautiful girl. Look at me again.

'I'll consider of it,' she teased, 'dependin' on the time, an' if it's ready, an' if we got the threads and the linsey woolsey.'

At which point the dear little amenable pony reached the village pound and the track to Chichester and missed his footing on the rough earth so that the cart gave a lurch and Johnnie was able to put out a happy arm to steady her, which naturally allowed him to tuck her against his side for protection. And oh, such a slender waist she had and such softly rounded arms and the smell of her sun-warmed skin was so enticing it made him feel dizzy.

'Seven miles,' he said happily.

The sun was already quite strong and the air was sweet with the scent of crushed wild thyme and spiced with the baked bread smell of the dusty stubble. As they plodded through the fields towards the distant spire of Chichester cathedral, which rose above the trees and tiles of the town, pale grey and bold as a bodkin against the misty blue of the September sky, a lark sprang up from the cornfield. They listened as it began to sing, sweet and sharp and with its familiar joyful abandon, and as song and flight rose to a blissful crescendo above his love-dazed head, Johnnie knew he had never felt so happy in the whole of his life.

'Sussex,' he said, 'is the prettiest place in the world.'

That was Mr Blake's opinion of it too. He and Catherine had walked for half a mile eastwards following the tattered edge of the beach, where the tamarisk trees leant sideways, their roots powdered with pale, dry sand. Sometimes there was an expanse of trodden earth to provide them with a pathway, sometimes there was barely any path at all and they had to clamber over the pebbles, but William was so entranced by the shifting patterns of the sea, the long stretch of honey-coloured sand and the extraordinary quality of the sunlight, that he didn't notice what was under his feet.

'It is a dwelling for the immortals,' he said, stopping to scoop up a handful of dry sand and examine it intently. 'Every grain of sand holds an eternity. The smallest pebbles catch light like fishes. We shall live here so happily, Catherine, shall we not, in our marine cottage, in the pure air, with skylarks singing hymns of joy each morning and the mundane shell of the sky in constant view. How could a man but be happy when the sun has risen so joyously?'

Catherine was wondering whether her loaf had risen sufficiently to be baked, for she was hungry after their long journey and they'd finished off yesterday's loaf for breakfast, but she agreed with him that their happiness was assured and wondered whether they might not be turning back.

'We must never turn back,' her husband said. 'Once the first steps are taken there is no turning back for any of us.' But he agreed that they might have walked far enough for their first morning and that they shouldn't leave his sister on her own for too long.

'Tomorrow we shall all three explore the village, for I hear 'tis a pretty place, and perhaps we may walk out into the fields a little,' he promised. 'Then I suppose I should take a turn to Turret House and visit Mr Hayley. What good fortune, my love, that he has seen fit to be my patron. Oh, we shall do very well here. Very well indeed. I must look for a spade. The garden is much neglected and needs turning over. There is sure to be one somewhere about. And if not, I'm sure Mr Grinder will provide one. He seems a most obliging landlord. His ale was quite excellent this morning.'

'I must find the best place to buy meat,' Catherine said, 'and where to go for such groceries as we need. Our stock of tea is very low and the sugar loaf has dwindled to nothing.'

'There is a city close by,' William said. 'We will walk there in a day or two and see what may be found. Mr Hayley speaks highly of it.'

The city was extremely busy that morning and even more pungent than usual for it was the day of the cattle market and besides horses and carts, well-dressed riders and gaitered farmhands, the streets were full of frightened livestock and consequently spattered with dung and puddled with piddle. Johnnie and Betsy could smell it long before

35

they reached the east gate, for they were immediately downwind. But they were well used to such farmyard smells and pressed on into the noise and effluvia without comment, secured the pony and cart outside the Nag's Head and prepared themselves for their shopping expedition in their usual sensible way, Johnnie strapping on his gaiters to protect his stockings, Betsy pinning up her skirt and easing a good stout pair of pattens over her boots.

The newsagent's was right in the centre of the town near the market cross and was so full of customers that it took some time for Johnnie to push his way to the counter. But *The Times* was duly bought and stowed away in his waistcoat and then they were off to the grocer's for coffee beans, cocoa nibs and a sugar loaf neatly wrapped in blue paper, to the chandler's for tallow candles and beeswax, and finally to the haberdasher's for Chichester needles and coloured threads and the exact quantity of linsey woolsey that Mrs Beke had specified.

At which point Betsy said she must make her next purchase on her own, 'being 'tis a secret.' So Johnnie took himself off to the Nag's Head for a pint of porter to slake his thirst and settled by the window to read the paper and watch for the return of his beloved. She was a long time gone, long enough for him to read all about the bread riots in London and how the Corn Market had been stormed and how handbills had been posted on the Monument, 'instigating insurrection'.

He saw the scarlet cloth approaching through the massed blues and browns of the crowd long before he realised who was sporting it so boldly. At first he thought it was a soldier's bright jacket but as it neared the window he realised that it was a woman's cloak and that the face framed by its thick hood belonged to Betsy Haynes. 'My stars!' he said, as she swept into the inn and strode towards him, gathering admiration from every man in the bar. 'Fancy you in a cardinal. You do look a swell.'

Her face was flushed with the warmth of her new garment and the triumph of its purchase. 'I been savin' for it for two whole years,' she told him. 'I've wanted it, and wanted it, for so long as I can remember. What d'you think of it?'

He thought it was the finest cloak he'd ever seen and that she was the prettiest girl in the town with her face framed by the bright cloth and her dark hair curling under the white frill of her cap, and he caught her by the hands as if he was going to pull her towards him and kiss her, which he might well have done if they hadn't been in a public place and he hadn't been afraid of being rebuked. But then the cathedral clock struck the hour to bring him back to his senses and to remind them both that they ought to be getting home, so he let go of her hands and tried to act with more decorum.

She took off her new possession and folded it carefully. Then she wrapped the resulting bundle in a length of brown paper and lowered it neatly into her wicker basket. 'I shan't wear it yet awhile,' she confided. 'I only put it on for you to see. 'Tis for high days and holidays and when the weather's cold.'

'Then I can't wait for cold weather,' he said, and was rewarded with a rapturous smile.

The return journey took longer than they expected, for halfway home they rounded a copse to find that their way was blocked by the massed backs of a flock of sheep, who having followed their leader through a gap in the hedge were now ambling about on the path in baaing confusion and wouldn't get out of the way no matter how loudly Johnnie shouted or how much he waved his arms. It was more than half an hour before the noise he was making attracted the shepherd who arrived with a couple of dogs to tease his charges back to the meadow. 'They got no sense in those funny ol' heads,' he explained, ''ave 'ee my woolly lovelies.'

'Tha's all very well,' Johnnie said. 'Now we shall be late back an' Mrs Beke'll have somethin' to say about it, you just see if she don't. I was s'pposed to be home midday to pick the plums.'

'Never you mind,' Betsy consoled. 'She *must* know how sheep go on.' And she put her hand through the crook of his arm and gave it a squeeze. Actually gave it a squeeze. He might not have found an excuse to kiss her yet, but what a jaunt this was turning out to be.

In the event Mrs Beke was still in good humour when they finally got back to Turret House and told them they'd done well and that the master would have good time to read the paper before his dinner. 'Take it straight up to him,' she said to Johnnie, 'and then you'd best see to those ol' plums, or Mr Hosier'll have somethin' to say, and we don't want that. Go down to the kitchen and empty your basket, Betsy, and then you can come to my parlour and we'll get the new petticoats cut and basted before the roast is done. We'll just have time enough. Well, hop along then the pair of you.'

Johnnie went back to his proper work happily enough. It was pleasant out in the garden in the warmth of noonday with day-dreams to fill his head and a good meal coming and the plums so ripe they fell into his hand. But only half of them had been picked when Betsy came running out into the garden to tell him he was wanted in the library.

'Now what?' Mr Hosier said crossly, wiping the sweat from his forehead with the back of his hand.

'If you please, Mr Hosier, sir, he's wanted to run an errand.'

'There's never any peace in this house,' the gardener complained. 'There's no sense in the man. How's he s'ppose we're to pick his plums, if we're to run errands morning, noon and night? The way he go on nothin'll ever get growed nor picked. 'Twill be no good him complainin' when there's no food for the table, which there won't be if he keep on this way. Well, go then, if you must boy, but look sharp about it.'

So Johnnie set the laden trug in the shade of the plum tree and followed Betsy back to the house, where he left his boots and apron by the back door, and climbed the stairs to the library.

His master was sitting beside the window with a letter in his hand and an enraged expression on his face. 'Ah!' he said. 'There you are. Good feller. It's a positive disgrace. Quite, quite insupportable. Something must be done about it.'

There was no obvious answer but then there rarely was when the master was in the middle of an outburst. 'Sir?'

'There's a letter on the table, d'ye see it?' Mr Hayley said. All signed, sealed and ready for you to deliver. You are to take it straight down to Mr Blake, the engraver, just moved in to Mr Grinder's cottage. You know where it is. Good feller. Tell him I must see him at once. At once. On a matter of utmost urgency. It's quite insupportable. Explain to him that I shall compose a ballad for the poor soul and he shall illustrate it for me and we will send her the proceeds in her hour of need. But no matter. 'Tis all in the letter. Post haste if you please. The sooner we begin the better.'

The day was growing more extraordinary by the minute. First a trip to Chichester, which he hadn't expected, and now he was to meet the mysterious Mr Blake, whose arrival had been the subject of endless speculation at The Fox. What sport! He strode through Mr Hayley's forbidding gates with the letter in his pocket and headed south for The Fox and the cottage in a state of happy anticipation.

There were very few people about, only old Mrs Taylor who was standing by the gate of her white cottage, smoking a pipe and pondering, and Will Smith who was grooming a fine stallion in the stable yard alongside the inn. The Fox itself seemed to be deserted, but there was smoke rising from the cottage chimney and the wicket gate was ajar, so someone was at home. He pushed the gate open and walked through into the garden plot, noticing how overgrown it was, and

41

noticing too that someone had been using the well, for the earth around its worn brick was dark with spilled water. Then as he could hear women's voices inside the cottage he stepped under the high thatch that shielded the door and thumped its thick oak with the side of his fist.

Feet approached, a latch clicked and the door was opened by a woman who was drying her hands on a Holland apron, rather a handsome woman, tall and slender with dark eyes and a bold face under a plain white mobcap. Wife or servant? It was hard to tell, especially at first glance. She had the air of a wife but the clothes of a servant, her dark skirt patched and none too clean, her black stockings darned, her shoes scuffed and down at heel, but her day-gown was better quality – he saw that at once – made of linen and patterned in pink and white. 'How may I help you?' she said and smiled at him.

He explained his errand.

'He's in the work room,' she said, 'unpacking. Go through. He'll not mind.' And she opened the door to her right and stood back to let him enter. 'William, my dear, here's a messenger come.'

It was very dark inside the room, for the thatch over the window was extremely thick and very little light penetrated the straw. After a day in sunshine, it took a little while for Johnnie's eyes to adapt to the darkness.

At first all he could see were amorphous suggestions, which gradually resolved themselves into a round oak table, a cottage chair and a stack of wooden boxes, but then a log shifted in the grate and the fire flickered into life and he caught the gleam of an eye and saw that there was a figure stooped over one of the boxes lifting something heavy from the sacking that enwrapped it, something heavy and gleaming like gold. A copper plate, catching the firelight as it rose.

'You have a message,' the engraver said, setting the plate against the wall. And he held out his hand to receive it.

Johnnie watched as the newcomer broke the seal with a stained thumb, smoothed out the paper and lifted it to the firelight so that he could read it. Not a rich man by any means, he thought. Mr Grinder's wrong about that. The man stooped before the fire was a labourer, his clothes and hands stained by his trade, and the room full of his tools, the table loaded with papers, ink bottles, a pot full of brushes, a tumble of paint-smeared rags. There were canvases propped against the whitewashed walls, two with strange pictures painted on them, all swirling blues and greys and long white figures like statues; there was a pile of books in one corner and a box full of papers in another; and standing at the back of the room, where the ceiling was high enough to accommodate it, a huge wooden structure like a cider press or – and his heart contracted at the thought – one of them newfangled instruments the Frenchies called a guillotine. My stars! Here's a man with a difference and no mistake.

The paper was read and put on the table next to the brushes. 'Tell your master,' the engraver said, 'that I will call upon him at my very first convenience and will be happy to undertake his commission. Explain to him that I am unpacking as speedily as may be.' And he strode to the door, calling to his wife. 'Catherine, my dear, we have our first commission. Did I not tell you we should do well here?'

So she *is* his wife, Johnnie thought, as he strolled back to Turret House, despite her poor clothes. My stars, I shall have some tales to tell in The Fox tonight.

Evening in The Fox was the high spot of the village working day, when the men left their labour in the fields and farms and big houses and gathered to slake the thirst of the day, to smoke a calming pipe and to enjoy the gossip. The church might think itself the centre of the village and so it was on a Sunday morning or when it came to weddings and christenings and burials, but the inn was the place for news. The old men had their allotted places in the chimney corners, the young found space on the settles, there was a fire of sea-coal, no less, and beers and ales aplenty, for Mr Grinder was a provident landlord, and barely an evening went by without plenty to comment on and exclaim about.

'So you been in to see the new engraver feller, then,' old Reuben Jones said, as Johnnie and Mr Hosier walked in that evening. 'Mr Sparkes was a-tellin' me this afternoon. Ol' Mrs Taylor seen you go in, so he say. So come on then boy, what did he say? D'you reckon he's a-goin' ter stay here?'

Johnnie laughed as he walked to the bar. 'You can't sneeze in this village without everybody knowin',' he said. 'Yes, I did see him, *an'* his wife, *an'* I went in the cottage. What you want to know?'

'We been at sixes an' sevens all day,' Mr Hosier complained. A-runnin' errands, here there an' everywhere. He got another bee in his bonnet, that's the size of it, an' we've all to be turned topsy-turvy to satisfy. Errands all day, I ask you. How's he s'ppose we're to grow vegetables if we're runnin' about all day long. Pint please, Mr Grinder.'

'I didn't see you do much runnin',' Johnnie grinned. 'The one what was runnin was me.'

'"Tis all the same, you or me,' the gardener said, holding out his hand for the beer. 'It all takes good time from the garden,

45

which he can ill afford, onny he don' seem to know it. You don't get vegetables grow'd if you're forever runnin' about.'

'But you spoke to him, Johnnie,' Reuben said, pushing the conversation back in the direction he wanted. 'You been in the cottage an' spoke to him. D'you reckon he's goin' ter stay?'

'You've the right of it there, Mr Jones,' Johnnie said, feeling important. 'I been in the cottage an' I've spoke to him.'

There was a rush of cold air and his father came clomping through the door in his muddy boots. 'Oi've spoke to him an' all,' he said, winking at his son. 'You aren't the only one, so there's no cause for you to go a-givin' yourself airs. Evenin' Reuben, How's the pigs?'

'Comin' along lovely, Hiram,' Reuben said. It was his job to look after the piggery on Outerwyke farm and he took it very seriously.

'An' how's the foot?'

'Mendin' tolerable,' Reuben said, glancing at his bandaged foot. 'Oi don't complain. So is he goin' ter stay, this engraver feller? We needs ter know.'

'More to the point,' Will Smith said, looking up from where he was lounging on the settle, 'could he have written this?' And he pulled the leaflet from the pocket of his breeches and held it up for Johnnie to see.

Johnnie took a swig of his beer and read it carefully. 'Tha's from Lunnon,' he said. 'They been handin' 'em out all over, according' to *The Times*. I read it this mornin'. Stuck to the Monument an' all sorts. There's riots there, so they say, on account of there's no bread. How d'you come by it?'

So the tale was told, in the usual happy length, and then Reuben and the potboys joined in to exaggerate the weight of the boxes they'd had to carry, and Hiram described how he saw the engraver step out of the gate and head off to the beach. 'Lunnoners are all the same.'

'He *is* a Lunnoner then,' Reuben said. 'I thought so last night.'

'Oh, yes,' Johnnie agreed. 'He's a Lunnoner all right. Tell you one thing, though. He aren't a rich one. You wait till you see his clothes.'

Reuben had reached the surly stage of his evening's drinking. 'Rich or poor,' he said, 'foreigners are all the same an' we don't want 'em hanging round here. Oi told 'ee we was in for trouble when ol' Dot-an'-Carry first come here, onny none of 'ee listened. An' what happen? First 'ee build that ol' wall ten foot tall for to keep us all out and then dang me if he don't go an' build that great tower. An' what for, Oi ask 'ee. Blamed if Oi know. 'Tis allus the same with strangers. You let 'em in they takes liberties. They turn

47

things contrariwise. This ol' engraver feller'll be just the same. You see if Oi ent right.'

Outside in the cold night air, the stars were sharp as frost and the moon hung above the village, whey-faced and waiting. A faint yellow candlelight warmed the windows of Mr Blake's cottage and from time to time a wisp of grey smoke rose from the kitchen chimney. It drifted in the still air, propelled by its own heat, thinning and dispersing until it was nothing but a ghostly shadow across the moon.

Chapter Three

Having given his word, Mr Blake walked up the lane to Turret House as soon as he'd breakfasted the next morning. It was a short walk and a pleasant one, for after the crush and noise of the London streets this small dusty village seemed like a kingdom of peace. He felt he was at home there and it pleased him that he could recognise some of his neighbours. He saw the ploughman and his little lad as soon as he stepped out of the cottage, and was warmed when they waved to him, and as he passed The Fox, there was Mr Grinder in his blue apron, standing by the door talking to an old man with a bandaged foot and Mr Grinder was all welcoming smiles.

'Off to Turret House, Mr Blake?' he said and it was more a statement than a question.

'There's work to be done,' Mr Blake told him happily.

'You've a good day for it,' the publican said. And the bandaged man nodded and grinned, showing his two remaining teeth.

It was an unusual sensation to be walking on trodden earth instead of paving stones and a luxury to have the lane to himself instead of sharing it with crowds and carriages and horses. After a few yards, when he'd passed a long barn to his right and a cottage standing in a very well-tended garden to his left, greeted a skinny old woman standing by her wicket gate, and a shabbily dressed young one brushing the dust from her doorstep, he realised that although his new neighbours were undoubtedly poor, too poor to be warmly dressed at any event, they were not starving as the poor in London had been these past twelve months and more. There was a strong smell of baking bread emanating from both cottages, the garden was growing vegetables and even ran to a fruit tree, hens were clucking somewhere nearby and he could smell a brew house as well as the various privies. He remembered the very different smell of Lambeth, the stink

49

of unwashed bodies and filthy clothes, the haggard faces and rank breath of starvation, the ragged children waiting patiently in line outside the Dog and Duck for a bowl of thin soup and bread made from potato flour, and his old familiar anger rose in him and he grieved that innocent children should be starving when profiteers were making a fortune from the very bread they needed so much and couldn't afford. And he thought of dear Thomas Butts who'd bought his engravings all through these dreadful famine years and was humbly grateful to him, knowing that without his open-handed patronage he and Catherine would have starved along with all the rest. He was grateful to Mr Flaxman too, who'd been another good friend to them and had arranged for him to come here to Felpham to work for Mr Hayley. There was, he decided, much for him to be thankful for, and thankful he *would* be, he was determined on it. His short walk was over. He had reached the gates of Turret House. We shall do very well here, he promised himself.

Mr Hayley's fine house looked prosperous and important, standing in its wide gardens, at the end of a long covered walkway, with its tall windows catching the sun and its high tower dominating the grounds. This is what it is like to be a celebrated poet, Blake thought, as he followed the path to the front door, and although the knowledge saddened him a little, he shrugged it away at once, jealousy being an altogether ignoble and harmful sentiment.

'My dear friend,' Mr Hayley said as his visitor was ushered into the library. 'You have come at the most opportune moment. But quite the most opportune. I have this very second completed the ballad and it is a fine work. I will read it to you.' His long handsome face was bright with enthusiasm as he took up a pose and began to intone.

It was a truly dreadful poem, dripping with false sentiments and warped by the need to find a rhyme. *'Angels could not thee save / when low beneath the wave / you lost your innocent life / cut by the ocean's knife.'* But Blake kept a straight face, listened to it humbly and, when the reading was finished, agreed that it was a fine work and that he would be happy to illustrate it and print it.

'Two engravings would suffice, don't you think,' the celebrated poet said. 'One of the widow leaving her cottage to seek her sick husband, looking back wistfully perhaps, with her son rocking the cradle inside the house of course, and the other of the boy aloft on the shrouds in the midst of the storm, almost at the moment of death, with the spirit of his father holding out his arms to him from the storm clouds. It must all be noble and in proportion, you understand, and fitting to the quality of the verse. I shall

51

need several copies for I shall sell it to all my friends. How soon could it be done? We must help this poor woman with all speed. With all speed. Her loss is intolerable. As soon as I read her story... My dear friend Counsellor Rose wrote to tell me of it. Did I tell you that? No? No matter. As soon as I read it I knew she *must* be saved and that I was the one to do it. We poets have a duty to our society. We shirk it at our peril.'

He is right about that, Blake thought, if about nothing else. A true poet must write no matter what it may cost him. He'd always known that, for poetry came to him unbidden and with a terrible urgency. Lines were forming in his head at that very moment, swift bitter lines forged in anger at the cruelty and indignity of poverty, lines that swelled and pulsed to be written, as he sat quietly in Mr Hayley's elegant chair looking up at Mr Hayley's learned books.

When a man looks pale
With labour and abstinence, say he looks
*   healthy and happy*
And when his children sicken, let them die,
*   there are enough*
Born, even too many, and our Earth will be
*   overrun...*
Preach temperance: say he is overgorged and
*   drowns his wit*
In strong drink, though you know that bread
*   and water are all He can afford.*

Mr Hayley's upper class voice pushed into his thoughts. 'You can do that, can you not?' he insisted. 'With the greatest possible expedition.'

So a dish of his favourite coffee with milk was taken, the two men parted amicably and Blake walked back to his cottage, commission in hand, weighed down by the pressing need to earn a living but with his own lines fresh and singing in his head. He would commit them to paper before he began work on the ballad. They would not be lost.

In the kitchen of Turret House, Betsy Haynes was plucking a fowl, the white feathers sticking to her fingers and floating into her hair. She would rather have been sewing the new petticoats, for stitching was cleaner work than dressing chickens, but Mr Hayley had invited company for dinner that evening and Mrs Beke was determined that he should have a fine table so they were all set to work in the kitchen. The one good thing to come of it was that Johnnie had been in and out of the place all morning delivering fruit and vegetables but they were all so hard pressed that even the delights of flirting with him were beginning to fade.

'Get out my light do,' she said to him, flirting and scolding at the same time, as he stood in front of her for the seventh time. 'I can't see what I'm a-doin' of.'

'I just seen that Mr Blake,' he told her, importantly. 'Walkin' out the gate with a paper in his hand. What do you think a' that?'

She didn't think anything of it. 'I got enough on my plate without Mr Blake,' she said. 'Go back to the garden, for pity's sake.'

'Shall you walk to church with me tomorrow?' he hoped.

'If I aren't drowned in feathers.'

'And shall you wear your new cloak?'

'I might,' she conceded. 'If 'tis cold enough.'

Outside in the garden it was certainly cold enough. A breeze had sprung up and was whipping the dead leaves from the elms and making the holly bush rattle. The sound reminded Johnnie that autumn was coming. In a week or two it would be Harvest Home. Maybe he could persuade his father to get him invited to the feast, the way he did last year, and then maybe he could get an invitation for her too and she could come with him and sit beside him in her red cloak and eat Mr Sparkes's harvest pie. And after that they might walk out together. Was it possible? Oh, he did so hope it was possible.

The breeze was blowing the leaves from the great elm behind Blake's cottage. They tumbled in the air like golden birds, scurried across the road, spotted his dark thatch with colour. Their brightness cheered him, despite the weight of the work before him.

'We can have fires in all the rooms now my love,' he said to Catherine as he stepped into the kitchen. She was concerned about the damp, which was rather marked. 'Here's a commission will keep us in fuel and vittles for a good long time. I shall start on it directly and you will help me to print it, will you not.'

She would indeed. Had she not always been his helpmate? 'I've found us an excellent butcher while you've been with Mr Hayley,' she told him. 'Meat is a deal cheaper here than in London and a deal fresher into the bargain, and there's fresh fish to be had when the tide's right. I've been talking to Mrs Haynes about it.'

The name was new to her husband. 'Who is Mrs Haynes?' he asked.

'Why, the woman who lives across the way,' Catherine told him. 'Our nearest neighbour you might say. Her husband is the miller's servant so she's up on all the local gossip. Oh, and there's a letter come for you from Mr Butts.'

Mr Hayley's dinner party that night was a huge success. The wine he'd chosen was excellent, the meal well cooked, and after he'd treated them to a reading of his latest ballad, his guests were full of praise, both for his literary skill and for his latest charitable endeavour.

'That widow woman will count herself blessed to have you as a friend,' Mr Cunningham said, sprawling back in his chair. 'Damme if she won't. When are we to see the finished print?'

'Mr Blake has given his word that it will be ready for sale by the beginning of October,' Mr Hayley said. 'All proceeds to go to the lady.'

'I shall take three copies.'

'You are pleased with your new assistant then, William?' another guest asked.

'I find him admirable in every respect,' the celebrated poet told him. 'Engraving, of all human works, requires the largest portion of patience and he possesses more of that inestimable virtue than I have ever seen in a man. Moreover, he is modest of his abilities and not a man to speak out of turn. If he does well with this commission, I shall make him my secretary. I might even set him to work to paint some portraits for the library. I have a set already planned.'

'He's a lucky man,' Mr Cunningham said. 'I hope he appreciates what you are doing for him.'

Mr Hayley preened. It was always a pleasure to hear his charitable nature being given due praise. 'I do what I can,' he said, modestly. 'Little enough in all conscience when I consider all the troubles of the world, but I am a man of principle. I do what I can.

More port, Mr Cunningham?'

Back in his damp workroom, William Blake had stoked up his log fire, lit two tallow candles to give him enough light to see what he was doing and was bent over the round table, engraver in hand, ready to start work. He had decided to print Mr Hayley's ballad using a new method, which he called wood-cut on pewter, in which the ground of the pewter was smoked and the outline cut into the darkened surface. He hoped it would make for greater clarity in the final printed work but of course there were risks entailed as he had never done it before and this was an important commission. He steadied his hands and made the first scraping incision, carving the first of Mr Hayley's trite words. I will start my own work tomorrow, he thought, and when the village is at prayers, Catherine and I will walk along the shore and take our own communion there. My sister will keep within doors I fear – she was never much enamoured of fresh air – but Catherine will join me.

After the heavy winds and high tide of the previous evening, the beach was scoured clean. The incoming waves rolled joyously into shore, their onward movement a rush of rhythmical sound, their tips frothed into snow-white foam above glass-green water, where the sunlight reflected, bright and bold as if the surface of the sea was a mirror. The sky above their heads was heaped with rolling billows of blue and white cloud, and was higher than he'd ever seen it, and the morning sun, half hidden by a cloud, sent out visible beams of pale golden light. It was all movement, freshness and promise. The very air seemed to sparkle.

And as he stood with his feet on the dry white sand, shapes rose from the surface of the sea, at first faint and transparent like steam or smoke but then as they rose higher and higher into the busy sky, elongating until they were six foot, ten foot, fifteen foot tall, and he recognised the forms of human beings, noble and benign, gazing down upon him with intelligent eyes and infinite compassion, and knew he was being blessed with another vision, and stopped, still and entranced, to receive it in all its glory.

Minutes passed and he didn't move. His breathing was so shallow it was a wonder he didn't faint, but his eyes were wide open and full of wonder. Catherine could see nothing but sea and sky, but she knew that a vision had come upon him and stood beside him quietly until he could recover himself sufficiently to tell her what it was.

'Isaiah!' he said at last. He spoke faintly, like a man in a fever. 'Ezekiel. I am given a fourfold vision. The Spirit of God moves upon the face of the waters. The Lamb of God descends through the gates of Jerusalem. As a man is born on earth so He is born of fair Jerusalem. We delude ourselves when we speak of three dimensions. Vision is fourfold.'

He was beginning to tremble as he so often did at the end of a vision. 'We will sit down, my dear,' Catherine said to him. There was a large piece of driftwood a little further up the beach. It looked fairly dry and would serve until she could coax him home.

He allowed himself to be led, his face still glowing from his enchantment. She knew he couldn't see her although his eyes were blazing. 'To justify the ways of God to man,' he said, 'is a mighty work for any man to undertake. Milton gives evidence of that. But no less will suffice. I must begin at once.'

'And so you shall,' Catherine assured him. Are you ready to walk my love?'

'Aye. I am,' he told her. 'To walk and to write.'

But she noticed that he was glad of her arm on their way back to the cottage.

His sister was aggrieved that they were so late. 'I've been waiting on you this last hour,' she complained. 'It's unkind to leave me so long. What have you been doing?' Then, as Blake walked past her towards his workroom, she noticed the pallor of his face and knew. 'Oh, not again!' she said. 'I thought he'd done with such folly.'

''Tain't folly,' his wife cried, defending him at once. ''Tis a vision.'

'Folly or vision, 'tis all one,' his sister said tartly. 'It makes him ill and does him no good. You shouldn't encourage him. Unless you wish to be married to a madman.'

'My William is not mad,' his wife said fiercely. 'He is a visionary.'

'He's a fool,' his sister said scathingly. 'And you're another to believe his nonsense.'

'I wonder at you,' Catherine said. 'If you can hold such an opinion of your brother, you do not understand him. His visions are no folly. They're the stuff of life to him.'

'They're unhealthy nonsense. Papa would have whipped him for imagining things.'

The two women were toe to toe, glaring at one another, too deeply into another quarrel for either to back down. 'And he would have been wrong,' Catherine said hotly.

'My father was never wrong. He did as any father would have done, took a stick to chastise a bad child, which is the right and proper way for a father to behave.'

'It was wrong,' Catherine said, fighting on. 'You should never hit a child.'

'This child was telling lies,' her sister-in-law said, 'pretending he could see God looking through the window, if you ever heard such nonsense, and him only four years old, and screaming blue murder into the bargain. Do you tell me that a child should be allowed to scream?'

'I tell you that a child should be loved, or how else is he to learn to love? A screaming child should be comforted not beaten. Any fool could tell you that.'

'What do you know of it? I see no children in this house.'

'Nor in yours neither.'

'You overstep the mark, Catherine. I will not be spoken to in this way. I shall speak to my brother.'

But William was working in his badly lit room and not writing but engraving. He looked so cast down and so weary that his warring women grew quiet at the sight of him. 'I cannot write,' he said wearily. 'I have to finish the ballad.'

Half a mile away, the congregation of St Mary's church were gathering on the church path in their Sunday finery. There was no rush to enter the building for, apart from the necessity to wait until the village worthies had made their more important entry, this was a time for parents with working children to become a family again, for daughters to kiss their mothers and fathers to extend a gruff welcome to their sons. The vicar was well used to delay for such Sunday rituals were long established in a place where so many children went straight from their own hearths as soon as they were twelve years old – or big enough to be considered twelve – to live and work in a great house.

Betsy Haynes had dressed with more than usual care for the service that morning, for she was wearing her new red cloak for the very first time and she wanted to cause a stir. She was the prettiest girl in the village so why shouldn't she cause a stir?

She did, but not quite in the way she'd planned. As she came skimming up the path with her hood over her cap and the scarlet cloth wrapping her in warmth, she knew she was the cynosure of all eyes and was cheerfully proud of herself. But then she reached the porch and came face to face with her mother and realised with a painful sinking of the heart that her mother was not pleased.

'Borrowed finery now is it?' she said and her mouth was down-turned with disapproval.

Betsy decided to confess at once. 'No Ma,' she said, lifting her chin, 'tha's mine. Paid for fair an' square. An' so warm you wouldn't imagine.'

Mrs Haynes was blue-eyed like her daughter but there the similarity ended. Where Betsy was all burgeoning curves, glowing skin and shining eyes, her mother was all uncomfortable angles, with bony hands and sharp shoulders, her face wrinkled and her eyes guarded, her mouth pulled sideways by disapproval. Now she looked as if she could cut the air by breathing it. 'And where d'you get the money from, if I may make so bold as to ask?'

Betsy was stung. 'I saved it from my wages,' she said. 'Two whole years it took me.'

Her mother snorted. 'What nonsense. An' we so short we can barely manage. If you'd money to spare you should have brought it home to us an' we'd ha' made *proper* use of it. I don' know what the world's a-comin' to, I don' indeed.'

Tears welled from Betsy's eyes. She couldn't stop them. To be scolded for thrift was so unjust. Thrift was one of the virtues. Wasn't it what the vicar kept dinning into them week after week? And anyway, they were *her* wages. Why shouldn't she spend them on a cloak? Other women did. Mrs Beke had had *her* cloak for years and years.

'You're gettin' above yourself, my gel, tha's your trouble,' Mrs Haynes scolded. 'You're forgettin' your place.'

'Times are changin' Ma,' Betsy said, fighting back. 'We don't have to know our place, no more. We can rise out of it if we wants. Look what they done in France, stormin' the Bastille an' openin' the jails an' choppin' off the king's head. If they'd know'd their place they'd never ha' done that, now would they?'

'And look what happen to them after,' her mother said tartly. 'Think a' that. They had *their* heads chopped off too, every last one of 'em. You don' want to go follerin' the Frenchies. They're a bad lot.' She glanced back at the path, her face hard. 'Now here's your father comin'. I don' know what he'll say about it, I'm sure.'

Mr Haynes was a man of some consequence in the village partly because he worked for Mr Cosens the miller and partly because he was so strong, tall, thickset and muscular, with fists like hams and shoulders that could carry a full sack of flour with no apparent effort. He had the reputation of being able to crack ribs if annoyed. But on this occasion he was in an affable mood and no help to his wife at all. 'Mornin' Betsy,' he said, as he joined them by the porch. 'You look pretty.'

It was praise but it was too late to soothe his daughter's lacerated feelings. Her occasion was ruined. She'd been scolded – and publicly scolded what's more – when she should have been praised and admired. As she followed her parents miserably into church and took her place at the back behind the worthies, she was cast into a gloom. She wished she'd never worn her cloak to church and never bought it neither, even though she looked extremely pretty in it – she couldn't help but know that – and felt warm and snug wrapped in its folds, which was something she'd never known at a winter's service before.

Watching her, from his place on the opposite pew, Johnnie was torn by her distress. He rarely paid much attention to the service and usually contrived to doze during the sermon but that Sunday the sight of her biting her pretty lip and surreptitiously wiping those pretty eyes kept him in a state of painful alert, and as soon as the praying was done, he made an excuse to his parents and slipped out of the church so that he could hide behind the yew tree and join her on her way out without anyone knowing. She was almost the last to leave, dawdling so far behind her mother that she'd only just stepped out of the porch when her parents had spoken to the vicar, said goodbye to their neighbours, walked through the churchyard and were out in the road and on their way home. All he had to do was put out an arm as she passed and pull her behind the shelter of the tree.

Then what a torrent of tears was shed and how angrily she detailed the undeserved unkindness of her treatment. 'I'd every right to buy it,' she wept. 'It was *my* wages. She disapproves of everything I do. She as good as told me I was a spendthrift. A spendthrift, can you imagine that? She knows very well I saved up for it for years and years and hardly spent a single mortal penny in all that time. I thought 'twas a good buy. I thought I looked pretty in it. But not her. Oh no! She just sniffed at me. She said I was gettin' above myself. You don't think I'm gettin' above myself do you?'

Oh, he didn't. He truly didn't. He thought she had every right to buy her cloak – it was her money – and she looked beautiful in it.

His admiration cheered her. 'Do I? Do I really? You're not just saying it?'

'Beautiful,' he said, devoutly. 'Like a princess.'

She found a rag in her pocket and blew her nose. 'It's so unfair,' she said. 'She's always a-goin' on at me. 'Tent my fault I'm pretty. To hear her talk you'd think I'd done it a' purpose.' Then another thought struck her. Are my eyes red?'

'Why don't we go for a walk,' he said hopefully. 'Fresh air'll clear them.' There was no need to rush back. People were expected to talk a little when they went to church. So she blew her nose again and they set off together to walk through the bean field behind the church, heading north to the barn and the village pound, and to his great delight she held onto his arm and allowed him to wipe away her tears with his thumb. And as they walked and he admired, she gradually calmed.

When they reached the barn, they stood indecisively in its shadow, not wanting to return. 'We could go further if you'd like,' he hoped.

'Best not,' she said, looking up into his eyes, but not flirting this time, simply looking, 'or they'll be wonderin'.'

The earth was so damp he could feel the chill of it through his boots. 'We shall take cold if we stand here long,' he said.

'Yes,' she said. But she didn't move. And neither did he. How could he? He was bewitched by the mere sight of her, with her mouth so soft and her eyelashes still spiky from all the tears she'd shed and her washed eyes not red at all but blue as the summer sky.

'Oh, Betsy,' he said. And as she still didn't move, he put his arms round her red cloak and, greatly daring, bent his head to kiss her. It was the merest touch, a gentle brush of lip against lip, but it was a commitment and it left him breathless. 'Oh, Betsy, my dearest dear.'

She stood before him, plagued by the oddest thoughts. Over the last year, she'd grown used to having young men make sheep's eyes at her. At first she was confused by it, because it was all so obvious and the other girls teased her about it, but after a while she learned how to flirt and then she found it flattering – for it showed how pretty she was – and comical too because they made themselves look such fools. But here with Johnnie everything was different. He wasn't making sheep's eyes and he didn't look a fool. He looked – well, strange really. Sort of intense. 'Twas just a kiss, she thought, and not very much of one, if the truth be told. She was used to kisses, for lots of young men had tried to snatch a kiss when they were alone with her – and had had their ears boxed for their pains, which had been splendid fun. But Johnnie was gazing at her as if he couldn't bear to take his eyes from her face. Was there really so much power in one little soft kiss? It was a sobering thought and really rather exciting.

'Oh, Betsy, my dearest dear,' he said again. The sky was huge and white behind her bright hood and a sea mist was rising out of the village to swirl across the field in long grey swathes. It reminded him of those odd clouds in Mr Blake's funny paintings. But it was horribly cold. 'We must go back now,' he said, trying to be sensible. 'But we'll walk out again, won't we?'

She began to recover, managed a smile, rallied and began to flirt. It was easier when you could flirt. 'Well, possibly,' she said. 'I shall have to see.'

Chapter Four

Sunday April 18th 1852

My dearest Annie,
Your most welcome letter arrived late yesterday afternoon, which I have to admit was a relief to me, for I was beginning to worry lest you had been caught in Friday's April shower and had taken cold. You will say that you are a good deal too sensible for such foolishness and your letter proves you right. So I will tell you simply that I am glad of it, and that as my work here goes on apace I shall soon be home with you again and then I can shield you from the showers in person.

I went to church this morning, partly for the sake of my soul and partly to pray for the success of my endeavours but mostly, I must admit, irreligious creature that I am, in the hope of seeing Mr Boniface again. You will be pleased to know that my hope was justified, for he was sitting in the pew immediately opposite to mine and smiled quite kindly in my direction. After the service I took the opportunity of conversing with him. Unfortunately, I learnt no more than I had done on Friday, for he said he could remember very little, 'on account of' he was 'only a boy at the time', not more than nine or ten or thereabouts, and most things went over his head. But as he seemed affable and plainly had a little time to spare, I asked him whether he thought his older brother might not remember rather more. 'I would like to speak to him, if it were possible,' I said. 'I am told he worked for Mr Hayley and would have known Mr Blake, would he not, being that Mr Hayley was his friend and patron. If he is still in the village, perhaps you would be so kind as to introduce me.'

The change in him was so marked, there was no doubt about it at all. In The Fox I could have put it down to a fevered imagination or over-much porter, but out in the churchyard, in bright daylight and sober as the most sober of judges. I could not help but notice it. 'That ent possible,' he said, 'on account of he's been gone these forty-eight years.' Then he turned on his heel and walked away from me.

His abrupt departure left me nonplussed for I could not be sure of his meaning without further questioning, and that was plainly to be denied me. Did he mean that his brother had gone away and is now living somewhere else, or did the poor young man take ill and die? It is most perplexing and more of a mystery than ever. But one thing is certain. This other Boniface was involved in the Blake's affairs in some way or another and his brother does not wish me to know of it. With perseverance I mean to find out what sort of involvement it was and what light

70

it throws on the character of our poet, for I am sure it will prove germane to my biography.

A few minutes later the vicar very kindly introduced me to a grizzled old man who said he'd been a potboy in The Fox in Mr Blake's day and he was more forthcoming and told me that Mr Boniface's brother was called Johnnie and worked as a gardener up at Turret House, and that 'our mad poet' *was a good neighbour and worked* 'uncommon long hours. Used to see the candle in his little window so late at night, you wouldn't believe it. Hard worker, we used to say. Not afraid to put his back into it. Unlike some I could mention. That ol' Mr Hayley never did nothing but ride about the countryside on his great hoss and build that great tower and that great high wall, which aren't fittin' in a village this size. Between you an' me, I never had much time for Mr Hayley, but your ol' Mr Blake was a different kettle a' fish.'

So if I have learnt nothing else, I now know that Blake was respected by the villagers and has a good reputation here. However, if I could discover the whereabouts of Mr Johnnie Boniface, providing he is still alive, I am sure I would learn a great deal more. I will make other enquiries, you may depend upon it, since an unanswered question is an irresistible challenge.

Meantime. I send you my fondest love. Stay well and avoid showers.

Your own Alexander G.

November 1800

It was well into the first week of November before the ballad of 'Little Tom the Sailor' was finished and printed, and by then William and Catherine were heartily sick of it. It had dominated their lives to the exclusion of everything else. His sister was bad-tempered with neglect, they were both exhausted and William hadn't been able to write a single word of his own nor touch a single canvas.

'Never mind,' Catherine commiserated, ''Tis done now and you are free of it. Tomorrow I shall build up the fire and you shall work as you will.'

But there was one more matter to be attended to before he could turn his attention to the poem that was burning his brain. Now that the commission was completed, his sister decided they no longer needed her help and said it was high time she returned to London and the rest of the family. So the next morning the fire remained unlit and the three of them set off to walk the seven miles to Lavant and the London coach.

It was a raw morning and despite the fact that they were wearing their ancient greatcoats and keeping up a very good pace, they were soon pink about the nose and so wrinkled with cold that they looked completely unlike their indoor selves. Winter had changed the landscape too. The ploughed earth was ridged and dark and damp, the trunks of the denuded trees speckled pale green with ancient lichen, the bushes sharp-twigged and rabbit-brown, and the cathedral spire, which had looked such a dazzling white against the blue of the summer sky, was a forbidding grey now that the sky had lost its colour.

'All is perception,' William said when his wife commented upon it. 'What is seen by one man in one place and time is not the same as that seen by another with a different perspective. Vision changes with the seasons and the time of day.'

His sister was unimpressed by such philosophical speculation. She walked doggedly, her mouth covered by her neckerchief. 'How much further is it?' she complained. 'I don't want the coach to leave without me.'

There was no need for her to worry. They were in plenty of time and for once she managed to get a seat inside the coach which pleased her so much that she said goodbye to them as if they were the dearest of relations and had never quarrelled in their lives.

'She means well,' William said as the coach finally rolled away from the inn. 'She has a harsh tongue, I grant you, but she means well.'

Catherine was glad to see the back of her,

but she didn't say so for fear of upsetting him. He could be touchy when it came to any criticism of his relations, as she knew to her cost, except for his brother John, of course, who they both agreed had been the very devil, failing as a baker, going on the run without paying his rates and then enlisting as a soldier the way he had. 'Have we time to find a grocer's shop?' she asked. 'The sugar loaf is down to a few grains and we've barely any tea to speak of.'

So they walked south into Chichester and, once there, explored the town from one end to the other, east to west and north to south and twice round the market cross in the centre, which was extremely old and rather the worse for wear, its stone tracery crumbling and stained, the stone seat that circled its central column worn into hollows by centuries of sitting. Catherine was charmed by the place. The town centre might be marked by a decaying antiquity, the alleys might smell as rank as any in London, but most of the shop fronts were in the latest style and extremely handsome, although the goods they were selling were unlike any she'd seen in London. The ironmonger offered scythes and sheep-shears among the spades, hoes and pails she'd expected; there were bee-hives and hay-rakes, churns and milking stools at the cooper's, and the glover's stocked some very sturdy country wear, huge leather gloves for hedgers, knee-caps for thatchers, country leggings and wooden pattens. But she also found several bakers', a chandler's, three butchers' and as many grocers', and after some debate as to quality and prices, finally bought the things they needed. And in the course of their long per-ambulation, William discovered to his great delight that it was a four-gated city.

'Think of that, my dear,' he said. 'Four roads to quarter the town, four gates to guard the entrances and a wall with four sides. 'Tis my Golgonooza no less. What could be more fitting?'

''Tis a pretty town,' Catherine said, 'even though the price of tea *is* exorbitant. But that's to be expected, I daresay, given the wealth of the citizens. Just look at that one – the one over there riding the chestnut. That waistcoat must have cost a fortune, what with all that embroidery an' all, and he wears it as if it was linsey woolsey. And look at the carriage that's coming. Brand new I'm cer-tain sure, and with two footmen up. There must be some very grand houses here-abouts.'

'We will take some sustenance before we return,' William said. 'There are some very grand hostelries hereabouts too. The bill of fare at this one looks possible. Then we must return home and I must take the ballad sheets to Mr Hayley.'

That worthy gentleman declared himself delighted with them. 'Absolutely delighted,' he said. 'You might not have completed quite within the time I specified – for we did say the beginning of October did we not? – but no matter. The print is excellent and sits well upon the page. Yes, yes, it is quite admirable. Quite, quite admirable. I shall start selling them immediately.'

Blake said he was glad to have been of service and thought how glad he was to get the wretched papers off his hands. Now perhaps he could continue with his own work.

But his patron had other plans for him. 'Now my dear friend,' he said, 'you must begin upon the Poetic Heads. They are the last and final embellishment that my library requires so they must be magnificent in every respect. You are just the man to paint them. I required spaces to be left for eighteen portrait heads as you see.' He waved an imperious hand at the ranks of waiting spaces.

'Milton, of course, and Shakespeare, that goes without saying, Dante, Homer, Chaucer, Dryden, my dear friend Cowper, myself, naturally, and my dear Thomas Alphonso who would most certainly have been among the truly great had he been spared, poor dear talented boy, don't you agree?'

Blake didn't agree with very much of it, but felt obliged to make the sort of vague noises that could be interpreted as acceptance. How was his work to be done if he had to paint eighteen pictures? It would take him months.

'There are sketches of most of these great men in my books,' Mr Hayley went on happily, 'which you shall borrow for your purposes. You can enlarge them into portraits as I require, can you not? Ah, my dear friend, what good fortune this is for you. It is a noble commission and will keep you occupied most handsomely.'

Temper was rising in Blake's chest, making it difficult for him to breathe and to control himself. I must say nothing, he thought. The man means well. He is trying to help me. It is a living. But he ached to write of Jerusalem and the four-gated city, to follow the progress of Eternal Man through the tribulations of the material world, through aspirations and fulfilments, until all the scattered fragments of his eternal nature are reconciled in the final glory of eternity. Having set himself such a monumental task, the thought of spending his time merely copying somebody else's sketches was demoralising.

'He acts like a prince,' he complained to Catherine when he was safely back home and could speak his mind. 'You must needs agree with him whether you will or no.'

'Try not to mind it too much,' Catherine said, kissing him. ''Twill pay the rent and keep us in vittles. That is how we must think of it, my dear. I will help you all I can.'

But even with her help, it was well into November before he had completed the first two portraits – one of Shakespeare, surrounded by the ghostly figures of his imagination and the other of Milton wearing a wreath of oak leaves – and there were sixteen more to go.

Winter and work progressed inexorably and often miserably. The cottage was damp and grew damper as the winds blew the sea mists straight across the fields and under their door. The chimneys smoked, the fires wouldn't take, and when it rained, as it often did, the thatch dripped dirty water on them whenever they went out to the well or to empty their chamber pots in the privy. They both had fevers, with coughs and rheums and miserably aching limbs, and, although William recovered after a week or two, Catherine grew worse and worse until her knees were so sore and swollen it was painful for her to walk. And the visions spoke with terrible regularity, rising from the shining pebbles of the beach to tower above the cottage, stern-faced and angry against the grey skies and the driven smoke of the chimneys.

'I am rebuked because I do not work upon the task they have set me,' Blake mourned, agonised by what he saw and heard, 'because I neglect the task to which I am called, because I have left the story of Eternal Man, of Albion and Jerusalem, to labour like a hired hand.' It was not a happy time.

''Twill be better come the spring,' Catherine tried to encourage. But the spring was far away. As he started upon the next portrait, which was the picture of Thomas Alphonso, it was so bleak and cold he declared he was fast giving up hope of ever being warmed by the sun again. And to make matters worse, that picture was more difficult than all the others put together.

Mr Hayley was impossible to please. The shape of the boy's head was wrong, it would be better if he were depicted in profile, his nose was too long, his eyes were the wrong colour and lacked life. 'You are inaccurate,' he cried, when William presented his third attempt. 'You have not caught the spirit of my darling boy. You detract from the grace of his character. It is imperative that you present a true likeness, that you show his soulfulness, his nobility, his intelligence. It must be done again.'

It was done again, and again, and again until William was crushed under the weight of so much criticism and disapproval. He wanted to please his patron because, however trying he might be, he had been extremely generous, but the longer this work went on the more impossible it became to do it.

'There's not a single line in the entire portrait that he will accept,' he said to Catherine wearily. 'I shall still be working on it come the summer.'

'Paint one of the other portraits,' Catherine advised. 'Dryden perhaps. Or Cowper. And present them together. Perhaps you have concentrated too long upon one subject.'

So Dryden was copied from the frontispiece of Mr Hayley's collection of his poems and the two canvases were carried up to Turret House and set up for inspection side by side. The stratagem worked. Mr Hayley was delighted with the head of Dryden and pronounced it 'quite capital' and the head of Thomas Alphonso, whilst not entirely accurate, was 'prettily done' and would 'pass muster'. And the next day when the Blakes went out to buy fresh meat and take the air, there was actually enough winter sunshine to warm their faces.

'There you are, you see,' Catherine encouraged. 'There are some good days, even in December.'

'But not enough of them,' her husband growled.

That was Johnnie Boniface's opinion too, for he was in an agony of frustration that was every bit as acute and painful as that of his poetic neighbour. After that first wondrous Sunday when he and Betsy had walked into the fields and exchanged their first gentle kiss, he'd lived in a fever of impatience until the next Sabbath and the chance to kiss her again. But despite deliberate patience and extraordinary self-control, he was disappointed.

For a start the service was much too long, and then, when it was finally over, they walked out of the church into a stinging torrent of rain. Still hopeful, he suggested they might take a stroll, but Betsy laughed at him and told him it was 'out of the question' and to have some sense, which, as the rain was buffeting against them as if it meant to push them off their feet and everyone in the congregation was scurrying off home as fast as their legs would carry them, he was forced to do. And then, of course, once they were back at the house, they were caught up in the preparations for dinner and kept apart by hot soup and roast beef and a ridiculous assortment of vegetables.

'If it clears this evening...' he hoped, as they passed one another on the way to the dining room, he bearing used dishes back to the kitchen, she carrying in the pudding.

But all he got was a scolding. 'Johnnie!

Johnnie! How can you be so foolish?' she said. 'Look at it, for pity's sake. 'Tis a-comin' down cats and dogs. 'Twill be raining all day. An' all night too I shouldn't wonder. There'll be no walking for any of us, not while this holds. We shall all have to bide indoors an' put up with it.'

He was in a state of such painful desire that it was all he could do to walk straight and his yearning wasn't satisfied by so much as a single kiss, or even the chance to stand and talk to her, for the rain continued all day, just as she'd forecast, and, as Mr Hayley would insist on going for his usual ride despite the weather and consequently came home mud-smothered to the thigh, by evening there was so much work to do cleaning the floors he'd trampled on and polishing his filthy boots and brushing his rain-soaked clothes and grooming his mud-spattered horse, that the entire household was kept at it until long past their usual bedtime and he didn't even get the chance to wish her goodnight.

'Maybe we could go for a bit of a walk this evening,' he hoped, when they met at breakfast the next morning. But he was laughed to scorn again. That night there were stockings to be mended and skirts to be patched and all three housemaids spent the evening sewing in Mrs Beke's parlour. The best entertainment he could manage for himself was to go mooching off through the mud to The Fox, where he was doleful company.

He became more and more doleful as the weeks progressed, for no matter how carefully he broached the subject, there never seemed to be a moment when a walk was possible. At first her answers seemed sensible. There wasn't enough time, it was too cold, or too wet, there was too much work to be done. But when the third Sunday had come and gone without so much as the hope of a hand to hold, he began to feel she was deliberately putting him off, almost as if she didn't want to walk out with him. That couldn't be true, could it? She'd allowed him to kiss her and she must know what that meant. The weather *was* bad. He couldn't deny it. It *was* too wet. But there wasn't too much work. In fact, there was hardly anything to do in the garden at all, once the beds were cleared, and all the indoor jobs were boring and repetitive – coal to carry, fires to tend, candle ends to scour from the sconces of a morning, errands to run, tables to clear – and none of them took very long. So he was left with plenty of time to think, and the longer he thought, the more troublesome his thoughts became. He mooched about the house, weak with longing for her, aching to kiss her. And oh he *did* so want to, constantly, every time he saw her, every time he thought of her, and in every single night of his dreams. His shirt was soon so sticky with love spillings, he was afraid Mrs Beke would comment on it when it turned up in the laundry, and took a cloth to try and wash the worst away. But there was nowhere to dry the offending garment when he finished with it – or at least nowhere where it wouldn't be seen – so he had to wear it wet and that gave him a cold and made him feel more miserable than ever.

Harvest Home came and went without the invitation he wanted, the winter set in with more and more rain, and on top of everything else, Mr Blake kept bringing up his wretched portrait heads and they were the very devil, nasty heavy awkward things, for they had to be hauled up the stairs to the library, a step at a time, and then either hung according to Mr Hayley's exacting instructions or, worse, manhandled down the stairs again to be redrawn.

'I hates the winter,' he said, as he and Bob, the boot boy, walked down to The Fox. It was miserably cold and the wind was moaning in Mr Blake's elm tree and scattering the rooks from Dr Jackson's garden. They fell and tumbled in the darkening air, cawing like handsaws.

'Be better after a pint,' Bob said. 'Porter puts a different complexion on things.' He'd just turned seventeen and considered himself an expert on matters alcoholic.

The inn was certainly an improvement on the servants' hall at Turret House: warm, companionable, booming with easy laughter, smelling of pulled porter and smoked tobacco, of horseflesh and pig sties and a hard day's sweat. The candle flames glowed like welcoming beacons, the warmth of the coal fire could be felt at the door, the scattered sawdust was soft underfoot. If it hadn't been for his constant frustration Johnnie could have enjoyed it a lot.

'Evenin' young shavers,' Reuben called from his seat in the chimney corner. 'We thought you weren't comin'. Oi jist been sayin' to your father, "Where's that young shaver a' yours?" Oi said, didden Oi Hiram?'

'We're late on account of we 'ad work to finish,' Bob told him. 'Work?' Reuben mocked. 'You don't know the meanin' a' the word, you young fellers. What work was that then?'

'Hangin' pictures,' Johnnie told him, 'an' don't go sayin' tha's not work 'cause we knows otherwise. We had two to put up this afternoon an' they weigh a ton, the both of 'em. It took me an' Bob here *and* Mr Hosier to get the last one up an' our arms was fair broke in half. If that aren't work I'd like to know what is.'

'He's still paintin' then,' Reuben said, 'that

ol' engraver feller. Oi thought he'd be over for a pint or two, now an' then. Tha's warm work that ol' paintin'. That Oi *do* know. Oi remember when we 'ad to whitewash the barn. You'd think he'd a' worked up a thirst by now.'

'I don't think he got time for a thirst,' Johnnie told him. 'On account of Mr Hayley's got his nose pinned to the grindstone. He's got all our noses pinned to the grindstone, come to that. Do this! Do that! Oh, I hates the winter.'

''Tis a bad ol' season but it passes,' his father said. 'Oi thought you was a-goin' to tell us 'ow the world wags. Aren't this the day ol' Mr Hayley go to Lavant to see Miss Poole an' pick up his letters and his newspaper?'

Johnnie agreed that it was.

'Well, then, what's the news? Or 'aven't you read it yet?'

News had little interest for his son, now that his senses were alert to other matters, though he admitted that he *had* taken a glance at the paper while he was in the library. 'Nothin' much so far as I can see,' he said. 'Bonaparte's in Egypt so they say.'

'Long may he stay there,' Reuben said, chewing his teeth. 'He can kill as many Gypsy-ans as he like, say Oi, jist so long as he leave *us* be. They're onny savages when all's said an' done, an' don't know no better. Anyways we don't want him hereabouts.'

'Amen to that,' Hiram said. 'But that aren't all the news surely.'

'I heard something this morning might interest,' Mr Grinder told them, and when they looked enquiringly at him, went on, 'We're to have a census.'

'An' what sort a' hanimal's that when it's at home?' Reuben asked.

''Tis a head-count,' Mr Grinder told him, polishing a row of beer mugs. 'They mean for to count all the people in the country, town by town and village by village.'

'Tha's a dang fool idea if ever Oi heard a' one,' Reuben scowled. 'We knows how many of us there is. You onny got to look round the village to see that.'

'Ah!' Mr Grinder said, 'but they wants to know what sort a' people we are, how many men could be took for the army, or press-ganged or some such, how many women and children would have to be took out the way if ol' Bonaparte was to invade – which he could do any day so they say – how many carts an' horses we got, how much grain we store.'

'Which is nobody's business but our own,' the miller said trenchantly.

'Not if it's to be took to feed the army,' Mr Grinder told him. 'They mean to build forts and beacons all along the coast, so they say, like they done when the Armada was coming, and there'll be troops stationed in every town, all a' which'll need feeding an' housing, not to mention stabling an' fodder for their horses, an' barracks an' cookhouses an' all sorts.

The candles guttered as his listeners stirred uneasily in their seats, the coal shifted in the grate and began to hiss and spit, the wind rattled the window. And somewhere in the distance they could hear a dog howling.

'Oi don't believe a word of it,' Reuben said stoutly. 'They'll be sunk mid-channel, that's what. Nelson'll see to that, you mark moi words. Sunk an' drowned dead, every last one on 'em.'

But the census was taken despite his disbelief and highly uncomfortable it was, for no fewer than four men arrived to gather information and, in the villagers' opinion, they wanted an inordinate amount of it – how many people lived in each house, how old they were, where they were born, what occupations they followed, how many of them would be available to join the local militia. There was no end to it. The complaints in The Fox were long and loud. 'Danged nuisances, every man jack of 'em, pokin' their long noses in where they aren't wanted.'

'An' all fer what?' Reuben said. 'Tha's what Oi should loike to know. Oi don't see no sense in countin' folk. Never did, never will. Oh, 'twill all be writ down. I grant 'ee that. They been scribblin' away at it ever since they come here. But what then? 'Twill all be hid away in some ol' cupboard somewhere, tha's what then, an' no one'll ever see sight nor sound of it again.'

Chapter Five

The Fox, Monday April 19th

My dear Annie,
I have spent the day poring over the census returns in Chichester, which is the nearest market town to this village and the place where all local records are kept, but all to no purpose I fear. I had hoped to find some mention of the mysterious Johnnie Boniface, but despite painstaking endeavour, I am no wiser now than I was at the beginning of the day.

The census of 1801 was no help to me, for it merely detailed the number of dwellings in the village (74 in all, so you see what a small place it was – it is twice the size now) and counted the number of inhabitants. There were 129 men and boys 'capable of active service', 8 men over sixty, 83 women and girls over seven years old 'capable of evacuating themselves' (which shows how real the danger of invasion must have been) and 81 incapable, including those with 'child at breast' who would presumably have needed some kind of transport to carry them to safety. There were 97 people described as being employed in agriculture and 41 in trade but none of them were named, so I found no record of the mysterious Johnnie and none of William and Catherine Blake either. Was he numbered among the 41 in trade I wonder? From what I have read in Mr Butts' letters, I believe he considered himself an artisan as well as an artist.

The census of 1811 was an improvement, since it gave names and addresses as they do today, but by then the Blakes had left and my quarry was gone too. I found plenty of Bonifaces, some described as fishermen, others as farm labourers, among them my farmer Harry, so they are obviously quite a large family hereabouts, and two were called John but neither were the right age. It is rather a disappointment.

However I met a clerk in the office who told me that he thought records of local events would have been kept by the local newspaper, and he thought I might find something about Mr Blake there, particularly if he had been sent to trial for sedition, which is what I believe to be the case. He very kindly gave me the address of their present offices and the name of a reporter whom I could contact, so the search will continue.

Your letter was awaiting me when I got back to The Fox and has encouraged me marvellously. I shall do as you suggest and send my notes to you for safekeeping. This is an important work that

*we are undertaking, my dearest, for William
Blake was one of our great artists and has been
ignored for far too long. I am blessed to have
your assistance in my endeavours.*

*This at midnight and somewhat wearily, from
your loving husband,*
   Alexander.

January 1801

That January the winter set in with a venge-
ance. The sea was the colour of swords and
rolled inexorably in to shore in long pon-
derous waves, while above it the sky was
ominously white, leeched of all colour by
impending snow. And what a snowfall it was,
goose-feathering the village for days on end,
and lying thick and heavy over fields and
gardens, blotching Betsy's bright cloak with
patches of icy dampness, freezing the breath
in Johnnie's lungs and the last remaining
hope in his heart. There was no chance of
walking out now, he thought miserably. It
was all very depressing.

But on that first snow-muffled Sunday
when the roofs were white-thatched and the
overnight fall had frosted so that it crunched
under his feet, he had a surprise. He'd set off
for church feeling thoroughly miserable.
There was no point in suggesting they might
walk to the barn, not that day, in that

91

weather. If a little light rain had been enough to deter his pretty Betsy, snowfall would be an impossible barrier. So when they emerged from the comparative warmth of the church into the chill of the air beyond the porch, he merely nodded at her, hunched his shoulders against the cold and prepared for the short trudge back to the house. But instead of nodding back as he expected and then giggling off with the others, she put a hand on his arm to detain him. Actually put a hand on his arm.

'We could walk up to the barn if you'd like,' she said. ''Tis dry enough.'

He was so surprised his jaw dropped. 'What, you and me?' he said. 'You mean, walk out like?' What an amazing girl she was! After all these months saying, no, no, no, all the time, and on the one day when he hadn't asked her, there she stood, actually asking *him*. Then he realised what a fool he must look, standing there gawping, and he closed his mouth and recovered himself enough to tease her. 'What's brought this about?'

That was a question she couldn't answer, at least not without revealing something rather shameful. The truth was, saying no to him had become a game. On that first Sunday she'd refused him because she'd been cold and tired and not in the mood for traipsing into the fields in the pouring rain, but, when she saw how put down he was, she'd had such a sudden and delightful sense of power that she couldn't resist a repeat performance the next time he asked. She was the prettiest girl in the village and she could reduce a young man to stammering simply by saying no. It was irresistible. True, as the weeks passed and he became more and more miserable, the game grew less and less attractive, but by then she'd established a pattern and, besides, he asked as if he expected rejection, so he only had himself to blame. She told herself he should stand up for himself and go in for a bit of argyfying. That's what *she'd* do if she was in his shoes. But her reasoning was unkind and in the privacy of her thoughts she knew it, and eventually she began to feel ashamed of the way she was treating him. At Christmas, when the hymns and carols were all being sung of goodwill and loving kindness, she made a bargain with herself. If he asked, she would go on saying no, that was only to be expected, but if he didn't ask, she would offer. It was perverse and she knew it but as it didn't seem likely that he would ever *not* ask, she wasn't unduly worried by it. And now this morning, just when she wasn't expecting it, he hadn't asked and he'd walked away from the church looking so cold and downcast that her heart was squeezed with pity for him. Not that she could admit it. Nor answer his teasing question. She'd made her bargain and she'd kept to it. Now there was nothing for it but to take refuge in flirting. 'Thought you might like to,' she said, flashing her blue eyes at him. 'Howsomever, if you've lost interest...'

'No, no,' he said, eagerly. 'I'd love to. 'Tis just...' And then, feeling that words would only fail him if he tried to explain, he offered her his arm.

They walked briskly, for it was much too cold to dawdle, and reached the barn before she could think how to respond if he asked for a kiss. But by then he was too breathless with hope and desire to ask for anything. It was the first time they'd been alone together since September and he wasn't going to spoil the moment by talking. He simply scooped her into his arms and kissed her, without a word and with such passion that they were both stunned by the sensations he roused.

She stood in his arms, round-eyed and wondering. 'Why Johnnie!' she said.

He had to answer the question on her face whether he would or no. 'I love 'ee, Betsy,' he said. 'I've loved 'ee from the first day I clapped eyes on 'ee.'

She was touched and humbled. 'Oh Johnnie,' she said again. And as her expression was so soft and welcoming, he dared to kiss her again. And again. And again.

They walked back to the house in a daze

of arousal with their arms round each other, their lips ruddy with kissing. 'We'll walk out again tonight,' he said. It wasn't a question. He was sure of himself now. He'd spoken and been accepted. They would walk out whenever they could.

That night was impossible because Mr Hayley had one of his dinners and kept his entire household on the run until well after midnight, but the next evening they stole away as soon as the servants' supper was over, put on all the clothes they possessed so as to keep warm, and walked down Limmer Lane in the moonlight, bundled and happy until they reached the shore. It was very peaceful away from the village and very dark, with the beach shrouded in snow and a full moon dropping a pathway of shimmering white scales across a sea so black that they couldn't see the horizon.

Betsy shivered. 'D'you think them ol' Frenchies'll invade us?' she asked, 'like everyone says?'

'I couldn't tell you,' he admitted. 'There's no knowin', is there.'

'My Pa thinks they will. He don't say nothing but he's got a cart all a-ready for me an' Ma to run away in.'

He held her close, all bundled up in her nice warm cloak and her two day-gowns and her three thick petticoats. 'I shall love you for ever,' he said. 'No matter what happens, if Boney invades, or the sea freezes over, or the moon falls out the sky, no matter what.'

'Idiot!' she said. But it was sweet to hear such things. 'Why would the moon go an' fall out the sky? Aren't it fixed up there?'

He remembered a nursery rhyme. *'The man in the moon came down too soon and asked his way to Norwich.'*

'Tha's poetry,' she said. 'That don't mean nothin'. Not poetry. You can't count that.'

'You'd better not say such things back at the house,' he teased, 'or you'll have Mr Hayley after you for blasphemy. He says poetry's the highest form of human endeavour.'

'Tha's on account of he's always writing the stuff,' she said sensibly. 'Why are we talking about Mr Hayley when we could be kissing? I'm gettin' cold just standin' here.'

So naturally she had to be kissed warm again.

In the next few weeks the snow gave them plenty of reasons to kiss one another warm but achingly few opportunities, for the cold weather increased the amount of housework that had to be done. Meals had to be served piping hot, fires stoked high, slush-smeared floors scrubbed clean, and such washing as could be done had to be dried in the scullery, which was a damp and inconvenient business. All of which meant less time for walking out, even after church. But they endured it patiently, telling one another the cold snap couldn't last for ever.

In February the snow finally thawed, but only because it was blown away by gales and piercing rain. The moon didn't fall but Nature seemed determined to keep them apart with too few chances and too much clothing. Johnnie ached to hold her in his arms without the layers of wool and heavy cotton that now lay squashed and pungent between them. He yearned to kiss her neck and stroke her pretty arms and fondle her remembered titties but there wasn't even the faintest chance of such delights with all that cloth in the way. He yearned for the spring, but what was the good of yearning? Nothing ever came of that. He would just have to bide his time, kiss when he could, dream of better things and be patient. But when you're nineteen and lusty, patience is impossible.

February kept his senses in a perpetual roar, cold though it was, March brought agonies of temptation, until one joyful Sunday, on a day of strong winds and bold blue skies, they spent nearly an hour in the shelter of the barn, and after kissing her until he was aching with frustrated desire, he persuaded her to allow him to put his hands under the warmth of her cloak 'on account of they're turnin' blue. Look at 'em.' For a well-behaved and warming interval they stood with his cold hands at her back, stroking and caressing, while he kissed her neck, which was a delight to them both and lifted him into such straining excitement that his member was as taut as a bowstring and it was a wonder it didn't spill into his breeches. But then, warmed and too strongly tempted to resist, he moved one tentative hand until it was cupping her breast, her lovely warm welcoming breast, and as she didn't scold, he began to fondle.

She sprang back from him as if she'd been stung, pushed his hands away and wrapped her cloak around her, pulling it tight for protection. 'No,' she said. 'No, Johnnie. You mustn't.'

He was baffled. 'Why not?' he said. 'We aren't doin' nothin' wrong.'

She stood before him, shielded by her cloak, her face flushed but stubborn. 'We are.'

'Who says?'

'The Reverend Church for a start.'

'He's the vicar,' Johnnie said, dismissing him with a sniff. 'He would. That's what vicars are for, to tell you off an' say you're sinners an' everything. You don't want to pay him no mind. Anyway, 'tis none of his business. Tha's just atween you an' me. Private like.'

He was persuasive but she was still worried. 'I shall get a reputation,' she said.

She knew very well what happened to girls who got a reputation. They were outcasts. They couldn't get work and people talked about them and said they were no better than they should be and they'd come to a bad end. 'Is that what you want?'

'No, you won't,' he said, lovingly, 'on account of I won't tell no one. I'd never do nothin' to hurt you, you know that. I won't tell a living soul.'

That was reasonable and what she'd half-expected him to say, but she was still bristling. 'No,' she said, 'you won't, on account of we won't do it.'

That made him smile. 'What never? How about when we're married?'

'It's different when you're married.'

'No,' he said, trying to convert her with argument, ''tis the same thing, married or single. There's no difference.'

'When you're married you're allowed.'

He'd opened his mouth ready to argue on, but she was walking away from him. 'Time we was gettin' back,' she said. The set of her shoulders was all straight-boned determination. There was no more to be said. At least for the moment.

But they had bitten the apple and now they would be tempted every time they were alone together. At first he merely stroked her lovely straight back, since that seemed to be permissible, but on the next occasion, when the wind blew cold and he was allowed to put his hands inside her nice warm cloak, he ventured to stroke her shoulders and her nice rounded arms, and the following Sunday, in a moment drowsed with desire and saturated with pleasure, he gentled his hands towards her breasts and was allowed to fondle them. This time she didn't push him away or make any protest. She hardly said a word, could barely keep her eyes open, she was so caught up in sensation. It was too sweet, too wondrous, too exciting to be a sin. The Reverend Church was wrong.

So their lovemaking continued and grew steadily bolder and was a joy to them both. They were careful not to touch one another when there was anyone around to see them and were pleased to think they were being so discreet. And the villagers told one another that young Boniface was sweet on Betsy Haynes and nodded with approval when they saw them walking out together.

Chapter Six

Felpham April 20th

My dearest Annie,

Your letter arrived this morning and made welcome reading. It is a great relief to me to know that my notes are being stored in such good order, particularly as I have no way of predicting which of them will prove to be significant when I come to write this biography. You are entirely right, my dearest, the only sensible way to deal with all the material I am gathering is to keep everything in a place where it is readily to hand.

I have spent the morning being entertained – and that truly is the word I must use for it – by a garrulous old woman who admits to being the village gossip and says she once worked as a housemaid in Turret House in Mr Hayley's time. Her name was Susie Howe in those days, but now she is Mrs Farndell and was very proud to tell me so, for the Farndells are bakers hereabouts and held in high esteem, having been the very first to follow that trade in the village.

She talked at great length about all manner of things and had a fund of stories to tell, most of them, I fear, apocryphal, but I wrote them all down and you will find them enclosed for what they are worth. My favourite is her assertion that Mr Hayley had two wives and kept one of them chained by the leg to a tree in a wood near his house in Eartham. She kept saying 'He was a poet you see, Mr Gilchrist sir, so you have to make allowances. They aren't the same as us ordin'ry folk. 'Tis on account of bein' poetical you see.'

I pressed her to tell me what a poetical person was like, for I couldn't resist the chance to tease, but she took my request perfectly seriously and said 'they look poetical, sort of noble and dreamy-looking' *and volunteered that Mr Hayley often sat in his library in his dressing gown until gone midday,* 'thinking up his poems. I daresay.' *I asked her whether Mr Blake was poetical too but she said 'not in the least' and declared that he was* 'a very ordin'ry man, funny looking, same as everyone else in the village' *although she had the grace to add that he was a* 'hard worker. I'll give him that.' *It is remarkable that all those who remember him here speak of him as a hard worker.*

Having hit upon the topic I most desired to pursue. I pressed her to tell me what else she could remember about him and she thought for a second or so and offered that he had a terrible temper. 'Many's the time I seen him storm out the house with a face like thunder.' *I questioned again to see if she knew the reason for it, but she simply said he and Mr Hayley didn't always get on, so I asked her whether she thought*

*it might have been poetic rivalry, which made
her laugh out loud.* 'No,' she said. 'How could
there be rivalry atween 'em? Mr Hayley was
a celebrated poet know'd for it all the way to
London, and your Mr Blake was just a
journeyman. They wasn't equals.' *As we were
talking so easily I asked her if she knew that Mr
Blake wrote poetry too and she surprised me by
saying that she'd heard of it.* 'That don't make
him poetical though,' *she said,* 'do it. Not
with a face like thunder.' *You see what pre-
judice there is against our William.*

*However she was far more sensibly forth-
coming when I asked her about the mysterious
Johnnie Boniface and talked about him for
nearly half an hour, waxing quite lyrical about
how handsome he was (tall and fair apparently
and 'strong-looking' with the finest grey eyes you
ever saw). If you had been here to hear her, my
darling. you would have suspected a romance
but apparently he was a one-woman man and
only had eyes for another one of the maids, who
was called Betsy. Naturally I asked her if Betsy
still lived in the village but she said she'd gone
away long since and she had no idea where she
was.* 'People comes and goes,' *she said, and
then (I am not making this up, my dear, it truly
happened) she closed her mouth and her face, as
if some inner voice was warning her not to tell
any more, and refused to say another word. It is
such a pity, for I had begun to hope that she
might tell me the present whereabouts of the*

handsome Mr Boniface. I cannot bring myself to believe that he is dead although I must accept the fact that it is a possibility. But whether he is or no, one thing is certain. This odd behaviour is one more reason to believe that I have stumbled upon a mystery that keeps mouths shut all over the village.

Meantime there is the newspaper office to visit, where I hope to learn more about the trial and I have arranged to call in at Turret House tomorrow morning, so there is much to keep me occupied.

Write back to me soon and tell me what you think of Mrs Farndell's outpourings, for, if nothing else, I know you will be amused by them and I value your opinions.

I am your most loving husband. AG.

Spring 1801

The poetical Mr Hayley was inspecting his garden, his long face turned towards the vegetable plot, his elegant head full of plans for his good friend and secretary, Mr Blake, now that the portraits were progressing so well.

'I shall find other commissions for you when the heads are completed,' he said. 'You will not be idle, I promise you. Not for a second. Have no doubt about that. And first you must come with me to Lavant and meet

Miss Poole. That is imperative.' The long rows of beans and peas were already in place, the fresh cabbages set. 'There are plenty of onions, I trust, Mr Hosier,' he said, pausing to address his gardener. 'Young Boniface working well? Good. Good.'

William waited until his patron was ready to continue his tour. He knew that further commissions were unavoidable if he was to earn a living here, but he had hoped they would take time to arrange. Even though he'd sat up late into the night and worked by candlelight, very little of his poem had been written. As they resumed their inspection he smothered a sigh. This man might walk with a limp but he rushed at everything he did like a bull at a gate. 'I would be honoured to visit your friend,' he said diplomatically. 'When would you wish it to be?'

'Why Tuesdays and Fridays of course,' Mr Hayley told him. 'I breakfast with the lady on Tuesdays and Fridays. You will find her the most agreeable company. The most agreeable. I have no hesitation in saying that of all the ladies who live in this county, she is the wisest and most agreeable.' They had followed the path to the extreme end of the vegetable garden. 'I am glad that is settled,' he said. 'I shall expect you at six o' the clock tomorrow morning and we will ride over together. You shall have Bruno. He was Thomas's pony and you couldn't want for a better ride.'

William didn't complain until he was back in the cottage with Catherine. But then he opened his mind at long and bitter length. 'How am I to work when he crowds my life with visits and commissions? Is it not enough that I toil in his library and slave over his portraits every hour of the day? Am I now to be required to breakfast with him, too? His demands are endless, Catherine. He acts as though he were an emperor, and I his slave. Now I am to ride horseback through the village and be made mock of, for I never rode a horse in my life and will fair badly at it. I tell you truly, I wish we had never come to this place.'

Just as he'd predicted, he found that first ride to Lavant very difficult and very uncomfortable, even though the pony was the gentlest animal alive. It stood still and patient while he struggled to mount, which he did with stomach-fluttering anxiety, feeling envious of his patron, who swung astride with irritating ease, despite his limp and the fact that he had a large black umbrella hanging over his left arm. They set off cheerfully and Blake was relieved to find that the pony plodded amiably along the bridle paths without need of a prodding heel or the slightest tug of the reins. Even so, he was ill at ease, aware of his lack of horsemanship and afraid that he would be mocked for it. To make matters worse, the dawn was only just beginning so it was cold out there in the fields, and the emanations that rose from the sleeping earth were dark and disquieting and writhed like serpents. He was glad when the sky developed streaks of pink and orange cloud and watched with relief as they lengthened and brightened until the sun finally blazed above the distant downs. He remembered the vision of angels he had once seen clustered about the risen sun and was heartened by the memory.

'We make good time,' Mr Hayley said to encourage him. 'Another half an hour and we shall see the house.'

And suddenly as they rode over the brow of a low hill, there it was, a large square red brick building with stabling to the north of it and well-tended gardens all around it, a rich, imposing, classical house, as fine as anything that Blake had ever seen. It was no distance from the inn where the London stage changed horses and he and Catherine had said goodbye to his sister. He'd noticed it then, but hadn't imagined he would ever be visiting the place.

They rode their horses up to the front door like princes, dismounted by means of a mounting block, for which Blake was heartily thankful, and handed them over to a groom, who doffed his cap and called them both 'Sir'. Then Mr Hayley gave the iron bell-pull a tug and a footman in full livery and with a white wig, no less, opened the door and admitted them into the wonders of the house. They were led up a curving stairway and ushered in to an elegant reception room where they stood, Blake awkward and Hayley beaming, as the lady of the house rose from her seat in the wide bay window and walked forward to greet them.

She moved with the total ease of one born to money and position, her propriety and grace as natural as breathing. She looked intelligent and was plainly kind, completely at ease and beautifully dressed, her brown hair unpowdered, curled above her forehead and caught up in an elegant Grecian bun above the nape of her neck, her hands long, white and unsullied by anything as unseemly as housework. Her day-gown, which was in pink silk and the very latest fashion, whispered as she walked across the room, the air that wafted before her was full of the scent of flowers. She had pink satin slippers on her feet and a kerchief of fine blonde lace about her neck. She emanated golden hospitality, a lady to her elegant fingertips, which Mr Hayley bent to kiss.

'My dear William,' she said to him, 'How very good to see you. And you have brought your friend, I see. How delightful!'

Blake was introduced, the footman ushered

them into chairs at the round table that filled the space of the bay window, the teapot was laid reverently before her, a dish of milky coffee was provided for Mr Hayley since that was his preference, covered dishes were carried in, emitting succulent steam, and their meal began.

At first Blake sat quietly eating bacon and eggs, sampling the three kinds of bread provided and listening to his patron as he described the 'immeasurable improvements' he had made to his library. 'Ten of my eighteen portrait heads are completed. Mr Blake has done the most excellent work. The library is transformed. Quite, quite transformed. It looks exceptionally fine. You must visit me, dear lady, when 'tis all done, and see it for yourself.'

She turned to smile at her silent guest. 'Are you pleased with your work, Mr Blake?' she asked,

''Tis not everything I would wish, ma'am,' Blake said diplomatically. It was easy to be diplomatic in the company of such a lady. 'But I believe I have executed the commission to the best of my ability.'

'There speaks a true artist,' she said.

The talk and the meal continued gently. The used dishes were discreetly removed by two footmen in white gloves. A dish of fruit was quietly provided. Mr Hayley, declining any further sustenance, offered to read his latest work, and took up his pose by the window ready to declaim. He made a fine figure, with the sunlight snow-dazzling on his grey hair, his maroon coat princely, his stock immaculately white and well folded, and the rolling countryside spreading behind him like a backdrop to his eloquence. 'Epitaph to a departed friend,' he boomed.

Blake listened with apparent politeness but now that he'd satisfied his appetite, his mind was busy taking in the detail of his surroundings – the silver teapot and patterned china, the expensive curtains, thick carpet, duck-egg blue walls with their large oil paintings, the row of chairs set neatly against the skirting boards, the high ceiling with its elaborately carved coving, even the number of new wax candles set about the room, ready to be lit that evening. It was, as he saw through all his senses, a well-ordered, comfortable home where this lady lived lapped in every luxury, and although he envied her good fortune, he acknowledged that it was probably deserved for she was gentle and kindly. It was a new experience to find himself admiring someone in the ruling class, for his usual angry view was that the riches of the great had been gathered at the expense of a half-starved workforce. But this woman was almost making him reconsider his views.

The talk turned easily from Mr Hayley's poetry and the trivia of domesticity to national and political events. 'I hear they have plans afoot for much building hereabouts,' the lady said, 'There are to be towers raised all along the coast to warn us of any approaching fleet and an army barracks outside the north gate in Chichester, not very far from here. The duke was telling me only the other evening. There are renewed fears that the French may invade.'

The emanations were sudden, dark and full of foreboding. They rose like black fire clouds, acrid and thickening, pierced by scarlet flames, bringing the sight and smell of blood, the screams of battle, twisted agony, unnatural death. The very light in the room was darkened by oncoming horror.

Mr Hayley spoke at once to reassure them all. 'Fear not, dear lady,' he said. 'I cannot imagine we shall ever see fighting upon British soil, not while we have Nelson and the Channel to protect us.'

''Tis thought likely this time, notwithstanding,' Miss Poole told him, 'and we should take cognisance of opinion.' She smiled at him and began to tease. 'You are like to have soldiers billeting upon you in Felpham, so I am told, or to lose your servants to the militia.'

'Arrant nonsense,' Mr Hayley said, stoutly. 'I defy any man to deprive me of my household and there's an end to it. If any come asking I shall send 'em packing.'

'I have always held it unwise to argue with any man who has a pistol in his hand,' the lady teased, 'I have seen how brutal soldiers can be, on many occasions, when they have been called to restore order to the streets of London, and highly unpleasant it was. You must have seen something of it too, Mr Blake, for you lived in Lambeth I believe before you moved to healthier climes.'

Blake admitted that she was right in both matters, having once seen a soldier shoot an apprentice boy through the head, but that was hardly a fit subject for a lady's breakfast table. 'I saw the Gordon riots when I was bound apprentice to Mr Basire,' he told her. 'The rioters ran down Long Acre as I was walking to his shop in Great Queen Street. I was caught up in the rush and swept on to the very gates of Newgate.'

'So you saw the riot itself,' Miss Poole said, looking at him with increased interest. 'Not a thing you would easily forget, I'll be bound.'

He was remembering it as she spoke, the dark hands swinging sledgehammers and pickaxes at the great barred gate, as flames leapt into the sky; roaring like beasts, the prisoners screaming in fear of being burnt alive, and crawling blackened and terrified through the broken gate, iron fetters still fastened to their ankles.

'I kept within doors on that occasion,'

Miss Poole said, 'discretion being the better part of valour, and I have endeavoured to be out of harm's way on every subsequent outbreak.'

Remembered terror still shook her guest, followed by remembered anger and then, close upon it, his familiar nervous fear, lest he lose control and say things to annoy or enrage.

'They were sorry times,' Mr Hayley observed, 'and no good has come of them. Which is all the more reason to oppose such folly now and refuse all talk of invasion and suchlike idiocies. 'Twas all talk of invasion the year before last and nothing came of it. 'Twill prove the same this year.'

'Well, well, you may be right,' Miss Poole said soothingly. 'We must await events. It may not come to it, as you say, but 'tis as well to be prepared and preparations are undoubtedly in hand.' She gave Mr Hayley the full bewitchment of her smile. 'Such a sombre conversation to conclude your visit, my dear William! I trust 'twill not prevent you both from taking breakfast with me on Friday.'

They were happy to give their word to the appointment, Mr Hayley because he saw he was forgiven for a possible transgression of good manners in having spoken too harshly in front of her, Mr Blake because he had contrived not to speak at all and was delighted to be considered even a lesser member of her circle.

'I am so pleased to have made your acquaintance, Mr Blake,' she said, when he bowed his farewell to her. 'I saw your engravings to "Little Tom the Sailor" and thought them very fine. Now I shall see your watercolours when I visit with Mr Hayley. You are a man of many talents. Do you paint in oils, too?'

He admitted that he did not, but offered, feeling rather daring, that he did write poetry.

'But how splendid,' she said. 'You must bring some of it with you the next time you come to breakfast and let me see it.'

His elation carried him halfway home, even though he was decidedly saddle sore and still rather afraid of falling.

'I have found a patroness,' he said to Catherine, when he was back in the cottage at last. 'She wants to see my poetry. I thought I might print some of the songs from "Innocence and Experience".'

Catherine rushed at him to kiss him and congratulate him and be told every last detail about this momentous meal. 'Did I not always say you would prosper?' she said. 'When do you see her again?' And being told it was in three days' time, 'We must set to work at once.'

So the plates were found and the most likely poem chosen, which took a very long time for there were many that he was sure would suit. In the end they settled on 'The Clod and the Pebble' and a copy was printed, painted and brought to perfection. Then there was still a day to wait in fidgeting impatience before he could place it before his new friend.

But when they had been greeted and led to the table, he had to wait his turn with such patience as he could muster, for Mr Hayley was cock-a-hoop with good news. He'd been hinting at it as they rode through the fields but now it was the moment to declare what he knew. There had been a sea battle in the straits outside Copenhagen and most of the Danish fleet had been destroyed.

'Such a victory!' he said. 'Incomparable. They are ringing the bells for it in London, I believe. Did I not tell 'ee Nelson would come up trumps? There ain't a man to equal him. So much for Armed Neutrality, say I. They'll find it hard to enforce their will upon us without a fleet. No, no, the alliance will founder now, you mark my words. There will be a peace struck in no time.'

On Tuesday it had been all darkness and foreboding, now the sun shone upon them in all its heat and glory as if it were already summer. Blake took his painted poem from the hip pocket of his old blue jacket and laid

115

it gently before his hostess, like the triumph it must surely be.

His hopes were not disappointed. She declared herself delighted with the illustration; admired his depiction of the ram and three sheep standing in line with a bull and a cow, heads dipped to drink at the stream where the clod and the pebble lay; enjoyed the contrast of the colours he had chosen – the clear blues of sky and water, the greens of tree and grasses, the cream of the fleeces – and finally asked if he would be so kind as to read the poem for her, which he did, most proudly, sitting in his chair with the paper held up to the sunlight. She listened with complete attention, her chin propped on her white hand, the little finger touching her lips, while he sang the words in his usual way. Then he waited, strained with a quite painful anxiety, to hear what her judgement would be.

'You are a fine poet, Mr Blake,' she said, when the last word had melted into the warmth of the room. 'Do you not agree, Mr Hayley? A very fine poet. You follow the precepts of Mr Wordsworth and Mr Coleridge, I see. Your simplicity pleases the ear as theirs does and the sentiments you express are as profound as any I have ever heard. How true it is that love can be both unselfish and selfish, soft and yielding as a humble clod of earth or hard and unforgiving as a stone. *"To build a heaven in Hell's despair"* is very fine. And all written in such a rhythmical style and with such balance. I congratulate and applaud. Are there any more of such lyrics that I may hear?'

He promised her another three by their next breakfast together.

'An exceedingly pleasant visit,' Mr Hayley said as they trotted away from her great house. 'I always say good news is the best condiment to a meal. What excellent fortune that we had such exceedingly good news to tell her. Dear Paulina. She is a first rate hostess. Quite first rate. She deserves no less. Did I not tell you you would find her the best of women? Oh quite, quite the best. She finds a good word to say of everyone. Many another would not have listened to your verses at all, you know.'

Blake turned his head sharply to look at him, aggrieved that his work should be so belittled, and as he did, a small sharp rain began to fall. It distracted him enough to make him glance at the sky instead, that being a safer target for his ill humour. A smoke-blue cloud was skimming across the downs towards them trailing tatters of rain like the fringe on a shawl. They were in for a shower. The pony twitched his ears, Blake tried to turn up his collar with one hand, but Hayley laughed and flung the reins over his left arm so that he had both hands free to deal with his umbrella.

''Tis as well I was prepared,' he said and opened the umbrella with a crack like a pistol shot, It was so loud it reverberated through the hills and the suddenness of it frightened his horse, which reared onto its hind legs. The movement was precipitous and Hayley was off balance. He was tossed sideways into the air, rose as if he was flying and landed on his back with the open umbrella upturned beside him.

For a stunned second, Blake sat lumpily on his pony, uncertain what to do. He knew he ought to dismount and go to his patron's assistance but what if he got down and then couldn't get up again? What if Hayley was injured? Where would he go for help? The horse had galloped off into the field, pranced a little, slowed to a walk and stopped and was now placidly cropping the grasses, as though that was what it had intended all along, but it would probably gallop away again if he were to try to approach it, and what would he do then? Fortunately, as he dithered, Hayley sprang to his feet.

'No cause for alarm,' he called. 'I am unhurt, as you see. Quite, quite unhurt.' He picked up his umbrella, held it over his head and went limping off across the field to collect his horse. There was some fidgeting and snorting, for this was a spirited creature,

118

but eventually it allowed him to remount. 'All is well,' he called. 'No harm done.' And set off at a gallop to prove his opinion.

Blake clicked the pony into a trot and did his best to follow, thinking what an extraordinary man his patron was. The rain had set in now and was stinging his ungloved hands and casting a gloom across the sky and his spirits. And they still had at least five miles to ride. Then he became aware that there was a cart approaching and he drew his pony aside to make room for it. The driver was a fair-haired young man, who tipped his hat to him by way of thanks, and as Blake nodded in return, he realised who it was. The boy called Johnnie, the one who'd delivered Mr Hayley's message on his first morning in the village, the one he'd seen working in the garden with Mr Hosier. And with a very pretty girl sitting beside him in a scarlet riding cloak.

'Who's that?' the very pretty girl wanted to know when they were safely past.

Johnnie gave her a kiss before he enlightened her. They were out of sight of both men and there was no need for caution. 'Tha's that ol' engraver feller,' he said. 'You know, the one what painted the pictures in the library.'

'He aren't no horseman,' she laughed, 'an' tha's a fact. He ride poor Bruno like a sack a' potatoes an' he don't look like a careful man neither, not with all that paint down his sleeve, but he got a good face.'

'You should see inside his cottage,' Johnnie told her. 'There's paintings everywhere you look in there, an' tools an' paintbrushes an' ol' rags an' everythin'. 'Tis a real sight.'

'I'd like to,' Betsy said, but then he started to kiss her with rather more passion, because they were trotting between two conveniently high hedges where they couldn't possibly be seen by anyone, and being kissed was so delightful, even in the rain, that she forgot about painters and painting and simply gave herself up to sensation.

It wasn't until two weeks later that she remembered her curiosity. Mrs Beke had made one of her pigeon pies for dinner that evening and Mr Hayley had sent it back to the kitchen without taking so much as a mouthful. She was very put out. 'Bein' abstemious is all very well,' she said, crossly, 'but this is downright wasteful. An' 'twas one of my best too. I shall throw it on the compost heap if that's all he thinks of it.'

Betsy was aghast at the thought of such a waste. The pie was too small to be shared among the servants but that didn't mean it should be thrown away. 'Why not send it to the painter feller instead?' she suggested. 'He'd love it, I'm certain sure. I could take it down for you if you'd like me to.'

'Do what you will with it,' Mrs Beke said. ''Tis all one to me.'

So Betsy warmed a pudding cloth, wrapped the pie in it, very carefully, and bundled it onto a hot tray. Then she set off along the winding path to see what she could discover.

The cottage was very quiet but there was a light in the little western window and smoke rising from the central chimney, so she walked through the wicket gate into the little garden, balanced her tray on one hand and knocked at the door. The woman who opened it smelt of onions like a kitchen maid but she greeted her politely. 'Good afternoon.'

Betsy explained her errand and held up the pie. ''Tis pipin' hot, ma'am,' she said. 'I been a-burnin' my hands bringin' it down to 'ee. I hopes you'll be pleased to accept it.'

Instead of being pleased, the lady seemed annoyed. 'Well, you'd best come in and set it down afore you get burned any further,' she said, but her voice was ungracious and her spine was stiff and she was looking away with the oddest expression on her face.

She thinks 'tis charity, Betsy understood, and hastened to put the matter right. 'The missus made it for Mr Hayley,' she explained, 'an' then he sent it back without so much as a mouthful took, an' she was so cross she was all for throwing it on the compost heap, an' I said not to waste it. If he was such a fool as to turn his nose up at such a fine pie, there'd be others who wouldn't.'

The lady looked at her quizzically. Then she threw back her head and laughed out loud. 'So that's the way of it,' she said. 'We're better than the compost heap. Is that what you're sayin'? 'Tis just as well Mr Blake is over in The Fox filling our jug for supper or dear knows what he'd say. Well, come along in and let us see this offering.'

She led the way into the room to her left and Betsy followed her. What else could she do? The place smelt of damp and onions, but that was only to be expected. Most cottages were damp, especially after a wet winter, and they all smelt of cooking. It was scantily furnished too, with just a table and two wooden chairs, but that was usual as well. There was a good log fire in the hearth and the table had been set for two, with bread on a board and a slab of cheese and two fat onions peeled and quartered on a dish beside it. There was ample space and obvious need for the pie and Betsy set it down, glad to be relieved of its weight.

'Let's see this culinary masterpiece then,' Mrs Blake said. And she unfolded the pudding cloth. The smell that rose from the uncovered pie was so savoury that both women sniffed appreciatively.

'Well, she's a fine cook, your Mrs Beke,'

Mrs Blake admitted. 'I'll give her that.'

'She got a bad temper, that's all 'tis,' Betsy explained. 'She can lose her rag as quick as blinkin', an' then we has things throwed about an' all sorts.'

''Tis a common fault,' Mrs Blake told her, bending to sniff the pie again. 'But this is wholesome, I must say. 'Twill make good eating.'

She'll take it, Betsy thought. She aren't a-goin' to refuse. And having satisfied herself that her errand was completed, she began to look round for the paintings.

'Is there something you lack?' Mrs Blake asked and her voice was sharp again.

Betsy blushed, for she knew she shouldn't have been gawping at the room. It was ill mannered to pry. But since the lady was obviously waiting for an explanation, she mumbled something about paintings.

'Ah!' Mrs Blake said. 'You wish to see his paintings. Is that it? Very well. Why should you not? 'Tis great work and should be seen by the world.' And she took a taper from the pot on the mantelpiece, lit one of the tallow candles that were standing in their pewter candlesticks on the table and led her visitor out of the room, trailing black smoke and a strong smell of grease. She continued past a steep staircase and into a second room of such a very different kind that it made Betsy catch her breath.

There were paintings and engravings on every one of the whitewashed walls, some in bold reds and golds, some in misty blues and greys, some in greens and browns, pictures of angels with huge soaring wings and men who looked like statues, pictures of trees like flames and flames like flowing hair, and laid out on a trestle table, a row of little printed pages with pictures twined in and around the words. She stood in the midst of them too overwhelmed to speak. It was like being in church.

'You like them,' Mrs Blake said, and now her face was plumped with smiles and pleasure.

'Oh, yes ma'am,' Betsy whispered. 'Very much.'

'I would that all the world could see with your eyes,' Mrs Blake said. 'He is a great artist and a great poet, but there are few who appreciate his worth.' She led Betsy to the round table at the far end of the room and held up the candle so that she could see the papers that were lying on it. They were covered in handwriting, not neat and flowing like the writing she'd seen on Mr Hayley's papers in the library, but crowded and crabbed together, with words crossed out and other words written in the margins. Oh, Betsy thought, if only I could read like Johnnie. I should so like to know what he's written.

But there was no time to piece out even a few of the words, which she could have done if she'd had a chance to think about them, for she knew how to sign her name and could make out the words in the prayer book. But her dinner would be waiting back at Turret House and no servant was ever late for dinner.

'If you please, ma'am,' she said. 'I got to be goin' now or I shall be late at table an' Mrs Beke'll *really* have something to say.'

'Well, well, we mustn't have *you* thrown about,' Mrs Blake said. 'Tell her we are glad of her pie and thank her for her kind thought.'

'An' thank you for lettin' me see the pictures,' Betsy said, as she was led to the door. Then, the formalities having been observed, she pulled her red cloak about her, and set off for the short walk back to the house. But although she knew she should have been hurrying, she dawdled back in a dream, for her head was so full of swirling visions of saints and angels that she couldn't have walked fast even if Mrs Beke herself had been there to nag her. Who would have thought to see such amazing things in Felpham?

'Johnnie,' she said, as she sat down beside him at the kitchen table, 'you must teach me to read.'

Chapter Seven

Betsy's reading lessons continued all through the summer and, although decoding letters was harder than she expected, difficulties only made her more determined. If Johnnie could pick up *The Times* of an evening and understand everything that was written there, then so would she. She'd keep on and on until she could walk into Mr Blake's cottage with a pie or a pudding and read whatever was lying about. Within a week she'd mastered over fifty words, within three she could read a short sentence and had discovered how to judge the moment when Mr Hayley would finish with the latest copy of the paper and put it into the canterbury. From then on, as soon as she heard his limping step, either on the stairs or retreating into the bedroom, she crept up the backstairs into the library to purloin her precious reader before anybody else could get their hands on it. Then she sneaked it away to the kitchen and hid it in the dresser until she had time to resume her battle with the print.

'Tell me what it says, Johnnie,' she would demand, pointing to any word that baffled her. And when she'd been told, she pondered it carefully, pronouncing it and considering it until it was fixed in her brain.

In the fourth week, she discovered that politicians speak in a language of their own. 'Yesterday in the Commons, Mr Pitt said these neg ... ot...' she read. 'Now what's all this Johnnie?'

'These negotiations are of the utmost delicacy and must be pursued with patience and perseverance if we are to achieve our objective,' Johnnie obliged.

The words meant nothing to her. 'I can't make head or tail a' that,' she complained. 'Why don't he speak English?'

'He does,' Johnnie told her. 'Tha's just *his* English, tha's all. Tha's the way they goes on in Parliament.'

'But what do it mean?'

He did his best to translate. 'They're trying to get a settlement with the Danes and the Swedes,' he said, 'and 'tis a tricky business seemingly. He says they got to be careful what they says and how they says it, otherwise they won't get what they want. Leastways that's my readin' of it.'

'What's per-sev-er-ence?' she said returning to the paper.

'You are,' he laughed. 'It means keeping on and on.'

Although he laughed at her, he was touched by her determination and proud of his unexpected skill as a teacher. He would look round at the other servants while she read aloud and feel smug when he saw how impressed they were, and after one amazing afternoon, when she stood in Mr Hayley's empty library and read a whole page from the book left open on the table, he was so full of himself that he actually bragged about how clever he was being and was teased for days afterwards, every time he walked into the kitchen. But better by far was the effect all this learning had on their courtship.

She was so quick and so passionate, kissing him almost before they were out of sight of their neighbours, allowing him so many new liberties when they *were* on their own that he lived in a state of perpetual arousal. Strolling into the fields after church was now a regular occurrence, and one they both looked forward to with intensifying pleasure. Sometimes, when it wasn't too wet – and it often *was* wet that summer – they took a stroll during the week too, eastward along the beach towards Middleton and the sand dunes, or south through the water meadows that lay alongside the two mills, or west towards the great houses that Mr Hotham had built for his wealthy friends. And every walk took them further away from the village and nearer to the moment that Betsy was both breathlessly awaiting and, it had to be admitted, secretly dreading.

Their passion was now so strong they kissed until their lips were sore and, as he lifted his head so that they could catch their breath, he groaned that he was driven wild for love of her and begged her to let him go further. Which she did, further and further, and with increasing pleasure until it was an agony to him not to go on to the final longed-for moment that he needed so much and urged so strongly.

As the summer bloomed towards harvest and the trees grew heavy-bosomed and the corn stood rustling and ready for reaping, it became more and more difficult to deny him anything, when his face was so pale with passion and his cock so hard she could feel it through both sets of clothes.

'Let me,' he begged, running his hands up her legs, his fingers moving closer and closer to the place where she ached so enticingly, and her heart shook and thundered, and her eyelids closed of their own accord, heavy with the weariness of long-deferred desire. Oh, how easy it would be to give in. 'Let me, Betsy, my dearest darling. Please, please let me. I die for the love of you.'

But what he was asking was wrong. The Reverend Church was always saying so, calling it 'fornication' and 'the sins of the flesh' and warning of dire consequences. And hadn't Sarah Perkins been forced to marry in a hurry only last year with the baby born a mere six months after the wedding – although 'twas a pretty baby and christened in the usual way so no harm seemed to have come of it. But she'd been talking to her friend Molly about it, for Molly had been back home for a day or two while Miss Poole was away in London, and Molly said the thing was a risk, on account of ''twas painful the first time and like to be painful for a considerable time after'. She couldn't say why that should be but she was sure 'twas true, having been told about it by no less a person than Sarah Perkins herself. It was all very worrying. And now Molly was back in Lavant again and there was no one to ask. Was it any wonder she spent so much time learning to read? But she was avoiding temptation and putting off the decision, that was all, and she knew it.

Eventually, one damp night in August, when their hair was spiked and their clothes spotted with the most aggravating rain, his frustration erupted into an outburst of bad temper. 'You're just hard-hearted,' he said. 'Tha's how it is. You don't love me.'

'I do,' she protested. Hadn't she told him so, over and over?

'You don't,' he said, his handsome face sullen. 'Oh, I knows you say so, but you don't, or you wouldn't keep on a-sayin' no. You knows what it means to me.'

'Have some sense, Johnnie do,' she said.

'We can't. 'Twouldn't be right. You know it wouldn't.'

'Why not?' he demanded angrily. ''Twould be right if we was married.'

It was a weary argument. They'd been over it time and time again that summer. 'But we're not,' she said doggedly, 'are we?'

He scowled. 'Then let's get married.' It was hardly the most gracious of proposals but he supposed he meant it.

But marriage held no charms for Betsy Haynes. Being married meant living in a tied cottage, which would probably be damp and dirty; with only cabbage and bacon to eat, and a baby every year. 'An' what would we live on?' she said. 'Tell me that. I'd have to leave the house. You *knows* that. He don't have room for married servants. An' what then? How would we manage?'

He was surly with anger. 'Other people manage.'

'We're not other people.'

'No, we're not,' he said, turning away from her. 'I'm off to The Fox.' And he strode away from her, walking quickly so as not to feel too guilty at leaving her. Well, what did she expect? He was only flesh and blood. 'Tweren't fair to go on a-teasin' him the way she did.

'Oh, tha's lovely!' she said sarcastically, piqued at being left. 'What am I supposed to do?'

'Do what you like,' he called back to her. 'I'm off to see my mates, what've got a deal more sense than you!'

Unfortunately his drinking companions were in a mood for teasing that evening and his sudden dishevelled appearance presented them with an easy target. They started on him at once, as he stood on the threshold shaking the raindrops from his shirtsleeves.

'An' where've you been my sonny?' Reuben asked. 'We been lookin' out for you all evenin'.'

'You knows where I been,' he said, still surly with frustration. 'I been teachin' Betsy to read. Same as I've been every night for weeks.'

He knew he'd made a mistake as soon as the words were out of his mouth. Sceptical eyebrows were raised dramatically on every side, the leers were scurrilous, and Reuben's goblin face gleamed through the smoke of his pipe wicked with intended mischief. 'You been a-doin' what?' he asked, as if he couldn't believe his ears.

Johnnie blushed and stammered. 'Teachin' Betsy to read.'

There was a chorus of mocking disbelief. 'Out in the rain?' they cried. 'Oh ho! Pull the other one, Johnnie!'

'So tha's what they calls it nowadays!' Reuben teased. 'Oi hopes she's a good learner.'

'You wanna watch out with some a' that ol' learnin',' the ostler warned, grinning at him, 'or you'll end up stood at the altar rail with a gun to your head. Tha's the punishment for lechery, as I knows to my cost.'

Johnnie struggled to think of something he could say to deflect them. 'That aren't the way of it at all,' he said. 'I'm helpin' her to learn, tha's all. I don't get no time for nothin' else.' And was greeted with hoots of disbelieving laughter.

He was very upset. It was unfair to tease him for lechery. He weren't no Jack the Lad, never had been, never would be. ''Tis all very well you shoutin' and laughin',' he growled. That just showed how coarse and silly they were. 'You don't know nothin' about it.'

That made things worse. 'You gonna tell us then, boy?' they yelled.

Reuben called for quiet. 'Hush up, you lot. Johnnie's gonna tell us what he been up to with that girl of his.'

'No, I'm not,' Johnnie yelled above the din. 'I'm not. On account of there aren't nothin' to tell.' But that just set them off into paroxysms of delighted hooting.

'Oh ho!' they yelled. 'Are you tellin' me you ent been doin' nothin'? Oh my eye!' 'Tha's rich, that is.' 'If that's what you been a-doin' Johnnie, Oi'd like to be a fly on the wall ter see you a-doin' of it.'

Johnnie's face flamed with embarrassment. Having spent the entire evening holding his passion in check he felt belittled by such unfairness. 'Twas wrong of 'em to mock him so. What he felt for Betsy wasn't lechery, never had been. Even the thought of it made him shudder. Lechery was a low, coarse, farmyard sort of activity. What he felt for Betsy was different altogether. He wanted to tell them how crude they were being but he couldn't find the words or the way. He wanted to yell at them to stop but they'd jeer even louder if he did that. He wanted to run away but his feet seemed stuck to the sawdust. He had never been in such a state of paralysed emotion. Fortunately, as he stood shaking and shamed and totally at their mercy, he was rescued by two new arrivals, Mr Cosens, the miller, and his friend and servant Mr Haynes who, being Betsy's father, had to be treated with some caution. Not that caution was needed that evening for they roared into the bar with the force of a gale, thick-set, broad-shouldered and so full of the latest news that they brushed all teasing aside, like the irrelevance it was.

'Evenin' my sonny,' the miller said, as Johnnie stood aside to make way for him. 'Pint a' porter, Mr Grinder, if you please.' He looked round cheerfully at his neighbours, rubbing his broad hands together to warm them. 'Heard the news then, have 'ee?'

They confessed ignorance, all heads turning his way.

'They're a-buzzing with it over Chichester way,' the miller said with great satisfaction. 'Seems ol' Bonaparte's got his invasion fleet all set an' ready for us this time. Sixty thousand men, so they say. They reckon he means to sail this summer. They're building look-out towers up Seaford way.'

Alarm flashed from eye to eye, beer was gulped for comfort, there was a sudden increase in the volume of tobacco smoke, but for a second nobody said anything. Then Reuben launched into bravado and rescued them.

''E won't get near us,' he said stoutly. 'Not with Admiral Lord Nelson to pertect us. 'Tis all talk, same as we had last summer an' the summer afore that. Anyway, they're s'pposed to be makin' some sort a' treaty to keep 'em out, aren't that right Johnnie.'

It was a great relief to Johnnie to be able to turn to the consideration of something else, even if it was invasion. 'Tha's what they says in *The Times*,' he confirmed.

'*Times* or not they're a-building towers,' the miller said, 'an' there's an army barracks going up in Chichester and soldiers every which way you look. Which I never seen afore. You mark my words they're a-comin' this time. There wouldn't be all this carry-on if there weren't something afoot.'

135

'Well let 'em come, sez Oi,' Reuben declared, puffing out his chest. 'We're more'n a match for a pack of ol' Frenchies. They won't get off the beach, will they boys?'

With one exception, his neighbours took their cue and were instantly full of fighting talk. 'Tha's right. They won't get past us, be they never so Frenchified. They needn't think it.' 'We'll see 'em off, right enough.' ''Tis a well-known fact one Englishman can see off ten Frenchies. Well-known fact.' 'We won't let 'em land, shall us boys, no we won't, an' there's an end on it.' 'Oi tell 'ee, Oi'll get my pitchfork out, tha's what Oi'll do, an' you won't see them yeller Frenchies fer dust.'

The exception was Johnnie Boniface. Being teased had sharpened his perceptions and now he stood in the shadows and listened with appalled understanding, annoyed by their stupidity yet aware that they were bragging to hide their fear. If the French landed it would take more than a dozen men with pitchforks to hold off an army of thousands and they must know it, no matter what nonsense they were talking.

After a few minutes, the boasting rose to such a beer-soaked crescendo of shouts and cheers that he couldn't endure it any longer. When nobody was looking, he slipped out of the door, thrust his hands into the pockets of his breeches for warmth and walked away – not back to Turret House, for Betsy was there and he couldn't face her just yet, but south along the narrow earth track to the sea.

There was a full moon that night and although it was intermittently hidden by rain clouds, there was enough light to find the way, and the occasional flurry of rain was cooling to his hot head. He passed Mr Blake's cottage with its yellow candlelight glimmering in the little western window, strode through the cornfield, where the wet corn whispered, and finally crunched onto the beach and stood on the damp shingle in the damp air to gaze out at the impenetrable blackness of the sea. There was a strong tide running and huge waves were rolling powerfully in to shore, one close behind the other, round-bellied as barrels, their crests white-tipped in the moonlight. They roared onto the sand, pushing in so fast that the second wave crashed into the first before it could retreat and they broke together in a swirling complication of froth, flying spume and small sharp leaping waves, that dashed madly against each other like fighting cocks, tattered, fell to pieces, and leapt up to fight again. There could be enemy ships out there in the darkness at this very moment, Johnnie thought. We'd never hear them with all this racket. He could imagine the weight of them, their prows carving the black water, could see the soldiers leaping into the shallows, wading ashore, muskets primed, swords sharpened, roaring drunk and fierce and implacable. If they come they could kill us all, every last one of us – me, Betsy, all those poor fools in The Fox – and we couldn't stop 'em. Oh, my darlin' Betsy, he thought, I couldn't abide for you to be caught by the Frenchies.

Someone was crunching across the pebbles to join him and, looking over his shoulder, he saw that the newcomer was his uncle Jem and knew that he'd be glad of his company. A sensible man Jem Boniface and one with a healthy respect for the sea, having been a fisherman for most of his adult life.

'Oi thought 'twas you, when Oi seen 'ee from the pathway,' Jem said as he arrived beside his nephew. 'Tha's a fair ol' toide a-runnin'. Bring the bass in a treat that will. Lissen to it takin' the shingle away. That'll all be scoured out lovely by mornin'.'

Johnnie listened to the rattle of the shingle and gave a grunt of agreement. 'They say ol' Boney's got his army on the other side, a-waitin' to invade us,' he said. 'D'you reckon they're right?'

'Couldn't say,' Jem said, calmly watching the sea. 'Tha's possible Oi s'ppose. No use worrittin' our ol' heads about it. If he's a-comin' he'll come, an' that's all there is to that. Might be hereabouts, might be further along the coast. Our worrittin' won't influence 'im one way or t'other. Won't be on a night like this though. Oi can tell 'ee that. He'll have to wait for toime an' toide same as the rest of us. Won't be on a low toide neither on account of that 'ud be too risky what with sinkin' sands an' all. That ol' Channel'll give him plenty to think about, that Oi *do* know. Howsomever, like Oi said, there aren't a thing we can do about it. Whereas bass can be caught. 'Twill be a good day for the bass tomorrow. Oi shall come down with my kettle net midday an' see what sort a' catch Oi can get. Tell your Mrs Beke Oi shall 'ave a treat for 'er, by afternoon, an' maybe she'll let you come along a' me, like she done last year.'

Johnnie thought about it. He enjoyed fishing with Jem. It was unpredictable and dangerous and made a pleasant change from endless toil in the garden. And as Mr Hayley was off visiting somewhere and Mrs Beke was always more agreeable when he was away, she might agree to it. 'I'll ask her,' he said.

'Be there one o'clock, prompt,' his uncle advised. 'Oi shan't wait for 'ee.'

'One o'clock prompt,' Johnnie agreed and set out to walk back to Turret House, much cheered by his uncle's good sense. The light was still burning in Mr Blake's window. He do work hard, he thought, as he passed. I wonder what he's a-doin'.

He was engraving a white horse and a noble animal it was. Later he would add a woman, standing her ground before it and facing it down while her child cowered behind her, weeping in fear, since that was the subject of Mr Hayley's latest ballad, but for the moment the horse dominated the page and his attention. It had taken the best part of the evening to draw it to his satisfaction and now he was weary and ink-stained and ached to sleep. If he could summon up the energy he would work on, for the engraving had to be completed by Friday, which was only three days away. Mr Hayley was due back from Bristol on Thursday evening, and intended to ride to Lavant the next morning to take breakfast with Miss Poole. And after that he planned to ride on into Chichester to see Mr Seagrave the printer, for this was the start of an ambitious undertaking and he was full of enthusiasm for it. He was going to write a new ballad and have it illustrated and printed every month for the next fifteen months, each one about a different animal. He would sell them in the first instance to friends like Mr Flaxman, Miss Poole and Lady Hesketh at half a crown a time, and eventually he would gather them all together, publish them as a quarto volume and offer them to the public at large. Two,

'The Dog' and 'The Eagle', were already finished and if everything went according to plan, so he said, he and Blake could make a handsome profit. But to Blake it was laborious work and, what was worse, it ate into the time he could spend on his own epic poem, which was roaring in his head.

He'd been in a state of simmering dissatisfaction for the last ten days and the weather was making things worse. The cottage was damp, chill winds blew knives under the door by day and roared like lions over the thatch at night, and his dear Catherine was ill again. She'd had three head colds one after the other and her knees seemed to have taken the cold too, just as they'd done in the winter, and were swollen and sore. She rarely complained but it hurt him to see how painfully she was hobbling about. And now, this morning, he'd had a letter from his sister Catherine to say that she was coming down to stay with them for a week or two 'to help about the house', and giving him orders to meet her on the afternoon coach at Lavant tomorrow, just when he could least afford the time. My poor Catherine, he thought, as he picked up his tools again, living here is hard for you. Perhaps we should return to London. There would be less work there and we would have to live on very little but at least I would have liberty to write my epic and you would not be so plagued with pain.

Catherine was in the kitchen, scouring the supper dishes and praying that the horse would be finished by Friday. She was keeping out of the way, providing food and drink at regular intervals but otherwise limping about her business in the rest of the house. When he set his own painting and writing aside and worked on a commission, he was very short-tempered and she knew better than to do anything to provoke him. Sometimes genius could be a prickly bedfellow and especially when it was put under pressure. There were so many commissions – twelve more ballads to illustrate, nine more poetic heads, a water colour of Jacob's ladder for dear Mr Butts, to say nothing of the painting for Lord Egremont, which Miss Poole had arranged. That was a very important commission, which certainly couldn't be refused, for Lord Egremont had a reputation as a connoisseur of painting and a country seat at Petworth, what's more, which was quite close by and near enough to make other commissions a possibility. She knew it was kind of Mr Hayley and Miss Poole to find so much work for him and it was a relief that he was earning his living so well, but, even so, how would he ever find time for the real work he wanted to be doing when they made such endless demands on him? My poor William, she thought, no wonder you're thinking of going back to London. It might be the best thing to do, especially if there's to be an invasion, like they all keep on a-saying.

While Mr Blake laboured, her father grew raucous with drink and her lover contemplated the sea, Betsy sat opposite Mrs Beke in her quiet parlour darning her woollen stockings while the housekeeper totted up the accounts. She held her work close to the candle so that she could see what she was doing, for Mrs Beke was very particular about neat stitching, but for all her peaceful appearance, she was thoroughly unhappy and her brain was spinning.

Quarrelling with Johnnie had upset her terribly. It wasn't like them to quarrel. They never quarrelled. But what could she do? It would be wrong to say yes. She knew that as well as she knew anything. She might fall for a baby or get a reputation. Anything might happen. And yet, she couldn't go on sayin' no forever. 'Twould be against human nature when he loves me so much. She'd have to say yes sooner or later. If only there was someone she could ask. Someone who'd know what she ought to do for the best. Because she did love him. In a perverse way, the quarrel had shown her that, if it had done nothing else.

There was a rush of feet in the corridor, a rap on the door, and as if she had conjured him up by thinking about him, there he was, standing on the threshold, his face flushed and eager, asking for 'Mrs Beke, ma'am'.

'My uncle sends compliments,' he said. 'And to tell you there's a good strong tide a-bringin' the bass in and he'll have some fine ones ready for you tomorrow one o'clock.'

The housekeeper took one look at his glowing face and understood the situation at once. 'And you want to work with him, as you did last time, is that the size of it?' she said.

If she was agreeable.

Mrs Beke was in a benevolent mood. ''Twill make good eating for Mr Hayley when he comes home a' Thursday,' she said. 'He's partial to bass. Very well. Tell Mr Hosier I'm agreeable to you going and be sure you set aside six of the very best for me. Betsy can collect them, can't you Betsy.'

Oh, she could indeed.

'That's settled then,' Mrs Beke said and she smiled quite kindly at her young lovers. 'Twas good to indulge them when she could. They were only billing and cooing when all was said and done and there was no harm in that. Besides, fresh caught bass would make a tasty dish.

Chapter Eight

The wind had dropped by noon the next day, swung round and become a gentle south-west breeze. The rain had passed, the sky was summer blue and heaped with clouds whipped into a froth like white of egg, the air was salty fresh, the tide high. There was still a heavy sea running with waves strong enough to drag a man down if he wasn't careful, but that was all part of the fun when there was bass to be caught, so there was quite a crowd on the beach come to buy the catch and to see how the two Bonifaces would fare. Betsy arrived with her pail even before they took the nets out, and sat on the pebbles where she would have a good view. And after a few minutes her friend Mrs Blake came limping across the shingle to join her.

'They got a good day for it,' she said.

'They have, ma'am,' Betsy agreed. Johnnie was removing his waistcoat and taking off his shoes and stockings ready to push the boat out and the sight of such careless undressing was making her feel amorous, just as if he was kissing her. Oh, their quarrel *was* over, wasn't it? She did hope so. Then he looked up, saw her, and came leaping up the beach, to drop his discarded clothes at her feet.

'Look after them for me,' he said, smiled into her eyes just long enough to make her breathless, and ran back.

'Isn't that your young man?' Mrs Blake asked.

Betsy went on watching him, as he and Jem began to push their dinghy into the waves. The first wave it met made it rear like a horse and it took both of them to hold it steady. 'Yes, ma'am,' she said breathlessly. 'He is.'

'He's very handsome.'

He was also very wet, for the wave had slapped against the side of the boat and broken all over him. Now his shirt clung to his chest like skin and his breeches were soaked and it was making her tremble to look at him. Oh, Johnnie, she thought, my dear, darling Johnnie. You're right. I can't keep saying no to 'ee.

The dinghy was launched at last and the two men rowed out until they were about a hundred yards offshore, took their bearings from the white mill and Turret House, turned the boat around and dropped the net. Then Johnnie rowed back through the choppy waves while his uncle paid it out and secured it in the shallows. It had taken less than a quarter of an hour.

'They're quick,' Catherine said. 'Now

what happens?'

'We wait,' Betsy told her.

Which they did, along with everyone else on the beach. But not for long. It seemed no time at all before Jem began to pull in the net and a matter of seconds before they saw what a fine catch he'd made. The two women could see the fish wriggling, silver-blue in the sunlight, and watched as the two fishermen disentangled them from the meshes, working carefully out of respect for their sharp fins. And at last, Jem looked up and called, 'Bass for sale' and there was a rush to the water's edge.

Betsy took six large bass and a handful of smaller ones and added a few herrings to make weight, Catherine asked for a bass large enough to feed three and was given a fine fat one for which she paid fourpence and which she declared a bargain, and Johnnie was so excited by the thrill of the catch and the freedom of the open air that he caught Betsy up in his arms and gave her a long damp kiss, right there on the beach with everyone looking. Oh, they certainly weren't quarrelling now.

She tried to remonstrate with him. 'Johnnie put me down for pity's sake do. What are you a-thinkin' of?' but it was all play and her shining eyes and happy smile gave the lie to the words. How *can* I deny him, she thought, when I love him so dearly? It aren't natural. Oh, my dear, darling Johnnie!

A love match, Catherine thought, admiring them. How quick and tender they are with one another. And she remembered the moment when she'd first seen her dear William, standing before her in the halflight of her father's impoverished room in Battersea and how she'd listened as he told her how shabbily he'd been treated by some heartless girl. She'd known even then that she loved him and would love him for ever. 'Do you pity me?' he'd asked. And she'd answered 'Yes, indeed I do.' How well she remembered it. And he'd looked straight at her and said, 'Then I love you.' She'd run from the room for fear of fainting because she was so happy. And now here was this girl, with the same flush on her cheeks and her blue eyes shining, caught in the same passion, loving and being loved in return. How rich our lives can be.

She picked up her pail with its writhing burden and they walked together towards the cottage, thinking much and saying little. 'He's a fine young man,' she said at last, 'and loves you truly, if I'm any judge.'

Betsy was surprised to be spoken to so openly but she agreed that Johnnie *was* a good man and that, yes, he did love her. 'Or so he says, ma'am, and I got no reason to doubt it for he's been larnin' me to read, an' it's not many men would have done that.'

'William taught me to read,' Catherine confided, 'and to write. When we married I could do neither and had to sign the book with a cross. 'Tis a great blessing to be able to read, as you will discover.'

They'd reached the wicket gate and Catherine had already turned towards it ready to enter her garden. Was another confidence possible? Betsy wondered. And decided that it was, 'I hopes you won't think me forrard if I tells 'ee something, Mrs Blake,' she said.

'If you tell the truth,' Catherine said, 'you cannot be forward and I believe you are a girl who would tell the truth no matter what might come of it.'

'Yes, ma'am. I believe I am.'

'Well then?'

It was time to confess. 'I'm a-larnin' to read, ma'am,' Betsy said, 'so's I can read some of Mr Blake's poetry. I been larnin' ever since I seen 'em on his table that time when I brought you the pie.'

Catherine was surprised and pleased. 'Well, bless my soul,' she said. 'If that's the case you'd best come in and let me see what progress you're making. I shall be interested to see what you make of them, indeed I shall.'

So the fish pails were left in the kitchen and the two women walked through into William's workroom.

Once again Betsy had the curious feeling

that she was in a church. There were more paintings in the room than there'd been the last time, bright against the whitewashed walls, and one, that looked half finished, was set up on an easel where the light from the shaded window could reveal it more clearly. Betsy recognised the subject at once.

'Tha's Jacob's dream, isn't it?' she said. For there was Jacob, lying fast asleep at the foot of the painting, although it wasn't a ladder that spiralled into the starlit sky above him but a set of wide stone steps that led up and up to a huge golden sun, and were thronged with people. Some of them were angels with great folded wings on their shoulders. For a man who never came to church he painted some very religious subjects.

'That's Jacob's dream,' Catherine confirmed. ''Tis for our dear friend Mr Butts and should have been completed these many months – would have been if he'd not had so much work to do for Mr Hayley. All those engravings over there are for Mr Hayley.'

But Betsy was looking for the poems, her heart jumping because she hadn't expected to be put to the test quite so soon and was worried in case she couldn't read them after all. There were three lying on the table, all beautifully printed in glowing colours, with trees and flowers curved around the words as if they were protecting them and little figures in the margins. One was called 'The

150

Garden of Love' so naturally that was the one she chose. It was painted in greens and blues as you would expect for a poem about a garden, but the three figures drawn above the words didn't seem to have anything to do with gardens at all, for they were kneeling in a churchyard in front of a grey tombstone, a man and a woman and a priest with a book in his hand. Intrigued, she began to read.

'*The Garden of Love*
I went to the Garden of Love
And saw what I never had seen;
A Chapel was built in the midst,
Where I used to play on the green.
And the gates of this Chapel were shut,
And Thou shalt not, write over the door;
So I turn'd to the Garden of Love,
That so many sweet flowers bore,
And I saw it was filled with graves,
And tomb-stones where flowers should be;
And Priests in black gowns were walking their
  rounds,
And binding with briars my joys and desires.'

'Do you see what he means?' Catherine asked, as Betsy raised her head.

'Yes,' Betsy said and as Catherine's expression encouraged her, she went on, speaking her amazement aloud. 'I think 'tis about how the priest says love is wrong unless you're married. The Reverend Church, he's always on about it. Sunday after Sunday. Thou shalt

151

not, like the poem says. He calls it the sin of fornication. He says we'll sweat in Hell if we – what's the word he uses? – succumb to it. But if I've took his meanin' – an' I might not have – Mr Blake don't think he's right. If I've took his meanin' he says love is a garden, what grows natural. He don't see it as a sin anyways.' Any more than Johnnie does. Now there's a thing.

'No, he don't,' Catherine said, smiling at her. 'He don't see things as good or evil and no more do I. We know that's how the Church thinks and what the Church says but the Church is wrong. We believe we are all composed of contraries, kindness and cruelty, love and hatred, meekness and anger. Every human quality you can think of has its contrary and we need them both if we are to be whole. Anger can be cruel and hurtful. We all know that. But used to good purpose it can be strong and cleansing too. Love can be cruel and selfish as well as tender and forgiving and unselfish. It depends on how 'tis used. Thinking in terms of good and evil is a nonsense. Sin and virtue are not opposites. They are contraries within our natures and we must acknowledge them both. If we condemn one and praise the other, we split our natures in two.'

It was such a liberating idea that Betsy could feel her brain swelling to accommodate it. What if Mr Blake and Johnnie were right and the vicar was wrong? What if there really was no such thing as sin? What if she was holding out against something natural and proper?

'But how are we to know if we're a-doin' right or wrong if we aren't told?' she said.

'We don't learn by being told,' Catherine said. 'Any child in school could tell you that. We learn by experience. If a thing is right we know it. Likewise if a thing is wrong.'

Betsy's brain was still spinning. She stood with the poem in her hand gazing down at it, deep in disturbing thought.

'Well, then,' Catherine said at last. 'Do you agree with the Reverend Church or William Blake?'

'I think,' Betsy said slowly, 'I'm not sure mind, but I think Mr Blake's got the right of it. Reverend Church, he reckons love's a sin. He's always on about it. And Johnnie says how can it be right if you're married and wrong if you're not? 'Tis the same thing you're a-doin' whether you've a ring on your finger or no. Leastways, that's what he thinks. An' that's what Mr Blake thinks too, aren't it? An' if Mr Blake is right, then so is Johnnie.'

'Stay there,' Catherine said, 'and I will find you something else to read.' And she left Betsy by the window and went to a chest of drawers where she retrieved another poem, this time written on paper in rather faded ink. 'Read that,' she said.

So Betsy read. *'Children of a future age,*
Reading this indignant page
Know that in a former time
Love! Sweet love! Was thought
a crime.'

'One day,' Catherine said, 'most people will share our opinion and love will be seen as it truly is, as a source of joy, as a bond between men and women, as something to be valued and treasured, not turned into a sin.'

Betsy still felt as though her head was swelling. 'Twas an idea of amazing proportions. She would have liked to talk on but Mrs Beke would be waiting for the fish. 'I must go,' she said, and remembered her manners. 'Thank you for letting me read the poems.'

'You must visit again and read some more,' Catherine said, as she escorted her to the gate and she watched as she walked slowly up the lane, carrying her heavy pail. Dreaming of her true love if I'm any judge, she thought, and wondered what progress her own true love was making on his journey to Lavant. It was the first time she'd let him walk in to meet the coach alone and now she regretted it, but truly her knees were too painful for a seven-mile trek. Never mind, she consoled herself, I've a fine supper for him, an' I'll do my very best to get along with Catherine this time.

At that moment, William Blake was enjoying the sunshine and the quiet of the open country. Walking was always a pleasure to him and peace gave him the chance to think. Having reached the halfway point, he was sitting on the grass beside the path, at the edge of a cornfield where the weeds grew high and rank, taking a rest before he completed his journey. Nettles clustered in stinging profusion beside him and there was a huge thistle a mere six inches from his face, its leaves grey with dust and its head thick with thistledown, white as an old man's hair. He watched it closely, sensing that there was more to it than mere weed, and it began to grow, swirling and elongating until it had become an old man in a long grey-green gown. He held a wooden stave in his right hand and a pen in his left, and his white hair was tangled by the breeze. He lifted up the stave like Moses bringing law to the Israelites and spoke in a slow sonorous voice, that ebbed and echoed as if he were speaking from a great distance.

'Do not return to London,' he warned. 'No good will come of it. You will starve if you go there. Your way will be barred.'

William said nothing, partly because he was overwhelmed by the vision and partly because there were now other figures crowding in upon him. His brother Robert, long dead and so much loved, smiling and holding out his arms in greeting, William Cowper, Thomas Alphonso, friends and relations he had almost forgotten and beyond them a host of angels, singing sweet as skylarks, and devils, huge-winged and shining and brighter than the sun. And he turned his head to the sun itself and saw that it was spinning round and round, round and round, hurtling towards him in a ferocity of golden flames and he knew that it was Los, the emanation of the eternal creative imagination in which all things exist, Los the material manifestation of Urthona, the creator of the sun and the moon and the stars, Los the great spirit who brings human souls to birth and releases them into death. And he stood to defy him.

Their struggle was long and terrible for the heat and power of this dread emanation enmeshed him and the light was so blinding he could see nothing beyond the flames. But he strove with all the energy he could summon, wrestling the fiery figure, refusing to submit, panting and determined. And after an endless time, there was a rush of hot air and it was gone like a bubble burst and he was alone on the pathway, pale-faced and exhausted, with the thistle crushed beneath his feet. And he knew that his fourfold vision was intact and that he was not to return to London and that the great work stirring in his mind was destined to be written.

After his triumph on the beach, Jem Boniface called in at The Fox that evening to quench a long thirst by spending part of his sea-fall on Mr Grinder's strong porter. His arrival sparked off a celebration.

'Best catch Oi ever 'ad,' he agreed as his neighbours crowded round to congratulate him. 'That ol' sea was fair jumpin' with bass. We could ha' caught 'em jest by puttin' our hands in the water. Oi never seen so many at one toime in all moi loife.'

'Shall you fish for 'em again tomorrow?' Mr Grinder asked, as he pulled the ordered pint.

Jem shook his head. 'No need,' he said. 'We got all we wants. Oi shall go after herrin' tomorrow. Let the bass live an' breed, tha's what Oi says, then we got plenty for the next toime they comes in.'

'I see Mrs Blake on the beach waitin' to buy,' Mr Haynes said. 'Sitting next to our Betsy. How d'you get on with *her?*'

''Andsome woman,' Jem told him, 'an' not one to haggle, which is more than Oi can say fer some. Oi sold her a good fat bass for fourpence an' she paid up like a good 'un.'

Others took up the praise of their new neighbour. 'She been here nearly a twelve-month now an' never a cross word to no one.' 'Allus got the toime a' day.' And Mr Haynes volunteered that his wife was on

157

'pertic'lar good terms' with the lady. 'They goes in an' out a' one another's houses for a gossip, as it does your heart good to see. She give us a dish a' peas from her garden only last week an' we give her some of our onions. Come up lovely them onions.'

'Oi seen Mr Blake this marnin',' Reuben said. 'Oi was up by the pound, an' he were off to Lavant to meet his sister off the Lunnon coach. He stopped to give me toime a' day so we stood an' talked fer a bit. He's a noice sort a' feller. Oi tol' him all about my piglets.'

That provoked laughter and some cheerful teasing. 'Thought you didden like strangers, Reuben,' Mr Haynes said. 'Thought you said they turned things contrariwise. Ur wasn't that what you used ter say?'

'Oi still says it,' Reuben said. 'But Oi don't mean Mr Blake. He's a different kettle a' fish altogether. He fits in fine. I mean newcomers loike ol' Dot-an'-Carry with his great wall an' that darn tower an' all, keepin' hisself apart, all superior loike. Not our ol' engraver feller. He's more of a workin' man, if you takes moi meanin'.'

It was generally agreed that Mr Blake was a good neighbour and a hard worker. 'He has to keep a-goin' all hours to satisfy ol' Dot-an'-Carry,' Mr Haynes said. ''Parrently, he got some bee in his bonnet he wants ter write ballads an' sell 'em to his friends an' Mr Blake's got to draw the pictures for 'em. Up half the night slavin' over it, so his wife says.'

'The light's on in his workshop till nearly midnight.' Mr Grinder offered. 'I do know that. I've seen it many's the time.'

'Well, there you are then,' Reuben grinned, pleased to be proved right. "Tis loike Oi says. 'Nother half please Mr Grinder an' one more for my friend Jem. Where's that nephy a' yours Jem? Oi thought he'd be in tonight.'

'Off with young Betsy Oi shouldn't wonder,' Jem told him, 'Billin' an' cooin'. Oi never seen a boy so moony over a girl as that one. Wouldn't you say so Hiram?'

His brother put down his tankard and wiped his mouth with the back of his hand. 'Tha's about the size of it,' he agreed.

'They got the weather for it,' Mr Grinder said, looking towards the window. The sky was gentling from blue to lilac and there was such an effulgent tenderness about it that it made him yearn to be young again. 'That's a rare ol' evening.'

Out in the fields to the north of the village the rare old evening gentled every copse and enriched every drying ear of corn. Black-birds sang in the hawthorn bushes as if it were spring again, mice foraged busily in the hedgerows and Johnnie and Betsy lay with their arms around each other, snug and

159

hidden in the mounded straw of last year's haystack. The farm hands had been carting the straw away to the stables all afternoon and they'd left a scooped out nest behind them that was completely dry and just the right size for a pair of close-cuddled lovers.

Johnnie was so given over to sensation that he could barely talk and he certainly wasn't thinking. He lay with his mouth in her neck, breathing in the warm, musky scent of her skin as he fondled her pretty titties, or lifted a hand to twist his fingers in the tangle of her thick hair, watching with fascination as the sunshine touched it with tiny strands of wine red and shining gold. From time to time he raised his head to kiss her, but kissing was both acute pleasure and acute pain, and he was soon straining with frustration and had to stop to regain his breath and his control. For once he wasn't begging her to let him go further. It was enough – or almost enough – to be here with her and to enjoy those liberties he had. He loved her too dearly to distress her. It puzzled him that she was lying beside him with her eyes shut and only opened them to look at him when his kissing stopped but they were the most loving looks and that was what mattered. She returned his kisses, her body was welcoming. It was enough. Or almost enough.

In fact, even as she kissed him back, Betsy's mind was spinning like a top, round and round over the same unmoving ground. She'd been thinking all afternoon, turning that poem over and over in her mind, remembering what Mrs Blake had said, trying to decide what it was she truly believed. After seventeen years of Sundays at St Mary's, she could hardly be unaware of what the Reverend Church thought about such things and, until Johnnie kissed her, she'd agreed with what he said, in a vague sort of way and without thinking about it very much. Yet, standing in Mr Blake's workroom with that extraordinary poem under her fingers, she'd been quite sure she agreed with him too, and she couldn't believe two opposite things at once. 'Tweren't possible. Either the vicar had the right of it and what she was doing was fornication and sinful, or Mr Blake was right and 'tweren't sinful at all but loving and natural. His words sang in her head. *'Love! Sweet love! was thought a crime'* *'And priests in black gowns were walking their rounds, and binding with briars my joys and desires.'* No matter what the vicar said, *that* felt true, lying here in the warm hay with Johnnie's lips rousing her to such pleasure. But she was remembering other things too, that it might hurt, the way Molly said, or that she might fall for a baby like Sarah Perkins. And what her mother would say if that happened she simply couldn't bear to imagine. Look how she'd gone on about the cloak.

Cross as two sticks. And then she remembered the sight of his long white legs on the beach, so white when his face and forearms were so brown. He was so loving and so handsome and she loved him so much. Her dear, dear Johnnie. Oh what *was* she going to do?

He turned towards her again, brushing her mouth with his lips, teasing her into pleasure, and she put her hands on either side of his head to draw him into greater and better pressure. 'Dear, dear Johnnie,' she said. And he groaned.

The little involuntary sound made her heart swell in her breast. She could feel it changing, enlarging, full of pity and heavy with love for him. The decision was made, there and then, and instinctively. 'Tweren't right to keep him waiting so long, when he loved her so much and had been so patient. 'Yes,' she said, gazing straight into his ardent eyes. 'Yes. Go on my dear, dear Johnnie. I wants 'ee to.'

It was a clumsy fumbling affair, for they were both virgins and neither of them had much idea about what should go where, but after several ignominiously stabbing attempts it was finally managed. There was little pleasure in it for Betsy. The sheer strangeness of it saw to that. But at least it didn't hurt her and she could see just by looking at him that it had made Johnnie supremely happy. He lay panting beside her, head thrown back, eyes closed, sweat filming his wide forehead and smiled like a seraph. 'I shall love 'ee for ever,' he said. 'You're mine now an' I shall love 'ee for ever.'

I've sided with the poet, Betsy thought. An' 'twas the right thing to do. Wasn't it?

Chapter Nine

The Fox Inn Felpham. Wednesday 21st April

My dear Annie.

I have been here for six days now and I have to admit I am beginning to feel a little disheartened. It is bitterly cold, the wind is blowing a gale, the reporter in Chichester has yet to answer my letter although I have written to him twice, and although I have heard a variety of stories about our Mr Blake no one has a word to say about his trial and I am no nearer to unravelling the mystery of Johnnie Boniface than I was at the beginning. It is very frustrating. There must be somebody hereabouts who can tell me what I want to know. It is not as if I am asking for anything other than a little information. You will tell me that a biographer must needs be patient and that it takes time to winkle out the truth, even in a court of law, all of which is true, as I know from education and experience, but my impatience grows notwithstanding.

This morning I visited Turret House. It is an elegant building and stands in large well-kept grounds with a covered walkway leading to the house, a fine lawn, a shrubbery and several neat gravel paths curving prettily between the trees, but the visit was a disappointment. Blake's portrait heads are all gone and the present owner knows nothing of Mr Hayley and less of William Blake. All she said when I tried to tell her about them was 'Fancy that'. I was so cross. Fancy that. What a foolish thing to say. I suppose I must have revealed my feelings, although I did all I could to control them, for she suddenly changed her expression and offered that her gardener was an old man and might know something. So even though I felt she was offering me a consolation prize, which made me crosser than ever, I set off into the grounds to find him.

He turned out to be a very old man, with the most weathered skin you ever saw, brown as a gypsy and with a shock of wild white hair, but friendly and forthcoming. He greeted me by name and seemed to know exactly what I'd come to ask him. 'You're the lawyer feller what's been askin' after Mr Blake,' he said. And when I told him I was surprised by how well-informed he was, he said nothing went on in 'a village our size' without the world and his wife knowing about it. So naturally I asked him about Blake and the trial. This, as far as I can *remember, is what he told me.*

First of all, he said he'd been a stable lad at The George and Dragon when Blake lived in the village. 'Turn a' the century so 'twas,' *he said.* 'He come here around September time in the year eighteen hundred. They was terrible times. Mr Gilchrist sir. Terrible. We had ol' Boney Part a-sittin' on the other side a' the Channel, ready for to invade us – which he would have done if it hadn't been for Lord Nelson – an' soldiers everywhere you looked, an' three bad summers in a row, rain, rain, rain all the time, and the crops so poor you wouldn't believe. He chose a bad time to come a-visitin'.'

'But the villagers thought well of him, I believe,' I prompted.

'He was a good man,' *he said.* 'Mad a' course. But he couldn't help that.'

I pressed him to tell me more, asking him what evidence he had for saying the man was mad, for truly I find the constant repetition of this myth more and more disturbing. He was perfectly at ease about it. 'Oh, he was mad right enough, Mr Gilchrist sir,' *he said.* 'Never made no secret of it. We all knew he was mad. Used to see things you see. Angels an' fairies an' prophets an' such, large as life and twice as handsome, walkin' about in the garden so he said. But he was a good man, like I said, despite the angels. Honest you see, sir. Worked as hard as any man in the

165

village, paid his bills reg'lar, allus gave you the time a' day, a good neighbour. Must ha' been or we wouldn't have stood up for him the way we did.'

At that point I truly felt that I was on the edge of discovery. 'Would this have been when he was brought to trial?' I asked.

His expression changed at once. It really is quite extraordinary how mention of that trial makes them close their mouths. 'Well, as to that sir,' *he said,* 'I couldn't say.'

I was annoyed with him by then and pressed him to tell me whether he meant that he couldn't *say or whether it would be more accurate to tell me that he* wouldn't *say.*

His face was still closed but he thought about it for a while and then said. 'There's some things 'tis best not to talk about an' specially to a lawyer.'

'You have a poor opinion of us I fear.' I said.

'Not of you personal, Sir,' *he said.* 'Just lawyers in general so to speak. That was the root a' the trouble last time, talkin' to lawyers. To tell 'ee true, there's times I wish I didn't know what I knows.'

That was too good a lead not to be followed. 'And what do you know?' I asked.

But he wouldn't be drawn. 'Well, as to that Mr Gilchrist sir. I couldn't say. I'll tell 'ee one thing though. What happened to Mr Blake was on account of that soldier an' his bad mouth.'

'But what of the trial?' I said. 'What do you know of the trial?'

'If you wants to know about that,' *he said*, 'the best person to ask is Harry Boniface. His brother Johnnie was very thick with the Blakes one time. Him an' Betsy both. She was on visitin' terms, or so they say. Many's the time I seen her a-talkin' to Mrs Blake. Ask old Harry. He'll tell you. Now I got to get on or the tatties won't get planted. You'll excuse me, sir.'

I had to let him go for I could see that was all I was going to get out of him. But halfway down the path he turned back and called out to me. 'I'll tell 'ee one thing. sir. He was a brave man, your Mr Blake. He could ha' gone back to Lonnon when 'twas all talk of invasion, but he never did. He stuck it out with the rest of us.'

I could not bring myself to answer him. To offer me a snippet I could have worked out for myself when he knew very well how much I wanted to hear about the trial was truly annoying. Is it not the most aggravating situation for a biographer to be in? Now I suppose I shall have to try another approach to the reluctant Harry.

This from your most loving but undeniably angry husband,

Alexander.

167

William Blake was putting the finishing touches to his engraving of the horse and the defiant mother, while his wife and sister worked in the kitchen, scouring the dishes. It had been an excellent meal and the two Catherines had talked to one another quite amiably so he was feeling easier than he'd done for several days. Making a decision had settled his mind. Even the need to produce a set of illustrations every month for the next year didn't seem so much of a burden now. And tomorrow he would be visiting Miss Poole again. I shall take her 'The Garden of Love' he decided. 'Twas a risky poem to choose but he believed she would understand it even if she might not agree with his opinions. Despite the rain and the damp this was a good place to live and if he applied himself for two more years he could earn sufficient to keep him in London for long enough to write a good deal of his own poem. He'd started it that very evening, while his wife and sister were setting the table for supper, and he knew that what little he'd done was good. Now, he thought, as he contemplated his finished engraving, tomorrow morning I shall test Mr Seagrave's opinion of this.

Will Smith the ostler was grooming a pretty pair of carriage horses when he passed the stable yard the next morning. 'Mornin' Mr Blake,' he called. 'You got a good day for it.'

'Yes,' William agreed. 'Indeed I have.' The rain was over, the sun was warm, his work was going well, and in an hour or so he would be taking breakfast with his dear Miss Poole. All *was* well with the world. 'That's a fine pair of horses.'

'Pair a' beauties,' the ostler agreed. 'Goin' home this afternoon though, more's the pity of it.'

'You will miss them.'

'I shall miss my earnin's more like,' the ostler said ruefully. 'These two's the onny hosses I've had this season. People don't come a-visitin' when there's talk of invasion. An' if *they* don't visit, I don't earn.'

Blake considered. The ostler was a hard-working man and it was miserable to be short of earnings, as he knew only too well, and here I am, he thought, too busy to do the digging and, for once in my life, earning enough to hire a gardener for an hour or two. 'Should you ever have need of an extra job,' he said, 'you might consider working for me. There's a deal of work to be done in my garden and I haven't the time for it.'

The ostler's face was instantly wrinkled with smiles. 'Thank 'ee kindly Mr Blake, sir,' he said. 'When would you like me to start?'

'Tomorrow?' Blake suggested.

Tomorrow it would be. They shook hands on it.

'And now I must be off,' Blake said, 'or I shall be late for Mr Hayley.'

That gentleman was already mounted and waiting for him, his handsome face pink with excitement, but instead of calling out that they must hurry or they would be late for their breakfast with Miss Poole, he waved his umbrella in the air and shouted, 'Such happy news, my dear chap! You will be astounded. We have a new commission, my dear friend, and such a commission. I simply cannot wait to tell you of our good fortune. My dear Lady Hesketh has suggested to me that I write a biography of my dear friend William Cowper, who was her nephew, as I dare say you know. Such an honour, is it not. She will kindly provide me with any information I might require and I have persuaded her that you are the man to engrave the illustrations. Such an honour. It is a first rate commission and good will come of it, for Cowper was a truly magnificent poet and his life, however sad, will be worth the telling. I shall set to work at once, this very afternoon.'

Blake was crushed by the news. 'I brought the engraving for your ballad of the horse,' he said. 'Are we not to take it to Mr Seagrave this morning?'

'Oh, that must wait,' his patron told him airily. 'All other work must be set aside. This is far too important. We must not disappoint my dear Lady Hesketh. That would never do. She ain't a lady to endure disappointment. Well, come along then, my dear fellow, make haste. We've a deal to do today and the sooner we're about it, the better.'

William mounted his pony and gathered the reins ready for his long ride. The joy had gone out of the morning. There seemed to be no end to the work this man required him to do. But he couldn't refuse it. He had to earn a living, especially with a sister to entertain and a gardener to employ. Ah Jerusalem, he grieved, when will you ever see the light of day?

Out in the fields beyond the pound, the reapers were at work, scythes sweeping in unison, gathering their delayed harvest. They'd been hard at it since daylight, so they were glad to stop for a minute and take a sip of ale and wave to the two poets as they passed. 'Mornin', Mr Hayley, sir. Mornin' Mr Blake.'

''Twill be a poor crop, I fear,' Mr Hayley said, pointing his umbrella at it, 'but what of that. A poor crop is nothing compared to the great work we are about to undertake.'

Blake thought of his own and greater work that would now have to wait even longer thanks to this man's benevolent stupidity

171

and he opened his mouth ready to say that a bad crop would mean high prices and that many would starve in consequence. But Mr Hayley wasn't listening. He was riding ahead and in the full flow of his self-congratulation. 'What joy it is to have such a commission!' he called. 'Deserved, of course, for it was entirely due to my endeavour that the dear man was given his pension and I think I may safely say that I knew him better than any man living. And loved him dearly, of course. What a perfectly splendid morning we have for our ride to Lavant! Are we not the most fortunate of men?'

The harvest was bad that year, but contrary to Blake's expectations, it didn't put up the price of corn. That stayed low for the third year in succession. But there were reports of more bread riots in London, where leaflets were distributed claiming that the soldiers were taking bread from the very mouths of the poor, and the men who farmed in Sussex were miserably out of pocket. Rough weather in the Channel had kept Napoleon at bay but it had ruined the corn. 'Seems we can't have peace an' a good crop together,' they said. 'There's no justice in the world.'

That was William Blake's opinion too. He'd come back from his breakfast with Miss Poole in a towering temper. 'Just when I was prepared to illustrate a ballad a month for him and I'd made up my mind to it,' he complained to Catherine, 'and bought the paper, what's more, which was a considerable expense to me, as he well knows, £30 being a much greater sum than I should have spent in any quarter. More than I should have spent in a year. However 'tis done now and complaint is useless. Though all the more reason to keep to our plans. But no, that is not the way Mr Hayley does business. Just at the very moment when all is prepared, when we were due to ride into Chichester and show my work to Mr Seagrave, what does he do? He decides to turn everything topsy-turvy so that he can write this life of Cowper. I try to be grateful for all the help he's given us but this last is insulting, insupportable.'

Catherine did her best to comfort him but his bad temper growled for days and that displeased his sister. 'It's no good going on about it, William,' she said. 'What's done is done. You earn good wages here.' And when her brother cast his eyes to heaven 'Good enough to employ a gardener at any event, which is more than I ever could. I see he's in the vegetable patch again this morning. Be glad of your good fortune.'

'Write to your brother James,' Catherine suggested. If he grumbled on paper his sister wouldn't hear it. 'You owe him a letter and Catherine can deliver it when she goes back home.'

But William was in the grip of his old enemy, nervous fear, and knew that he couldn't trust himself to speak or write on personal matters without giving way to black fury. 'I shall work on Cowper's portrait,' he said. 'The sooner 'tis done, the better.'

It took him longer than he expected because the sketch Mr Hayley had given him to copy was small, poorly printed and difficult to interpret, but it was done at last and taken up to Turret House with considerable relief. The celebrated poet pronounced it 'Capital!' and, after treating his 'esteemed friend' to a reading of the latest chapter of his new work, he sent the drawing and the chapter to Lady Hesketh for her approbation. 'She will be delighted,' he promised. 'You can depend on't.'

He was wrong. Lady Hesketh was very far from being delighted. Lady Hesketh was *not pleased*. The chapter had *'omitted several matters of* extreme importance', which she corrected at length and with much underlining, but the drawing was worse. That sent her into a paroxysm of fury. *'The Sight of it has in* real truth *inspired me with such a degree of* horror,' she wrote, *'which I shall not recover from in haste! I cannot restrain my pen from declaring that I think it is* dreadful! Shocking!'

Both men were upset but they covered

their feelings, each in his own way, Blake by silence, Hayley by declaring that the lady had right on her side. 'She was his aunt – we must take that into our considerations – and her sensitivities are extreme, as you would expect of such a lady. I will amend the text as she suggests and you will undoubtedly wish to comply with her wishes in the matter of the drawing, will you not?'

'The lady is a fiend,' William said, when he was back in his cottage and had recounted the whole miserable episode to the two Catherines, 'worse than Satan and Beelzebub put together. She bullies and berates us as if we were foolish children and she was a schoolmaster or a stern father. 'Twas a monstrous letter. I could see the chastening rod in her hands. This will prove worse than the portrait of Thomas Alphonso.'

But however much he might rage against her, the lady's instructions had to be carried out. The portrait was drawn three more times and rejected on every occasion. The rewritten chapters were criticised, yet again. It was painful work. And living with anger and anxiety made it worse.

There was altogether too much anxiety in Felpham that autumn, especially when moon and tide were propitious for an invasion. Even Jem Boniface took to watching the sea, and he was renowned as the most phlegmatic man in the village. Chichester was thronged with troopers; plans for the evacuation of women and children were circulated to all the churches; carts and horses specified to carry them away 'in the event'; and to make matters worse, rain continued to clog the ditches and churn the trodden paths into quagmires, so that the sky seemed perpetually dark and every soul was cast into depression. It was quite the worst time to be courting.

Johnnie and Betsy made light of cold weather. They were young and strong and sure that a bit of rain never hurt anybody. They slipped away to their haystack for as long as it was there to welcome them and even when it was really too damp and cold to be used as a love nest, and had been diminished to a mere mound of straw which offered them no cover at all. What did such difficulties matter? Love was an increasing delight and love was all they thought of. They were caught up in the magic of it, living from one rewarding moment to the next, taut with desire for hours and hours and then so drowsed with pleasure they could barely summon up enough energy to walk back to the house. Their bad start was soon so far behind them they'd forgotten all about it. Now it was all new pleasures, new sensations, new experiments. When they'd first made love, Betsy had been afraid that she would fall for a baby like Sarah Perkins and had told him so, but now he'd learnt a new trick that he assured her would prevent such a thing. It was a difficult trick and at first it wasn't easy, but soon he was playing it well, pleasuring her first before he fell away from her to groan into his own pleasure. Their working days crawled by, lightened by an occasional glimpse of one another and by the even more occasional chance to snatch a kiss as they passed in an empty corridor or found themselves alone together in an empty room.

But eventually it was plain that summer and autumn were over. The fields were swathed in such thick sea mist that Betsy shivered, even when she was wrapped in her red cloak, and as October shrank into November and all the leaves fell and the first frosts of winter broke the ploughed earth into an easy tilth, and even the most pessimistic villager was prepared to allow that Boney wasn't going to invade that year, they too had to admit to an inescapable truth. It was much too cold to be courting out of doors. Soon they were miserable with chill weather and lack of lovemaking, feeling that they were doomed to celibacy until the spring came round.

'Which aren't to be endured,' Betsy said, as the two of them walked in the rain-soaked garden at the end of their working

177

day. 'Oh, Johnnie, Johnnie, my dear, darlin' Johnnie, what are we a-goin' to do? We can't keep on like this, not nohow for I can't abide it. What are we a-goin' to do?'

'I don't know,' Johnnie confessed, sighing into her hair. 'Except get wed, I s'ppose.'

But Betsy Haynes hadn't changed her mind about the wedded state. After the luxury of life in a big house, marriage would be a bad exchange. Marriage made you poor and kept you tethered to a damp room in a dark cottage, wearing shoddy clothes and living on cabbage and bacon, with children to look after. Much better go on as they were. 'I don't see why we should,' she said. 'Time enough when we has to.'

'Least we'd have a bed of our own,' Johnnie said. 'That'd be somethin'.' Even the thought of being in a bed with her was making him yearn most painfully.

'We got beds of our own *now*,' she pointed out, 'onny we aren't allowed to sleep in 'em together.'

'Which we couldn't, could we,' he said, trying to be reasonable, 'not when you're in with Nan and Susie and I got Robert alongside a' me. They *would* have somethin' to say if we was to go climbing in together. P'rhaps we *should* get wed. I'm willin' if you are.'

But she was sure that marriage wasn't the answer, however often and however lovingly he might offer it, and as their celibacy continued, she said so over and over again. 'We can't Johnnie. What would we live on?'

That was a serious problem, for as a married couple they would have to manage on whatever wages they could earn and provide their own food and rent, to say nothing of work-clothes and boots and such, and even if he went on working for Mr Hayley and was fed and clothed, what would become of her? A gardener's wage wouldn't keep a wife. 'I could take a job on one a' the farms,' he said, rather sadly, because he'd never wanted to be a labourer. 'That'ud give us a cottage which'ud be something. Father'd find a place for me I daresay.'

'No,' she said, 'you mustn't. It aren't right. Leave that to them as likes it.'

'No one likes it,' he told her. 'They does it on account of they has to. 'Cept ol' Reuben, with those pigs of his'n.'

'*And binding with briars my joys and desires,*' she quoted bitterly.

'What?'

''Tis that poem I read. The one Mr Blake wrote. The one I told you 'bout. He don't reckon to keepin' lovers apart. He says love is right and proper an' should be allowed. He's a good man. I wager if we was *his* servants he'd let us sleep together. He'd give us the bed for it.'

Johnnie scowled. Poetry was a nonsense at the best of times and at this particular time

179

it was just plain annoying. 'But we aren't his servants,' he said, crossly, 'so there's no point a-thinkin' about it. We works for Mr Hayley an' there's an end to it.'

'So what are we a-goin' to do?'

There was no answer. They were going round and round over the same hard ground, exhausting themselves and getting nowhere, like dogs in a treadmill. And as one frustrating day followed another, they began to quarrel.

'Don' keep on a-sayin' such things,' they shouted at one another. 'What's the good of it?' ''Tis allus the same. It makes me fair sick to hear it.'

Finally on one dank, dark evening in early December, when they were walking pointlessly round the grounds, feeling cold and dispirited and unhappy, he lost his temper with her altogether and shouted at her that if she couldn't find anything sensible to say she'd be better to keep her mouth shut.

She was mortally upset. 'How can you speak to me so?' she cried. 'I thought you was s'pposed to love me.'

'I do,' he yelled at her. 'I do, It's just you will keep on so.'

'I don't keep on so.'

'You do. Look at you now.'

'Oh, so it's my fault. Is that it?'

'I didn't say that.'

'Yes, you did. You just did. This very minute.' And she began to cry. 'You don't love me no more.'

Her tears washed him from anger to remorse in an instant. 'Don't cry,' he begged. 'Oh, please Betsy, don't cry. I didn't mean it. Truly.' And he tried to put his arms round her.

She shook him off, distressed to hysteria. 'Don't you touch me,' she cried. 'If I aren't to talk, I aren't to be touched. Nor kissed neither. You don't want to kiss me, anyway. ''Tis all show. Tha's all. An' I'll not have that. Not when you don't love me no more.'

His hands fell to his sides, limply as if they didn't belong to him. He was lost and drifting. He couldn't even keep her face in focus. It was as if she was disappearing, her features filmed by shifting clouds. 'I *do* love you, Betsy,' he said, blinking back his tears. 'I do. More than anythin' in the world. I shouldn't have said what I said. I wish I hadn't. Oh, please don't cry. I can't bear it.'

At which she fell into his arms and they wept together.

The truth of it is we should be lovin' not talkin',' he said, when they were calmer.

But she wasn't listening. 'Hush,' she said, putting her hand over his mouth. 'There's someone a-comin'.'

There was a dark shape scuffling towards them along the path towards the stables. Not the coachman, nor Mrs Beke, which was a relief, and not the butler either, not that he was ever out in the grounds at night. Someone smaller and slighter and approaching them slowly, as if he weren't quite sure he should be there. Then the clouds rolled away from the moon and there was enough light to see that it was Eddie, the new stable lad. It was a considerable relief for he was an amiable boy, newly hired to muck out the stables and groom the horses, thirteen years old, pug-nosed, straw-haired, hard-working and no harm to anybody.

'Evenin',' he said, shyly. 'Tha's nippy out.'

They agreed that it was and Betsy wiped the tears from her eyes, as surreptitiously as she could, and hoped he wouldn't notice.

It was a vain hope because he noticed everything about her. He'd fallen in love with her the first time he saw her and, although he'd never had the slightest hope that she would notice him – after all she was a beautiful young woman of seventeen and he was just the boy who mucked out the horses – he'd loved her quietly ever since. He soon found out that she was as good as engaged to Johnnie Boniface and after that he'd followed their love affair with vicarious yearning. She was a goddess to him and, as she turned her face towards him in the moonlight, her tears smote him like glistening swords.

He spoke to her before he could stop to wonder whether it was proper. 'You all

182

roight?' he asked. 'Oi mean, there's nothin'
up or anythin' is there?'

'We're cold,' she told him, and added with
moon-touched honesty, 'an' there's nowhere
we can go to be alone together. Tha's all.'

He stood before them on the dark path,
scruffy in his stained breeches, his fustian
shirt and his dirty waistcoat, smelling of ale
and horses. And he thought of the words
he'd just heard Johnnie saying and understood her perfectly and galloped to her
rescue.

'You could come up the stables, if you'd
loike,' he suggested. ''Tis warm there. Or
warmer, anyways. What Oi means to say is,
'tent so nippy as out here. You'd be more
than welcome.' He was blushing but they
wouldn't notice, would they? Not with only
the moon to light him.

They were touched by his offer. ''Tha's
uncommon kindly,' Johnnie said. 'Onny we
got to be gettin' back or Mrs Beke'll have
somethin' to say an' we can't have that.'

He was abashed to realise that he'd been so
clumsy they'd misunderstood him and
rushed to explain. 'No,' he said. 'Oi don't
mean now. Not tonoight. What Oi means ter
say is, you could come in tomorrow maybe,
or sometoime when you wants...' No he
couldn't say that. He was blushing so deeply
he knew they must see it this time. 'What Oi
means ter say is, when you needs a place for

to...' Land sake's he was makin' it worse. He plunged into another explanation, speaking so quickly the words tumbled over one another. 'Oi got a little room over the hosses. You goes up a ladder. 'Tis quite safe. There's only ever me an' the hosses on account of Mr Turnball's got his cottage. What Oi means ter say is, Oi wouldn't mind, if you was to go there sometoimes. Oi never gets ter bed afore twelve on account of Oi goes to The Fox most nights with Mr Turnball an' he stays all hours.'

They were surprised and touched. 'Tha's real kindly,' Johnnie said. 'But we couldn't do it. What if they was to find out? We wouldn't want to get you into trouble or nothin'.'

But Betsy was looking hopeful and Eddie was thrilled to be playing Cupid and anyway risk was part of the game. 'No fear a' that,' he told them. 'You'd need to be pretty slippy but loike I said, Oi'm in The Fox most nights. Mr Turnball he treats me to a pint a' porter an' then I plays shove ha'penny. An' you'd be more than welcome.'

So two nights later, when their work was finally done, and they'd watched Eddie ambling off to the inn, they took possession of their second love nest. It was a small cramped space above the stables, smelling strongly of horses, and just big enough for a straw mattress and a cane chair with its legs cut off. There was a shelf nailed to the wall where Eddie kept his candle and a hook next to the shelf where he hung his breeches and the ceiling was so low that they couldn't stand up once they'd climbed through the trap door. But what of that? Why would they want to stand up? They had a small semi-circular window at floor level through which they could see if anyone was approaching, it wasn't exactly warm but it was private and, as Johnnie was quick and happy to say, looked like the perfect place. They flung themselves down on the straw and tumbled into one another's arms. Let it rain, let the wind roar, let battles rage, let the whole world go hang, they didn't care. They were alone and hidden and could do as they pleased.

For the next two weeks they loved whenever they could. Their only problem was that there was so much work to do in the house that it was only on rare occasions.

'I could do without so many a' these silly dinners he will keep havin',' Betsy complained, as they walked round the empty dining room setting the table. Mr Hayley's dinner parties were a weekly occurrence now that the celebrated poet had his new prestigious 'Life' to read to his friends, and they required a lot of effort from his staff. Every servant in the house, with the exception of the coachman and the gardener, was commandeered to cook, serve, fetch and carry.

Even Eddie had to do duty replenishing coal scuttles and feeding fires and Betsy and the other kitchen maids were kept scouring the dirty dishes until well after midnight. 'There's too much of it altogether if you asks my opinion. It's not needful.'

But their master was in his element, declaiming his great work as he stood before the fire, with all his well-fed guests listening attentively, or at least with polite approbation, and ready to applaud when the reading was finished. It lifted his spirits to be acclaimed and especially on days when he had received yet another blast of disapproval from Lady Hesketh. She really was excessively difficult to please and she seemed to have taken against poor Mr Blake so thoroughly that he was afraid he would have to tell the poor chap he couldn't continue with the portraits and that would never do when he'd gone to so much trouble with them. Her last letter had been quite vitriolic.

'*I have to say I have* very serious doubts,' she'd written, '*as to Mr Blake's abilities and I am not the only one. Those of my friends with pretensions to* Taste *find* many defects *in his work.*'

'We progress,' he told his friends when their applause had died down. 'My dear lost friend is a subject of the most affectionate interest to me and I am sensible of the honour I have been done by being chosen to write his life. I labour day and night.'

'What a blessing that you have a secretary to assist you,' Mr Cunningham said. 'And to provide the illustrations, what's more. Are they progressing, too?'

'Oh, indeed,' Hayley lied. 'Yes, indeed. Everything is progressing most admirably. You would be amazed to see how patient he is and how open to suggestion.'

'A good fellow,' his friends agreed. 'He is lucky to have such a patron.'

'I am thinking of teaching him to read Greek and Latin,' Hayley confided. 'I believe it would afford him some amusement and might furnish his fancy with a few slight subjects for his inventive pencil, without too far interrupting the more serious business he has in hand, of course. The 'Life' must continue, as I am sure he understands. That takes precedence over everything else. But to study these languages of an evening would make a pleasant diversion. I shall mention it to him tomorrow.'

The mention was greeted with such a long, stunned silence that for the blink of a second Mr Hayley wondered if he had offended his good friend in some way. 'You are surprised, my dear fellow,' he said kindly, 'and cannot find the words to thank me. Have no fear. I do not look for thanks.

187

That is not in my nature. 'Tis enough that I am able to provide you with suitable employment and to put some slight but, I may say, well-earned reward in your way. Let us start as soon as possible. Would this evening suit?' And he waited happily for his reply.

Blake was still too stunned to speak. To be offered the chance to learn Latin and Greek was such a wonder he could barely take it in. He'd yearned to know these languages for so long, and always felt that his way to them was barred and would remain so. And now this amazing offer had been dropped before him. If he applied himself well he could read the gospels in their original Greek, he could read Homer and Sophocles, Virgil and Ovid in the purity of their original languages, unsullied by translation. It was a gift of incomparable, unlooked-for richness and offered at the very moment when he'd been angry with this man for dominating his time with trivial nonsense. 'I'm beholden to 'ee,' he said at last. 'This evening would suit me very well.'

Chapter Ten

The Fox Inn, Thursday April 22nd am.

My dear Ann,
  It is seven of the clock and your letter has just been delivered. I must say your rebuke was both unexpected and surprising. I have not yet washed and dressed, in fact the day is scarce begun, but I feel I must hasten to send you a reply, for there truly is no need for your concern. I have no intention of losing my temper on my next visit to Mr Boniface, as you put it. We may have been married but a short time as yet, but you should know me better than that. I may be angry from time to time — who would not when confronted by so much positively bovine intransigence as I have had to endure in this village? — but I am perfectly capable of keeping my feelings under control. You must understand that when a man is on a mission — as I have been ever since I saw our Blake's wonderful illustrations of the Book of Job in that dingy print shop — he will feel all matters pertaining with some passion. I knew then, and am sure now, that I had discovered a genius and that it was my business — nay, my life's work — to reveal that genius to the world. So is it any wonder that I

189

react with passion when I hear yet another foolish person castigate him as 'mad'. What is madness? Do not prophets and heroes invariably seem 'mad' to the respectable mob?

On a happier note. I must tell you that, in the same post as your missive, I received an answer from the reporter who tells me he would be agreeable to see me tomorrow morning at ten of the clock and will answer such questions as he can. This morning I have arranged to see an old lady who was taught to draw by William Blake. So much may come of that.

I will write again this evening by which time I should be in a better humour. AG.

Winter 1801/2

William Blake spent a lot of his time teaching drawing that winter and enjoyed it far more than the mere copying he had been required to do until then. It earned him an extra wage, which was undeniably welcome, good invariably came from good teaching and true learning was a rewarding occupation. How well he understood *that*. Now that he was learning to read Greek and Latin, the very flavour of his life had changed. After the labours of their day, he and Mr Hayley spent as many evenings as they could in the scholarly seclusion of the library, where he astounded his patron by the speed of his

...ing, and on the rare occasions when ...y paused from their studies, felt bold ...ough to commiserate with him for the ...uculence of the formidable Lady Hesketh.

'I believe it is her purpose in life to disapprove of everything I draw,' he said one evening. The third sketch of Cowper's head had been returned that morning with yet another furious letter. 'Nothing ever suits. First she says I have made him look "too enthusiastic", then it is "not a true likeness", now she detects "wildness" in his face and orders it to be removed, as if I can paint wildness in or out at her command. There are times when I wish she would draw the portrait herself and have done with it.'

'She is a hard taskmaster, I allow,' Hayley agreed. And added, lest his powerful patron be criticised too harshly, 'Let us return to the Iliad, my dear friend.'

Homer was a perpetual delight to them. To sail the wine-dark sea with their familiar heroes, when outside the house an eldritch wind battered the thatched roofs of the village and howled down the chimneys and whipped the bare branches of the elms like flails, to fight with courage and passion before the walls of immortal Troy while the paths of the village were ridged with mud and manure and the water meadow was a soggy marsh, to be enticed by the sirens' song when the Reverend Church could

barely make himself heard above the co...
and sniffs of his congregation, was to er...
a world of pure pleasure.

There was a disadvantage to all this learning, of course, as Blake knew and acknowledged, especially late at night when he was
striding home to his cottage. It meant leaving Catherine on her own for far too many
evenings and, although she didn't complain,
he was aware that she was often lonely. Of
course he was also aware that most of the
village wives were lonely of an evening
because *their* husbands were in The Fox.
That was part of village life. But even so, he
felt ashamed to be neglecting his loyal
Catherine. They had always been partners
and equals, and neglect was unkind.

So he was relieved when he came home
one night to hear that she'd had a visitor.
'Young Betsy Haynes called in this evening,'
she said. 'Said she'd come to keep me company.' And feeling that she ought to explain
who she was, she went on, 'Mrs Haynes'
daughter, the girl that wears the red cloak,
pretty girl, you must have seen her about.
Works up at the house.'

William remembered her clearly. She was
the girl he'd first seen in the cart with Johnnie Boniface, the pretty maid who brought a
pot of milky coffee to the library, when their
studies were over for the night and Hayley
had rung for sustenance. 'That is kind o...

her,' he said.

It was also artful. And necessary. For although she and Johnnie had been most discreet, she was afraid that Mrs Beke was beginning to have suspicions about them. Three nights ago, Susie had reported that the housekeeper had been watching from the window of the front parlour just after Betsy went out. 'All hid behind the curtains, loike she didden want anyone to see 'er.'

'She might ha' jest been a-lookin' at the garden,' Betsy hoped.

'In the dark?' Susie scoffed. 'What for would she be lookin' at the garden in the dark. She wouldn't see nothin' in the dark, now would she? Ho no, she was a-lookin' out fer someone an' someone pertic'lar, what's more. Tha's my readin' of it, anyway. An' there was onny one person what went out a' the grounds that night, an' that was you. Off to see your Ma or some such, wassen that the story?'

'We must take more care,' Johnnie said, when he was told about it next evening. 'If you says you're a-goin' to see yer Ma you'd better go an' see her in case she go a-checkin' up on you. An' I'd better nip down The Fox now an' then, just to put in an appearance like. An' we shall have to be together more slippy goin' in an' out the
le.'

their precautions were too late. Mrs

Beke had already spoken to Betsy's mother. She'd been pondering the situation for several days, ever since Betsy had asked her – for the third time – if she had her permission to 'just slip out for a minute or two to see my Ma'. There'd been something so artfully innocent about her that the housekeeper's suspicions had been alerted at once. She'd given her permission, as if it were of no consequence, but, as soon as the girl was gone, she'd left the kitchen and taken up a position by the window of the unlit parlour, as Susie had reported. There was enough moon to give her a clear view and that red cloak was as bold as a flag. She'd watched as Betsy trotted through the garden and slipped through the wicket gate. So she's gone where she said she was going, she thought, which is something I s'ppose, but she's up to no good, as sure as eggs is eggs. I shan't say nothing to Mr Hayley yet awhile. He's got enough to deal with what with writing that 'Life' and answering all those awful letters from that dreadful Lady Hesketh. There's no point worrying the poor man needlessly. I'll just keep an eye on things for the time being and have a word with her mother as soon as I can meet up with her.

The meeting was contrived the next day when Mrs Haynes came out of her door the very moment Mrs Beke just happened to be passing by.

'Good morning to 'ee, Mrs Haynes,' the housekeeper said. 'I trust I see you well.'

'You do, Mrs Beke,' Mrs Haynes said. 'Thank 'ee kindly. I had a cold a week or two back but 'tis quite gone now.'

'We were quite concerned about you up at the house,' Mrs Beke said smoothly, 'with your Betsy visiting you so often.'

Mrs Haynes took this information as it was intended but she was too shrewd to allow Mrs Beke to know it and she certainly wasn't going to quarrel with it. 'She's a good girl,' she said, automatically defending her young. 'She keep an eye on me, which is more than some young 'uns do. I hope it don't trouble you that she comes down so often.' She spoke calmly but her thoughts were furious. She's up to something, she thought, an' I'm bein' warned of it. This is what comes of her buyin' that dratted cardinal. I allus said no good would come of it. It's give her ideas. She smiled at her adversary. 'An' are you well yourself, Mrs Beke?'

'Mustn't grumble,' Mrs Beke said, smooth as butter. 'We all have our troubles in cold weather, do we not.' And she too was thinking, Well I've warned her. Now she knows an' 'tis up to her to keep her daughter in order. 'I mustn't keep you, Mrs Haynes.'

So the two women parted, each bearing her secret knowledge away from the encounter, Mrs Beke with satisfaction at a job well done, Mrs Haynes with considerable bad temper, thinking, Oh, won't I have something to say to that minx on Sunday.

She fed her bad temper for the rest of the week and by Sunday she was primed to scold. 'And where was you when you was s'pposed to be a-visitin' me?' she said crossly as her daughter came tripping up the church path to greet her, bright in that dratted cardinal. 'Tell me that.'

The attack was so fierce it took Betsy's breath away, as her mother's outbursts very often did, but at least she was prepared for this one and had an answer ready. 'I was with Mrs Blake,' she said sweetly, 'a-keepin' her company.'

Her mother was so surprised her mouth actually fell open. 'An' why on earth would you want to do that, child?'

'She's on her own, with Mr Blake allus up at the house,' Betsy explained. 'I thought she'd like someone fer to talk to.'

It sounded so plausible Mrs Haynes could almost believe it. 'Well, why didn't you tell Mrs Beke all that, instead a' lettin' her come down to me to tell tales?'

'I didn't think she'd like it,' Betsy said. 'We're s'pposed to be in the kitchen of an evenin'.'

'Then tha's where you *should* be,' her mother said, 'instead a' gaddin' all over the village.'

But at that point Mrs Beke strolled down the path towards them, stout and impressive in her own red cloak, and the conversation had to stop so that they could pretend to be neighbourly. The two cloaks dipped towards one another, swaying like red bells, bonnets nodded, smiles were fixed and held, polite greetings murmured, then Mr Haynes arrived at his usual speed and they all filed into the church and took their places on the pews. There was barely time for Betsy to send a warning eye-message to Johnnie before they were singing the first hymn.

It was a difficult service for the text of the sermon was 'Honour thy father and mother' and the Reverend Church was in full flow, threatening hellfire for the least trace of disobedience. He went on so long that Reuben Jones fell asleep with boredom and snored so loudly that his wife had to jab him in the ribs to wake him. And then when they were finally allowed out into the chill air again, and Betsy was looking forward to a few minutes alone with her lover, her mother spoiled it all by saying she was sure Betsy would want to walk back with her parents for once, 'If you're as concerned about the state a' my health as Mrs Beke was sayin'. I see she's a-watchin' us.'

Mr Haynes was rather alarmed. 'You're not poorly again are you, Mother?' he said, his broad face wrinkled with concern. 'I thought you was over that cold long since.'

'I'm as fit as a flea,' his wife said briskly, and gave Betsy a meaningful look, 'as well she knows. Well, come along then, don't stand about.'

So Betsy had to leave her Johnnie waiting by the yew tree and walk home with her parents with as good a grace as she could muster, which wasn't easy. Fortunately they passed Mr and Mrs Jones at the corner of Limmer Lane and Mrs Jones was in an entertainingly bad mood, berating poor Reuben for snoring in church. 'Did 'ee ever hear the loike?' she said to the Haynes. 'Snorin'! What people must think of 'ee Oi cannot imagine. You ought to be ashamed, so you should, not a-standin' there loike a noddle, with that stupid grin on your face. Oh, Mrs Haynes what must you think of us?'

Mrs Haynes was diplomatic. ''Twas a mortal long sermon,' she said. 'I was about ready to drop off mesself.'

'You ask me,' Reuben said, defendin' himself, 'our Mr Blake's got the roight oidea. You don't see him in church. An' fer why? On account of he's a non-affirmist or some such an' he don' reckon to the clergy. Tha's why. He say they're jist human same as all of us an' they 'aven't allus got the roight of it, an' we don't need to pay 'em no mind.'

'An' if you ask me,' his wife said, 'tha's blasphemous. Oi wouldn't ha' thought our

Mr Blake would go around sayin' such things. He's too gent'manly fer such a carry-on.'

'An' so he is,' Reuben said. 'Onny man Oi ever met what'll tell 'ee the truth straight out. Which is more than can be said fer some. Are we standin' about here all day, woman, or are we gettin' back? My chilblains are killin' me.'

Left on his own in the churchyard, Johnnie felt neglected. He knew that Betsy hadn't really deserted him, that she'd walked off with her parents because they'd told her to, but even so he couldn't help sighing. After so many months walking out together without let, hindrance, notice or responsibility, it was sobering to think that they were being watched and judged. He waited until his parents left the church, walking quietly down the path with young Harry striding between them, and then stepped forward to join them.

'Well, here's a surproise,' his father said, grinning at him. 'She 'aven't never stood you up, that young Betsy of your'n, for that Oi'll never believe.'

He hastened to tell them that 'no she hadn't' but he looked so shamefaced his father was concerned. 'Oi thought we'd be a-hearin' weddin' bells by now,' he said, as Johnnie fell into step beside him. 'You been walkin' out long enough.'

'It aren't for want of askin',' Johnnie said, sensing criticism. 'I been on an' on at her but she wants to wait. She's worried where we'd live an' how we'd manage.'

'Tha's allus a worry,' Hiram said. 'Allus was, allus will be. 'Tis the nature a' matrimony to my way a' thinkin'. You jest got to take a deep breath an' get on with it.'

But no amount of deep breathing would solve Johnnie's problem for him and now he had an additional one. 'If you've told your ma you're a-visitin' Mrs Blake,' he said to Betsy later that day, 'then you'll have to do it. Otherwise she'll smell a rat.'

Betsy had worked that out too. 'What with one thing an' another,' she said, miserably, 'I reckon we're a-goin' to be kept apart all winter.'

'Not if we're slippy,' he promised. ''Tis just a matter a' givin' 'em what they're aspectin'. If I go to The Fox an' make sure they all sees me a-goin' an' you go to Mrs Blake's likewise, we can slip back quiet-like in an hour or so, an' no one the wiser.'

She wasn't convinced but she knew it had to be done. There was no other way. So the next evening, when Johnnie strode off to The Fox with Eddie and Bob the boot boy, she wrapped herself up in her red cloak and went visiting. It turned out to be more enjoyable than she expected for when she arrived Catherine was cutting out the cloth for a new shirt for William, so naturally, not being one to sit idle while others were working, she offered to help to baste the pieces together and Catherine took the offer so gladly, telling her she was an angel sent from heaven and had come at just the right time, that she was warmed by a delightful sense of her own virtue. After that the two of them sat by the fire and tacked the shirt together and talked like old friends.

Before long they were discussing William's poetry. 'He don't get to write much nowadays what with all the work he's got to do for Mr Hayley,' Catherine said, 'painting heads and illustrating ballads and such-like, but we're printing off another three copies of "Innocence and Experience" as there isn't a copy in the house and that pleases him. Perhaps you'd like to see it?'

She would indeed, so the printed poems were gathered from William's workroom and laid out on the kitchen table for her inspection. Feeling greatly honoured, she chose a poem about a lamb and another called 'The Shepherd' and read them, slowly and carefully. When she finally raised her head from the paper, Catherine said she must read one called 'The Tyger' as well, 'because these poems are about the contrary states of our human souls'.

'What a lot of questions he asks,' Betsy observed as she read. 'This is all questions, all the way through. Why do he ask so many?'

'Why does anyone ask questions?' Catherine said. 'Why do you?'

'On account of I wants to know the answers,' Betsy said. That was simple.

'Exactly so.'

'But Mr Blake, he must *know* the answers, surely, bein' a poet.'

'If you asked him he'd say he doesn't know enough of the answers,' Catherine told her. 'The more questions you ask the more answers you find.'

It was an extraordinary thought to carry back to the stable but not one that Johnnie wished to entertain. 'We 'aven't got time fer poetry,' he said, kissing her neck. 'That can wait.'

But although he kissed her thoughts away, they were only gone temporarily and the next evening when she carried the usual pot of coffee up to the library, she found herself gazing at Mr Blake's animated face and wondering what other weird ideas were bubbling in his head.

The following evening there was a dinner party which went on until long past midnight and the night after that the household was kept busy running for Doctor Guy and cleaning Mr Hayley's clothes. He'd taken another fall from his horse and had come home from his afternoon ride covered in mud and bleeding from a gash on his chin.

''Tis all the fault of that dratted umbrella of his,' Mrs Beke complained. 'Why he must take it with him everywhere he goes is beyond my comprehension.'

'And mine,' Johnnie whispered to Betsy as they left the kitchen together, he to run down to The Fox to buy a bottle of brandy for the invalid, she to carry his dirty linen to the laundry room. 'We've lost another evenin' thanks to that umbrella.'

'Never mind,' Betsy said. 'There's always tomorrow. Least we got somethin' to look forward to.' And as she walked away with the muddy jacket hanging over her arm she was thinking of the other things she was looking forward to. Tomorrow she would see Mrs Blake and read another poem.

It was a disappointment to her that Johnnie showed so little interest in what she was reading, especially when he was the one who had taught her to read in the first place. She tried to tell him on several occasions but if she started when they arrived in the stable, he only grunted and kissed her with more passion and if she tried to talk about it afterwards, when they were dressing ready for their sprint to the house, he told her she looked good enough to eat and to hurry up or they'd have Eddie back. Eventually she decided he simply wasn't interested in poetry but by then it didn't matter because she'd found another audience.

After she'd been visiting Mrs Blake for about a fortnight, she returned to the kitchen one evening to find Susie complaining that the master had dropped ink all over the library table. 'An' how he thinks we're to clean it all off, I do not know.'

'You should see Mr Blake's table,' Betsy told her. 'Tha's a mass a' stains. Inks an' paints an' I don't know what-all. It comes with bein' a poet.'

'I never knew he was a poet,' Susie said. 'D'you hear that Nan? Tha's two poets we got in our village. Who'd ha' thought it? Is he a celebrated an' all?'

Betsy said she didn't think so, but he ought to be. 'He writes poems about all sorts a' things,' she told them. 'I been a-readin' of 'em.'

'What sort a' things?' Nan wanted to know.

So she told them. And from then on she reported to them every time she'd been to the cottage. 'We been reading about the sweep boys, this evening. Terrible what they do to 'em. They shaves their poor heads, an' gives 'em hardly anythin' to eat so as to keep 'em small, an' lights fires under their poor feet when they get stuck in the chimernees, an' I don't know what-all.' 'Tonight I found a poem about how if you're angry you ought to spit it out an' have done with it, on account of if you keeps it all hid an' don't say nothin', it grows an' makes you cruel.' 'The one I found tonight was about a school boy an' there was somethin' he'd wrote in the middle of it I thought was really good. How did it go? *"How can the bird that is born for joy, sit in a cage and sing?"* That was it. He don't reckon you should put birds in cages, an' no more do I.'

'He do write some odd things,' Nan observed.

'You should see 'em,' Betsy said. ''Tent just the words an' the ideas he has, 'tis the drawin's. He draws 'em an' all an' they're so pretty you wouldn't believe. I read another one tonight about a newborn baby and he'd drawed her a-sittin' on her mother's lap inside a great red flower with an angel a-lookin' at her.'

'My stars!'

Christmas came and went in a flurry of snow. The subterfuge continued. Blake and Hayley continued their studies, Eddie played endless shove ha'penny while Johnnie and Betsy made love, and Betsy read more and more of Blake's poetry and grew steadily more fond of his wife. Mrs Beke made it her business to meet up with that lady – entirely by chance of course – and having established that Betsy really was making regular visits to the cottage, she relaxed her vigil, confiding to the butler that as Johnnie Boniface was spending so much of his time in The Fox, even if Betsy *was* just over the road from him, they weren't likely to be getting up to any mischief. 'A word to the wise,' she said, 'that's all it took. Mrs Haynes is a sensible woman.'

Chapter Eleven

The Fox Inn. Felpham. April 22nd midnight.

My dearest Annie.
    Such a day I've had of it. I have gathered material without pause and I am sure that most of it will prove useful. Blake's pupil was a treasure. She lives in a comfortable house on the southern edge of the village, which she bought when she was newly widowed and it was newly built. She was ready and waiting for me when I arrived and had all her childhood sketches arranged on the parlour table so that I could see them at once. She said Mr Blake had been hired by her parents to teach her and her two sisters to draw: 'they thought we should be accomplished, you see,' *and maintained that he was an angel, being kind and patient and painstaking, with never a cross word. She remembered*

206

him vividly. He'd shown her some of his own drawings so that she could see how to use shading to shape her subject and when I asked her what she thought of them, she said. 'Mr Gilchrist, he was a genius.' *I told her that was my opinion too and she positively beamed at me. She was altogether the most agreeable and amiable person I have encountered since I arrived here. Unfortunately she knew nothing of the trial, having left the village with her family some months before it happened,* 'when invasion was expected almost hourly' *but she knew he stood accused of sedition and that the penalty could have been five years in prison or transportation had he been found guilty.* 'Which would have been a crying shame, for I truly believe that incarceration would have been the death of him.' *I agreed with her that it would indeed, and asked if she knew who had given evidence on his behalf. She told me she was sure it had been the villagers who lived near his cottage or who were in The Fox at the time of his supposed transgression, but could not supply any names or details. However she volunteered to ask her neighbours to see what else she could discover. Best of all she remembered Johnnie Boniface and knew that he had moved away to London and was, so far as she was aware, still alive and prospering, adding* 'his brother Harry would tell you more about him.' *After our talk we took tea like old friends.*

I walked on to my visit with Harry Boniface

in high good humour and you will be pleased to know that all business there was conducted with courtesy and to good purpose. I found him in the milking shed examining one of his cows but I waited with commendable patience until he was finished and then questioned him delicately and said nothing untoward. As he seemed easier than he had been the last time we spoke I ventured to ask him whether his brother was well. He told me that he was but, when I pressed him for a possible introduction, he said he lived in London nowadays and wouldn't be willing to discuss the trial, even if he could remember it, which he thought unlikely. ''Tis all over an' done now Mr Gilchrist sir, an' best left that way.' *You see how they turn all questioning aside, I own I was disappointed by yet another rebuff, but I kept my counsel and said nothing. Perhaps the reporter will know more of the matter, or perhaps I shall find something in the archives. Newspapers are not always kept for posterity, I know, but some matters are considered of sufficient interest to merit storage and a trial for sedition should come into that category. I must live in hope.*

However, once I had stopped asking him about his brother, Mr Boniface was more forthcoming and told me several useful things about William Blake and his wife. He said they were an affectionate couple. People remarked on it. 'I seen 'em many's the time, off for a stroll hand in hand like sweethearts,' *he said.* 'Did your heart good to see 'em.' An' a' course they stayed here, when 'twas all talk of invasion an' most people wouldn't come near the place. You got to admire that.' *I said it must have been a difficult time and he said it was and one they would never forget,* 'although I don't know which was worse, waiting for Boney to invade or having soldiers all over the place, swaggerin' about an' gettin' drunk an' all. It was a soldier made all that trouble for your Mr Blake. Name of Scolfield, as I recall. He's the one you should be talkin' to.' *I asked where I might find him. But he couldn't say.* 'Could be anywhere,' *he said.* 'Dead even. They was fighting at Waterloo not many years after, an' a-many fell there.' *It seemed only too likely so I didn't pursue the topic. But he offered one final piece of information without being prompted.* 'We had one good year while your Mr Blake was here,' *he said,* '1802 it was. They had a peace treaty, as I remember, beginning a' the year. I think it was atween Denmark an' Sweden, but whoever they were it stopped all the fuss about invasion. Not for long mind. It all started up again a year later, but 'twas good while it lasted. Your Mr Blake dug his garden over lovely. He was a very handy man, you see, an' very conscientious. Turn his hand to anything. A good neighbour.'

If only I could discover which of his good neighbours gave evidence for him. There is a story behind this secrecy and I know it as surely as I know anything. It is all very aggravating but I am not aggravated. I do assure you. I am calm as a saint.

It grows late and my candle is little more than a stub. It gives out so much smoke and so little light that I have to stoop over this paper if I am not to write amiss, which I would not wish to do, for it would be the second time this day, would it not. I fear that when I wrote to you this morning I may have written harshly and if that is so, I am sorry for it. I would not wish to distress you, not for all the world.

This from your most loving husband.
Alexander.

P.S. You will find my notes enclosed as usual. I would be glad to know what you think of them, for you know I value your opinion above all other. A. G.

Spring 1802

Spring came in gently that year as if it were determined to be a blessing. The winds of March were little more than a breeze, the sea lapped into shore, milky blue and quiet as a cat, the April showers were as soft as kisses. In Dr Jackson's apple orchard, the blossom grew abundantly and set well, in the Blake's garden the first spring vegetables pushed through the earth as strong as green spears, and in Mr Sparke's piggery, Reuben's sows produced three large and healthy litters, to his ebullient delight.

'Tha's set us all up for the winter an' no mistake,' he said from his usual seat in The Fox Inn. 'Be no shortage a' good bacon this year.'

'You'd think he give birth to 'em hisself, the way he go on,' his friends teased. The fading light of that April evening softened their faces, smoothed the earth-stained roughness of their clothes to shadowy gentleness and transformed the dull gleam of their pewter tankards into a gilded shimmer.

'Oi darn near did with the last litter,' Reuben said. 'If Oi hadn't ha' been there she'd've overlaid the lot of 'em.'

'Stranger things've happened,' Mr Grinder told them from behind the bar. 'There was a woman once give birth to a litter a' rabbits so they say. Evenin' Mr Haynes. How's that ol' sail a-goin'?'

'Took us the whole blamed afternoon,' Mr Haynes told them, wiping his hands on his breeches. 'You never see such a to-do. 'Tis back in workin' order now though.'

They told him they were very glad to hear it and it was no more than the truth, for a broken sail on their main flourmill would have affected all their fortunes and now that the London swells were coming to the seaside again, their fortunes were looking up. Nelson's victory at Copenhagen hadn't simply broken the Northern Alliance, it had had a beneficial effect on trade and travel as well. The rich were taking excursions to the continent again and many were spending a few days at the seaside en route. There were carriage folk at the Dome and others lodging for a night or two in all the inns in the village. Mr Grinder already had a couple staying in one of his upper rooms and there were four more booked to arrive at the start of June.

Mr Haynes kicked through the sawdust to the bar. 'An' how's your visitors then, George?' he said to Mr Grinder.

'Off to dine with their friends at the Dome,' the landlord said. 'Proper old gadabouts. They've had our Will on the run since crack a' dawn.'

'He'll be glad of the work though,' Mr Haynes said.

'He's not complaining,' Mr Grinder agreed.

He wasn't digging Mr Blake's garden for him either. 'Can't be done Oi'm afeared,' he explained to his fellow William. 'Oi'd help if Oi could but Oi'm run off me feet.'

So Catherine and William tended the vegetable plot themselves, which was no hardship to them when the weather was so balmy, the earth so pliable and the path beside their gate so full of cheerful activity. Felpham was in holiday mood and there was a daily chattering procession to the sea. Elegant ladies, wearing *bergère* hats of woven straw tied under the chin with summer ribbons, fancied that they were shepherdesses as they teetered two by two towards the pebbles in their silken dresses and their pretty leather shoes, while their husbands walked at a more considered pace and a little behind them, solemn with the importance of their money-earning masculinity. Crowing infants sat in wickerwork baby carriages brandishing rattles, their little pink faces shaded against the sun by the prettiest lace-edged parasols, while their nursemaids sweated in serviceable fustian as they trundled them along the earth road or paused to call the older children back to the safety of their skirts. 'Don't go too far, Master John.' 'Take care, Miss Phoebe. We don't want you drownded.' And all of them waved to the Blakes as they passed and bade them 'Good morning.' It was a warm, light-hearted time.

There was plenty of work for everybody. Mr Hayley gave countless dinner parties for his visiting friends, Mr Grinder hired another chambermaid and two more potboys and Eddie was offered a job as second ostler at the George and took it happily.

'Be a nice change from just muckin' out,'

he told his friends at Turret House.

Betsy wished him luck like everyone else, though privately she thought it was an unwelcome change and would have miserable consequences unless she and Johnnie could persuade the new stable lad to be accommodating. But for the moment the sun was shining, there were haystacks aplenty and, although they had even less time to themselves than usual, at least they had privacy out in the clear air and the warm fields.

So it was a surprise to everyone when the quarrels began.

The first was because Reuben Jones stood on a rake and bruised his foot. Ordinarily he would have accepted that he'd been clumsy and joked his pain away, but on this occasion he roared round the farmyard blaming everyone in sight for being 'such danged fools as to leave the danged thing a-lyin' about.'

'You might ha' know'd someone'ud get hisself hurt!' he yelled.

'With you in the yard,' his workmates retorted, 'how could we be off a' knowin'?'

At which he grabbed a fork and jabbed at them like a man demented, and they skipped out of his way, laughing and egging him on and driving him to more and more ridiculous excesses, until the farmer arrived to restore order by roaring.

The second was a stand-up fight between Mr Grinder's two new potboys, which began in the bar over a tip they were both claiming and yelled into the street where it gathered a cheering crowd. That was a more bloody affair, with split lips, torn knuckles and a broken nose, and it didn't stop until Mrs Grinder came out in a temper and told them they were worse than a pair of turkey cocks and threw a bucket of cold water over them.

And then that same afternoon, Mrs Beke removed the new stable lad from her kitchen by his ears and the coachman came storming into the house in high dudgeon and dirty boots to point out that the lad was his responsibility and to advise her to desist if she knew what was good for her. And Mrs Beke declared that she had never been spoken to in such a way in the whole of her life and gave him such a blazing piece of her mind it was a wonder the kitchen didn't burst into spontaneous conflagration.

From then on there seemed to be a quarrel every other day. Mrs Haynes said she thought the village was bewitched, 'I never see such a pack,' she said. 'Allus at one another's throats. I don't know what's got into them. You'd think they'd have enough to do without all this carry-on.'

William Blake certainly had more than

enough to do. Now that the 'Life of Cowper' had been written – even if it wasn't entirely to Lady Hesketh's satisfaction – Mr Hayley had returned to his ballads and had instructed his 'engraver' to produce the illustrations for the next four, which he was sure would sell 'in great quantity'. The drawing of 'The Elephant' was already completed and now he was working on 'The Eagle', 'The Lion' and 'The Dog'. It was very annoying when what he really wanted to do was to complete his half-written epic 'Vala' and begin work on the new poem that was burning his brain with constant fire.

Unfortunately the ballads didn't sell at all well, which was a disappointment to both men. Hayley was aggrieved because he felt his excellence was being unaccountably scorned, and Blake was angry. He was the one who had bought the paper for this venture, so he stood to lose his investment, and he hadn't wanted to illustrate the things in the first place. For the first time since his arrival in the village he spoke out to his patron, accusing him of putting too much work his way and depriving him of the time he needed to work on his own poetry.

The celebrated poet was considerably put out. As he explained to Mrs Beke afterwards, at some length and with much injured passion, he'd gone to a deal of trouble to persuade his friends to offer Mr Blake commissions, so it was ungrateful and hurtful of him to complain of it, indeed it was. For some weeks the two men were cool with one another and for two weeks Hayley went to breakfast with Miss Poole without his secretary. Then, in July, just when he hoped they were beginning to patch up their differences and they were both breakfasting with Miss Poole again, he was summoned to Bristol to report to Lady Hesketh.

He travelled with as much support as he could muster – his coachman, naturally, his valet and two of the chambermaids – so he required both carriages, which meant that Johnnie was commandeered to drive the second one, he being more knowledgeable about Mr Hayley's horses than the new stable lad, who didn't seem to be knowledge-able about anything except porter. The arrangement didn't suit the stable lad, who went about his labours in a black sulk, and it didn't suit Betsy either. She said she couldn't see the necessity for two carriages and sighed and complained until Johnnie kissed her and promised he'd be back like greased lightning.

In fact they were gone for ten days and she missed him miserably on every single one of them. What was the good of all that sunshine if she couldn't be out in the fields with her darling?

Mr and Mrs Blake, on the other hand,

were glad of warm weather. Catherine's knees didn't ache so much when the sun shone and William could enjoy his rides to Lavant to take breakfast with Miss Poole. When Hayley announced his impending visit to Bristol, he assumed that the breakfasts would be put into abeyance until his return, but Miss Poole had another opinion of it. 'You must come without him,' she said to Blake. 'I must have company of a morning, and he'll not mind, will you Mr Hayley.'

So the new stable boy was left instructions and managed to saddle Bruno on his own and to lead him out to the mounting block as if he'd been doing such things all his life and William took an easy ride to Lavant to keep the lady company. It was one of the most pleasant meals they'd taken together for they talked of poetry throughout and of William's poetry in particular.

'I have heard so much about Mr Hayley's "Life of Cowper" and his collection of ballads,' she said, 'but very little about your work, Mr Blake,'

'I fear I have written very little of late,' he had to confess.

She pressed him. 'But something, I am sure,' she said, 'for I cannot believe that your talents are without expression of any kind.'

So he told her about the poem he'd been writing before he came to Sussex and tried to explain what it was about. ''Tis the story of mankind and the manner in which our lives are passed here on earth,' he said, 'an account of our hopes and despairs, our trials, our triumphs and disappointments.' The explanation didn't satisfy him, for it was too brief and over simplified, but she understood it well enough to question him.

'Then you are writing an epic, are you not?'

He agreed that he was.

'Mr Hayley is of the opinion that the epic is the highest form of literature,' she said, 'as he has doubtless told you. I take it that your story is written in the mythological style.' And when he told her that it was, she urged him to explain the major figures to her. 'I have heard much about the great mythologies, naturally,' she said, 'the gods of Greece and Rome. Do these appear in your epic, or do you use the Christian mythology?'

'Neither, ma'am,' Blake told her and added with pride, 'I have minted a new mythology of my own.'

She was surprised and impressed. 'Have you so?' she said. 'In that case, you have set yourself a mighty task.'

So he told her about Vala, 'who is the eternal female, a goddess of beauty and nature, the lily of the desert, veiled in beauty and yet wearing the veil of moral virtue, which is woven by laws.'

'Which is why you have called her "Veil-a".'

'Exactly so but I spell it VALA.'

'A woman of great beauty and moral virtue,' Miss Poole said, leaning her chin on her hand, as she considered what he had said. 'She sounds a magnificent creature. Does she represent truth and goodness, too? Is she the pattern of perfection?'

They had reached the heart of his thinking. 'No, ma'am,' he said. 'She is composed of contraries, as we all are. I do not believe in opposites, Miss Poole. There is no right and wrong for me, no good and evil. To think that is to distort the truth. We are all things at once, love and hatred, kindness and cruelty, pleasure and pain, never all good, never all bad. I try to reflect that condition in everything I write.'

''Tis a dangerous doctrine, Mr Blake,' she said smiling at him, 'and there are many who would take exception to it, especially among the clergy.'

'I know it,' he said, smiling back. 'But I must write what I know to be true.'

'Is there a god, Mr Blake, to match your veiled goddess?'

'There is.'

'Composed of contraries, too, no doubt. What do you call *him?*'

'His name is Lover,' he told her. 'But not spelt as you would expect. I have spelt him

L U V A H, to show that love is delight and despair, pleasure and pain, selfish and unselfish and all shades between.'

'The clod and the pebble,' she said, remembering.

Their conversation continued for another hour after the meal was over, which was most unusual. 'We will talk again on Friday,' she promised when they finally parted. 'You must bring me what is written of your great epic and read it to me. I should like to hear it.'

He was ecstatic to have found such under-standing and returned home in a state of such euphoria he fairly bounded through the wicket gate into his garden. The two Catherines had spent the morning hard at work washing the dirty linen and when he arrived they were out in the garden draping the wet clothes over the walls and bushes to dry.

''Twas a pleasant visit, I see,' his wife observed, hanging his shirt on the flint wall, where it dangled an inch above the young corn like a man in a faint.

'Our lady Paulina,' he said, calling her by Hayley's pet name for her, 'is a woman of quite splendid intelligence. She has asked to see all that I have written of "Vala".'

She did even better than that. For when he returned for their second tête-à-tête, she told him very firmly that he must complete his great work. ''Tis insupportable that poetry of such quality be left unfinished,' she said. 'I trust you will return to it at the very first opportunity.'

He returned to it that very afternoon, using the unsold copies of Mr Hayley's ballads as rough paper, and working with such speed and satisfaction that it was all he could do to absent himself from his mythical lovers for long enough to eat his supper.

His sister made her wry grimace. ''Tis as well I leave you tomorrow,' she said to Catherine, 'for he'll be monstrous company 'til that's done. We shan't have a word out of him.'

His wife was surprised when he walked his sister into Lavant the next day without a word of complaint and kissed her goodbye quite fondly, but he made up for his restraint on the way home, complaining bitterly that he'd lost a morning's work and that every moment was precious. 'My tormentor could be home tomorrow,' he said, 'and if that is the case, I shall be dragged back to his engravings and there won't be a word written for weeks.'

But as it turned out he had another four days of freedom and by the time the two Hayley carriages bedraggled back to Turret House, a very great deal had been written.

Chapter Twelve

August 1802

William Hayley was in high good humour when he got back to Felpham after his visit to Bristol. The 'Life of Cowper' was selling well and had received ecstatic reviews and Lady Hesketh was satisfied at last.

'It is well thought of, you see,' he said to Blake, as they set off to Lavant for their next breakfast with Miss Poole. 'A fine work. Paulina will be pleased.'

She praised him fulsomely, as he expected, and said that it was no more than he deserved. Then she praised Blake too, when he'd told her how much progress he was making with his work. 'He is composing an epic, Mr Hayley,' she said.

'I am glad to hear it,' Hayley said generously. 'The epic is the highest literary form known to man.'

Unfortunately, it wasn't quite high enough to take precedence over his next commission. Later that morning, when they were back at Turret House, he asked Blake to join him in the library for a few minutes before his return to the cottage and, once there, told him he had an excellent commission for him. Lady Hesketh, 'a woman of exquisite taste and ever mindful to enhance my reputation' had suggested that he should produce another edition of his famous poem 'The Triumphs of Temper'. 'Her advice is sound,' he said, 'so I shall comply with her wishes. Naturally, my dear friend, you are just the man to provide fresh illustrations.'

To his credit his dear friend didn't rage or argue, much though he wanted to, but accepted the commission with as good a grace as he could summon up. A new design would pay well and it would give him scope to draw an original figure or two, which would be no bad thing. But to his chagrin he discovered that six designs had already been chosen. All that he was required to do was to copy and engrave them. Even then he kept his nervous fear under control and merely asked the name of the artist who had drawn the originals. It was a crushing blow to be told that it was Maria, the sister of their mutual friend, Mr Flaxman, a pleasant enough woman, as he knew having met her, but one with no artistic talent whatsoever. He received the information like the insult it was.

'You try me too hard,' he said to Mr Hayley. 'Indeed you do, sir. 'Tis not to be borne.'

'I provide you with gainful employment,'

Mr Hayley pointed out, his face stiff with displeasure. 'Which you would do well to remember.'

The rebuke provoked an outburst of anger. 'How can I forget when I am burdened on every side?' Blake cried. 'I labour for you day and night, sir. I have no time to call my own. 'Tis the devil's work to treat me so.'

It was a long quarrel and a very loud one. The household walked on tiptoe and held its breath so as not to miss a word. And that night in The Fox it was rehearsed and savoured with great enjoyment. 'At it hammer an' tongs they was,' Mr Hosier reported. 'I could hear 'em out in the garden.'

'Who'd ha' thought our mad poet would go off like that?' Mr Cosens asked, puffing smoke. 'I allus thought he was a mild sort a' man.'

'Oi would,' Reuben said, nodding knowledgeably. 'Oi knew he was a firebrand first time Oi see him. You can tell by that oiye of his'n. That's the fiercest oiye Oi ever see. Loike a sabre.'

'He got a good pair a' shoulders on him,' Mr Haynes observed, 'what's more to the mark if you're a-fightin'. If it come to fisticuffs I'd back him against anybody.'

But a fierce eye and a pair of broad shoulders were no help to Mr Blake in his present predicament. He could rage all he liked and put his tongue to every bit of low abuse he could bring to mind, but the engravings had to be done. He was short of money now that the ballads weren't selling and even as anger swelled in his brain he knew he had no option but to do as he was bid. It was corrosive knowledge. Two days after the quarrel he took a fever and was ill for more than a fortnight. And when he finally struggled from his bed and declared that he was ready to work again, Maria's wretched drawings lay on his round table to taunt him.

''Tis beyond endurance,' he said to Catherine as he prepared the first plate. 'I have neither the energy nor the will for it. And now here's September come and neither of us well.'

But no matter how he felt the work had to be completed. He laboured miserably as darkness seeped into the cottage and the cold air chilled his bones. It was late October before even two engravings were finished and he knew they were poorly produced and would print badly. How could it be otherwise when the originals were so clumsily drawn? He trudged them up to Turret House, hunched against a north-east wind, knowing he had taken too long with them, feeling cold and crabby and determined to be justified in his anger. And was then given even greater justification when the prints were taken from him at the door and he was not invited in.

'You see how it is,' he said to Catherine on his return. 'You see how he treats me.' He was white with fury, his blue eyes blazing. ''Tis not to be endured.'

But he had to endure it just the same. He had no choice.

The weeks passed and the quarrel dragged on. There were no more rides to Lavant and the comfort of Lady Paulina, no evenings in the library studying Greek and Latin – not that he could have expected such a thing after such harsh words had been exchanged – worse still, no news of any other commissions to keep him going through the winter. He had made a grievous mistake and now he was paying for it, betrayed by his own terrible nervous fear, caught up in the perpetual dilemma of any artist, with time to write his own poetry but with no money to clothe them and keep them fed.

His inability to provide for them was anguish to him and Catherine, watching as he scowled and sweated over his great work in a room half lit and poorly heated, knew it and grieved for him. In the end she put on her bonnet, pulled up the collar of her greatcoat and walked up the lane to see if a gentle approach would mollify their powerful neighbour.

He received her politely but was beyond mollification. He would, he said, endeavour to procure such commissions as he could for her husband, since he had given his word to Mr Flaxman that he would be a helpful patron and he had always been a man of his word, but he was of the opinion that they would be better advised to keep a sensible distance between them. 'I am a man of extreme sensitivities,' he told her, 'and was much hurt by your husband's belligerent attitude.'

She tried to argue William's case, pointing out that he had always suffered from nervous fear, 'as so many artists do, Mr Cowper among them,' and that he often said things he did not truly mean. But Mr Hayley was adamant. The rift had occurred and the rift would continue. He would remunerate Mr Blake for the work he was doing and pay her to run off the copies he required, but that was all.

The walk back to the cottage took her considerably longer than the walk out because she was so dispirited and, when she rounded the bend in the path and saw that William was waiting for her outside the wicket gate, her heart contracted with distress. He was in a black temper, demanding to know where she had been, and when he was told, he erupted into such a vitriolic attack that she recoiled from him as if he was spitting fire.

How could she belittle him so? What was

she thinking of? There was no talking to Hayley. She must know that. He was a man without compassion, a man full of spite and jealousy. Bad enough he should be imposing his will upon a fellow poet, is he now to be allowed to come between a man and his wife?

She retreated from him, withdrawing to the kitchen where she busied herself preparing supper. It was impossible to reach him in a mood as deep and black as this one and she had more sense than to try. She peeled the potatoes and listened. And presently she heard him stomping into his work room, where he thwacked at the logs with the poker, scraped a chair into position before the table, rustled a paper. Then, to her relief, there was silence, and she knew he was working and hoped that his work would heal him.

But the words he wrote in the days that followed were bitter and dripped from his pen like gall.

God is not a Being of Pity and Compassion
He cannot feel Distress: he feeds on Sacrifice
  & Offering
Delighting in cries and tears & clothed in
  holiness & solitude
But my griefs advance also, for ever and ever
  without end
O that I could cease to be! Despair! I am
  Despair

Created to be the great example of horror &
   agony.
To be all evil, all reversed & for ever dead.

For the next few days the cottage was
shrouded in his misery. Then he roused
himself sufficiently to write to Thomas
Butts, his dear old friend who had stood by
him through the lean years in London and
was often the only one who had commissioned work from him. The first letter was
hard to compose because he owed his old
friend at least two pictures and hadn't
written to him for more than a year, so he
began with an apology. But that done, he
wrote with greater fluency, although with
extreme gloom, telling his dear Mr Butts
what unsuitable employment Mr Hayley
had provided and how he was constrained
to do the work, insulting though it was, and
how exceedingly unhappy it made him. 'I
should be employed in greater things,' he
mourned.

Thomas Butts wrote back by return of
post, like the good man he was, and offered
a commission for two more paintings, tact-
fully neglecting to mention that the two he
had ordered before the Blakes left for
Felpham had yet to be delivered. 'You must
not despair,' he comforted. 'You are a great
artist and one day the world will know it.'

His friendship was so staunch it began to
lift Blake's depression. He wrote again. And

again, swinging from despair into a mood of exaggerated bravado and self-justification. 'I have Spiritual Enemies of formidable magnitude,' he wrote. 'I have travel'd thro' Perils & Darkness not unlike a Champion. I have conquer'd and shall still Go on Conquering. Nothing can withstand the fury of my course among the Stars of God. I am under the direction of Messengers from heaven, daily & nightly.' And when that letter was written, he walked down to the empty beach, where his messengers were waiting, and listened to the power of their voices and was comforted.

But now the first snows of winter were beginning to fall and, even with Mr Butts' commission, he was still parlously short of money and his poor dear Catherine was suffering from aching bones again. 'We will stay here until our tenancy has run out,' he told her. 'The rent is paid and we cannot afford to waste twenty pounds. Then we will go back to London, I promise you. You will have better health there and I shall be beyond the power of my enemies.'

The first snowfall brought misery to Johnnie and Betsy too. They had been happy lovers all through the summer and far into autumn, sneaking into any barn that lay open to them, but now the farm dogs were ready for them wherever they went and the barns were too cold for comfort and they were facing another winter of enforced celibacy.

'It aren't to be endured,' Betsy said, just as she had the previous year. 'We can't go on like this, Johnnie. We must do somethin' about it.'

But what? That was the problem. There was nowhere that either of them could think of, except the stable room and that had a new tenant now in Sam the stable lad, who wasn't disposed to be friendly, not since Johnnie had been preferred as the second coachman. The evenings passed in a misery of frustration. They were back to drifting about the garden shivering and complaining.

In the end Betsy said she thought they should risk the stable room. 'He'll never know,' she said. 'We could be gone long afore he come back, now couldn't we. What's to stop us? He don't want it in the evenin's. He's always in The Fox.'

Johnnie tried to be sensible. 'I can tell 'ee what's to stop us,' he said. 'He could come back unexpected an' catch us, that's what's to stop us.'

'No fear a' that,' she said. 'He spends every evenin' in The Fox, drinkin' hisself silly. I knows on account of I been watchin' him.'

'But what if he don't?'

'We'll keep an eye out for him,' Betsy said,

'through the little window. Anyways he won't come back. He's too fond a' porter for that.

It was risky, even so, and Johnnie knew it, but she was so persuasive and so pretty and he wanted her so much that, in the end, he stifled his fears and, two nights later, which was the next opportunity they had, they sneaked up the ladder to their old love nest, she pink-checked with excitement, he shivering with anxiety and repressed desire. The place was almost exactly as they remembered it. They snuggled into the welcoming mattress as if they were returning home, loved long and lustily – and were back in the kitchen, calmed, satisfied and tidy, a clear half hour before the stable lad came whistling into the garden.

'There you are, you see,' Betsy said, when Johnnie strode into the kitchen with the vegetables next morning. 'I was right. Nothin' ventured, nothin' gained.'

'There's no stoppin' you,' he said, admiring her, and was just about to suggest that they went to the stables again that evening when Mrs Beke brisked over to check the potatoes so the arrangement had to be left till later.

Now that they'd proved they could take risks with impunity, they used the stable room whenever they could. Johnnie was still worried about it because they hadn't asked permission and were probably trespassing, but as the weeks went by he stilled his conscience with argument. 'Tweren't as if they were doing anythin' wrong, now was it. 'Tweren't as if they were harmin' anyone. All they were a-doin' was just usin' an empty room when nobody else wanted it. Betsy was right. There weren't no harm in that. As the days shortened and the regulars at The Fox drank deeper and longer, they stayed in their nest for longer and longer too, reluctant to step out into the cold again for their dash to the house. They were so happy there, so warm in one another's arms, so sure of themselves.

Christmas was celebrated with a twelfth night party that kept them all up and hard at work until two in the morning and two days later, there was a heavy fall of snow, which lay so thickly outside the stable door that they were afraid of leaving tracks and had to postpone their happy evenings until the horses had come out to churn everything up and the paths had been marked by hooves and footprints. Even then a visit was more risky than usual, for, as Johnnie pointed out, if fresh snow fell while they were inside, they would leave tracks when they left.

'We shall have to walk backwards, tha's all,' Betsy said, laughing his fears away.

'Then 'twill look as if we come up here an' went away again.' She had an answer for everything.

So the cold nights passed in warm delights and the snow thawed and no footprints had led to discovery. ''Twill be spring soon,' Johnnie said one evening as they lay recovering in one another's arms.

'It don't sound much like spring to me,' she said, as the wind roared in the elm trees. Then her body tensed and her voice changed to whispering alarm. 'Oh, my God! Oh, my dear good God!'

There was a head protruding through the trap door, its face creased with malevolent triumph. They could smell the ale on its breath and the grease on its cap, feel the heat of its anger, see the gleam of its eyes in the too-revealing moonlight. The stable lad had come home.

'Ho,' he said. 'Oi know'd there was somethin' a-goin' on. Well now, Oi've caught 'ee. Caught 'ee good an' proper. You wait till Oi tell Mrs Beke. She'll have somethin' to say, you see if she don't.'

Johnnie tried to find an excuse. 'We came in out the cold, Sam,' he said. 'Tha's all. 'Twas onny for a minute.'

'Out the cold moi oiye,' Sam said. 'Oi ent green. Oi got my wits about me. Oi knows what you was a-doin'. You was up to no good. She got her skirt right up round her waist, this minute. An' ho yes, you can pull it down now miss, but Oi seen what Oi seen. You don't fool me. Oi shall tell Mrs Beke, tha's what. See what *she* thinks.'

'No,' Johnnie said, 'there's no need for that, Sam. I can explain.'

'You comes in here,' Sam said, 'you takes moi job off a' me, drivin' that there carriage, what Oi ent forgot, an' now you thinks you can come in here an' take moi room an' all. Well, 'tis moi room, Oi'll have 'ee know, an' you ent welcome in it.'

Johnnie was in command of himself now, his breeches fastened, sitting on the edge of the bed, leaning forward towards his adversary. He would have stood up if such a thing had been possible but sitting straight was the next best thing. 'Now look 'ee here,' he said. 'I haven't took your job. I was asked to drive the carriage, just the once, on account of I knew the horses better than you did. You'd onny just arrived, which you got to admit.'

Sam sneered. 'If you thinks you can fob me off with a load a' fool talk about hosses,' he said, 'you got another think comin'. Oi'm off to see Mrs Beke an' then we'll see.'

'No,' Johnnie said. 'Wait.'

But it was too late. The stable lad was already running through the stable. They watched through their little window as he sprinted across the black lawn, dark legs scissoring.

236

Betsy was still lying on the bed, too stunned to move. 'What are we goin' to do?' she cried. 'Oh, Johnnie what are we goin' to do? I shall be dismissed sure as eggs is eggs.'

Johnnie was surprised by how calm he felt. 'We're goin' back to the house an' up to bed, same as usual,' he told her. 'There's nothin' we can do to stop him now. We'll just have to weather it out.'

They tiptoed back to the house and crept up the main stairs in their stockinged feet, because the servants' stairs led out of the kitchen and it was quite possible that Mrs Beke was in her parlour, listening to the stable lad, and the one thing neither of them wanted at that moment was to have to face her. They knew it was wrong to retire without her permission and wrong to use the main staircase, but they were in so much trouble already, two more, lesser sins were easily committed. But there was a night to get through, and the night was hag-ridden and full of stinging questions. What would she say? And worse, what would she do? What possible excuse could they offer?

Betsy tossed and turned so often it was a wonder she didn't wake her companions, but no amount of restless movement provided her with any answers. She knew their lovemaking was right and proper and that it was only a sin according to the priests, but she could hardly expect the housekeeper to agree with her, and using Sam's room without telling him was definitely wrong – Johnnie had said so all along only she wouldn't listen. They'd be punished as sure as eggs was eggs. She couldn't see any way to avoid it.

Johnnie had an even worse night than she did. He should never have agreed to use Sam's room. He'd known it was wrong all along. You can't go breaking into someone else's room. He had an unpleasant feeling that using the stable was trespassing and there were laws to cover trespass. He didn't know what they were nor what the penalties would be but if you crossed the law you always suffered for it. By the time the dawn broke he was haggard with anxiety and lack of sleep.

He put on his jacket and his gardening boots and apron and went out into the grounds. If there was a punishment waiting for him, the sooner he faced it the better.

Mr Hosier was up early too and busy in the outhouse, gathering implements. He didn't seem particularly cross and gave his helper a grin. Was that a good sign or a bad one?

'So wha's all this I hear 'bout you bein' up to no good with our Betsy?' he said, but he spoke amiably and didn't wait for Johnnie to answer. 'Find a better place next time. Tha's my advice to 'ee. Never piss on your own doorstep. Now then, see if you can find the twine. 'Tis about here somewhere onny I'm danged if I can see it. That ol' wind's done a power a' damage last night. All his honeysuckle's throw'd every which way an' what he'll say if he comes down an' sees how 'tis, I dreads to think. Ah! Tha's it! You found it. Good feller.' He picked up a pair of shears, ready to start work. 'If I was you,' he advised, 'I'd marry the girl.'

Johnnie swallowed hard. 'I *have* asked her,' he said.

'Oh, well, tha's settled then,' Mr Hosier said, smiling at him. 'Come along. No time to loose.'

Johnnie was weak with relief. It was all right. A storm in a teacup, that's all. No real harm done. Praise be! He'd get the honeysuckle tied up and then he'd find some excuse to go up to the house and tell poor Betsy. He followed Mr Hosier into the garden feeling quite light-hearted.

But he was wrong, of course. Harm was being done at that very moment. Betsy had risen early too and come down to the kitchen to show willing by lighting the fire, fetching the water and setting the table. It didn't do her any good as she could see the minute Mrs Beke walked into the kitchen, for that lady was wearing her sternest face and her breath streamed before her in the cold air like a dragon breathing smoke.

'Ah, there you are, Betsy Haynes,' she said, rubbing her hands to warm them. 'And what have you got to say for yourself, pray?'

Betsy winced. It was no good pretending she didn't understand.

'We didn't mean no harm, ma'am,' she said.

'I wonder at you, Betsy,' Mrs Beke said. 'I truly do. I thought you had more sense. What your mother will say when she hears of it, I cannot imagine.'

Betsy's heart took a palpable lurch downwards. The one person she didn't want to hear of it was her mother. There'd never be any end to the scolding if *she* heard. 'Please don't tell her, ma'am,' she begged. ''Twon't happen again, I give 'ee my word.'

'No,' Mrs Beke said sternly. 'It won't. An' I'll tell 'ee for why. It won't on account of I shall make sure it don't. I can't have that sort of carry-on in this house an' there's an end of it. The master won't stand for it. I don't know what you were thinking of, I really don't. You'll get yourself a reputation you go on like this and then what'll happen to you? Have you thought of that?' She was into her stride now, happily unleashing her anger. 'To say nothing of falling for a baby. If you haven't all-a-ready. Which wouldn't surprise me given what young Sam was telling me last night. 'Tis a scandal and if we're not careful 'twill be all over the village.

240

You should be ashamed of yourself. You've been acting like a common slut.'

'I haven't fell for no baby,' Betsy said, trying to defend herself.

Mrs Beke snorted. 'We all says that and a fat lot of good it does us. You could ha' fell last night. Have you thought a' that? No, course not. You young girls are all the same. You haven't got a happorth a' sense between the lot of you. Bit a' sweet talk and you give in directly. An' don't think he'll marry you, neither, for they never do. If they can get what they want without benefit of clergy, why should they bother making vows? Oh no, *you* won't be walking up no aisle and don't 'ee think it.'

'You're wrong,' Betsy said stung by so many insults. 'He'd marry me tomorrow. He said so.'

'Ho, yes?' the housekeeper mocked. 'I don't exactly see him a-standing there beside you, though, do I? If he loves you he should be here standing up for you.'

It was true. He should. Oh, why isn't he here?

'Oh, no,' Mrs Beke went on, 'you mark my words, you won't see him for dust now 'tis known. You'll be dropped and forgot, same as all the others. You've let yourself down and your mother down and me down and Mr Hayley. You're a bad wicked girl, that's what you are. A bad wicked girl. I don't know what's to become of you.'

There were feet approaching on the servants' stairs, a murmur of girls' voices. The rest of the household was arriving. The sound of them panicked Betsy into instant and active alarm. 'I'll tell 'ee what's to become of me,' she said wildly, striding to the coat cupboard to find her cloak. 'I'm a-leavin' this house. Now, this minute. Tha's what I'm a-doin'. I ent staying here to be insulted. I'm off.'

'Go then,' Mrs Beke said. 'Best thing.' But she was talking to the air. Betsy had already flounced out of the door.

Chapter Thirteen

By the time Johnnie Boniface walked into the kitchen with three cabbages and a string of onions as peace offering and excuse, Betsy's departure had been discussed at length and with great excitement for the last two hours. Most of the kitchen staff had heard the row on their way downstairs and the boot boy had run over to the stables to see if Sam knew anything about it and had heard the whole story. There hadn't been such excitement in Turret House since the master cracked his head open the last time he fell off his horse and came home streaming blood.

Johnnie was embarrassed by all the knowing glances he was given but he tried to appear unconcerned. There was bound to be a bit of teasing, that was only to be expected. But when Susie looked up at him, she had such a scurrilous expression on her face that he blushed furiously before he could stop himself

'Ho-ho,' she said. 'You're a dark horse an' no mistake, Johnnie Boniface. We all knows what you was up to last night.'

'What's no concern a' yours,' he said, trying to speak lightly. 'Where's Mrs Beke?'

'Upstairs with Mr Hayley, takin' instructions for dinner,' Susie told him. 'Oi'd ha' thought you'd've been asking where Betsy is.'

'Well, she aren't here,' he said. 'I can see that.'

'Run off,' Susie told him.

His heart contracted with alarm. 'What d'you mean run off?'

'Took her cloak an' gone,' Nan told him. 'We don't know no more of it than that. Took her cloak an' rushed off.'

He stood before them, one earth-stained hand on the cabbages, thinking hard. Off in a temper, that much was obvious, so she must have been scolded. Oh, my poor dear darling, he thought, knowing how she must

243

have felt, imagining her running from the room, tears streaming from those dear blue eyes. She could never stand a scolding. I should have been here to protect you and tell them 'twas all my fault. I should have come straight here the minute I finished talking to Mr Hosier and stood up for you. Too late now. The damage was done. But where would she go? Not to her mother's. That'ud be the last place. Nor to the mill neither. If her father knew he'd tell her mother, sure as fate, for he wasn't a man to keep secrets. The Blake's maybe. That was likely. I'll get through my work as quick as I can and go down and see.

Catherine Blake was pleased to see him because she thought he'd come with a message from Mr Hayley but as he stood before her, awkwardly shy in his muddy boots and his stained apron, she realised that there was no message and that something was amiss and invited him in. 'We must be quiet,' she warned, 'for William is at work.'

They sat by the fire in the kitchen and he told her what had happened, speaking frankly but as quietly as he could. 'I'd ha' married her long since,' he said, 'onny she wouldn't agree to it. An' now she's gone, an' I don't know where she is, an' I don't know what to do, an' that's the honest truth.'

Her advice was quiet and practical. She hadn't been out of the house since yesterday afternoon, so she hadn't heard anything about anybody, but she promised to see what she could find out. 'Someone's certain to know something in a place this size,' she said, 'and if she's still here, which I'm sure she is, she'll come to church on Sunday, now won't she. Bound to. Everyone goes to church of a Sunday except us and Mr Hayley. So you'll see her then if not before.'

'But that's four days away,' he protested. How could he wait for four days when anything could have happened to her?

His distress was endearing. 'You could be back together long before then,' she reassured. 'Meantime I shall listen to the gossip and if I hear anything, I'll come straight up to Turret House and let you know. Take heart, she'll not have gone far.'

'I will find her,' he said, as they parted on the doorstep. 'Never fear.' But he was comforting himself, not reassuring her, and they both knew it.

The next three days were the most miserable he had ever spent. In what little spare time he had, he walked about the village in a harsh rain, seeking out old friends and neighbours and talking nonsense to them until he could find the right moment to wonder if they'd seen Betsy about. None of them had and most were surprised to be asked.

'Oi thought you was walkin' out,' old Mrs Taylor said. 'Now don' tell me you've been an' gone an' quarrelled for that Oi *won't* believe. Not when Oi've seen 'ee so lovey-dovey. Though I has to say tha's been a bad ol' year for spats an' argyments. I never seen a worse one.'

Naturally he assured her that they hadn't quarrelled. 'I wouldn't quarrel with her for the world.' But it hurt him to have to admit that he didn't know where she was.

'You'll see her Sunday,' Mrs Taylor promised. 'She won't miss church, now will she. What would her mother say?'

But Johnnie was beginning to feel he would never see her again and had nightmares about her, perched aloft on the London stage, her red cloak flapping in the wind, stony-faced, as she drove away from him. And Sunday took an eternity to arrive.

It was a dank brooding day and the sky was cold and colourless. The sun rose reluctantly, white as whey and giving little light and no heat, and below it the village was mud-smeared and waterlogged, paths puddled, bare branches oozing oily moisture, thatches dark with damp, doors and gates wet to the touch. As he walked the few hundred yards from Turret House to St Mary's church, Johnnie had to will himself not to shiver.

There were very few people waiting by the porch, it was too cold for that, only Reuben Jones, who was chewing his gums, and his wife, who was stamping her feet, and Mr and Mrs Haynes, who nodded at him but didn't speak. He loitered just inside the porch, out of sight of his neighbours but near enough to see his darling if she came along the path.

And suddenly, there she was. He'd know that red cloak anywhere, even if it *was* moving in an unfamiliar way. It hurt him that she wasn't tripping up the path the way she usually did, bright and happy and looking about her. Now she walked wearily with her head bowed and her hood hiding her face. Oh, my darling love, he thought, and stepped forward to greet her. But her mother was before him and her mother was so loud with accusation and concern that he stepped back inside the porch again and kept out of the way.

'Where on earth have you been, you bad girl?' she said. 'We been worried out of our lives. Look at the state a' you, hair all anyhow, filthy dirty, an' look at the state a' your hands. What've you been a-doin' to yourself?'

'I been milkin' cows,' Betsy said, flatly. 'Don't fuss, Ma. I had words with Mrs Beke but tha's all done with. I got messell a new job up Middleton way. I'm doin' all right.'

'You don't look all right to me,' her mother said, holding her by the shoulders. 'You look half starved. What dairy? Not one that feeds you seemingly. Nor one what has water for washin'. I never seen you in such a pickle. This is what comes a' buying that dratted cardinal. I knew we'd have trouble the minute I saw it. Didn't I say so, Father?' But as her daughter's lip was trembling she stopped scolding and became practical. 'Ah well,' she said. 'Least said soonest mended, I s'ppose. Let's get this service over an' done with, an' I hopes he don't bore us with a long sermon, that's all, an' then we'll go home and I can feed you up. Good inner lining, that's what you need, an' a salve for your poor hands.' And she tucked Betsy's chapped hand in the crook of her arm and walked her towards the porch, moving so quickly that Johnnie only just had time to dart inside and hide himself on the pew next to his father.

It was an excruciatingly long sermon and he watched her through every boring word of it, aching to comfort her and tell her he loved her. But she kept her head down all through the service and didn't even look up when she was singing the hymns and when the final blessing had been given she left the church with her mother and father walking like guards on either side of her. He watched them until they'd left the churchyard, feeling bereft.

'What's up wi' your Betsy?' his mother said, coming up behind him. 'She don't look herself.'

He told them as much of the story as they needed to know, that she'd quarrelled with Mrs Beke and got herself another job working in a dairy, that she'd gone off 'a bit sharpish' and hadn't told anyone where she was going.

'Oi did hear somethin' a' the sort from ol' Reuben, yes'day,' his father remarked, 'onny I thought 'twas one of his tales. Must ha' been a bad sort a' quarrel.'

'Tha's been a bad year for quarrellin' altogether,' Annie said, and seeing how miserable her son looked decided to rescue him. 'How's that ol' garden a-goin'?'

He escorted them back to their cottage and talked gardening all the way, which was a relief. Then he gloomed back to Turret House and his Sunday dinner. It was a difficult meal, all meaningful glances and no talk, for Mrs Beke and the butler were watchful as hawks and listening to every word and, to make matters worse, Sam was determined to be the centre of attention and told endless tales of all the difficult horses he'd had to handle when he was working in Bersted and how well he'd managed them.

'Ent a crittur born Oi couldn't master,' he bragged, sneering at Johnnie. 'Men nor

249

hosses. 'Tis all one to me. Oi got the measure of 'em.'

Johnnie glared back at him, feeling miserably impotent but thinking, you just wait, Sammy Porter. I'll catch you one night on your way back from The Fox and I'll punch those grinning teeth right down your throat. But for the moment there was nothing he could do or say and he was glad when the meal came to an end and he could excuse himself and go back to the clammy clay of the garden, even if there wasn't any work to be done there.

For the rest of the day he brooded in the grounds, walking up and down the covered way, round and round the lawn, standing among the vegetable plots, occasionally treading in the soil around the onions with a professional heel, or brushing the cabbages with a professional hand, as though he was testing their quality, lost in miserable thought. Something had got to be done. He couldn't allow his darling to work at a dairy and only see her on a Sunday when she was too tired to talk to him. I'll write to her, he decided, as the white sun sank and the colourless sky wrinkled towards darkness. I'll find someone to give me pen and paper, there must be someone, Mrs Blake maybe, and I'll write her a letter and tell her how I love her and how she must come back, and I'll take it over to the dairy – there's only the one in Middleton – and leave it where she'll find it. That's what I'll do. The thought of taking action lifted him out of his melancholy and he went back into the house for his supper much cheered.

Catherine Blake provided pen and paper willingly. 'You can have a page from Mr Hayley's ballads,' she said. 'They didn't sell, for all his grand talk, and we bought the paper, so 'tis ours to do as we please with.'

It took him a long time to compose his love letter but she didn't hurry him. 'Good writing is worth the effort,' she said, 'for the written word is powerful, as anyone who writes could tell 'ee.'

Johnnie looked down at his careful handwriting and hoped she was right. I'll take it straight to the farm now, he decided, and did.

But whatever magic there was in his writing it didn't move Betsy. She arrived at St Mary's on Sunday looking as doleful as she'd done the previous week, holding her head down and not looking at him. This time he lay in wait for her when the service was over and stood right in front of her as she left the church so that she had to speak to him whether she wanted to or not.

'I wrote you a letter,' he said. 'I put it in the dairy by the churns. Did you find it?'

She looked at him briefly and so sadly he

251

felt as if he had been punched in the chest. 'Yes,' she said, dully, 'but there's no use in writin' letters. I works at the dairy now an' tha's that.'

'No,' he said, standing squarely in front of her and willing her to look at him. 'That's not that. I won't let it be.' Her mother was bristling at him but he couldn't stand by and say nothing.

Again that sad, flickering glance from her blue eyes. 'I 'aven't got time to walk out,' she told him, ''tis all work in a dairy. On an' on, no end to it.'

'Then leave.'

She shrugged her shoulders, hopelessly, looked away from him, stared into the distance. 'I got a livin' to earn,' she said. 'Like I told 'ee, tha's that. Best ascept it. There aren't a thing we can do about it, not now. 'Tis over an' done. You're at the house, I'm at the dairy. 'Tis over an' done.'

'No,' he said. 'I won't let it be.'

''Tis no good 'ee goin' on,' Mrs Haynes said to him. 'She's much too down for argyment. Leave it, eh? That'ud be best.'

'No,' he said. 'I can't. Betsy...'

But she was walking away, not looking at him, holding on to her mother's arm, drooping with misery and defeat. She was at the dairy. Love was over.

No, he thought, as he strode back to Turret House, hot with fury. No, no, no. I won't

let it be. Tha's askin' too much of me altogether an' it aren't to be borne. I love her.
I can't leave her in a state like this. 'Twould
be cruel. He was torn with distress for the
rest of the day, snarling at anyone who
spoke to him and kicking the trees, and he
slept extremely badly that night, dropping
in and out of nightmare, but by morning he
had decided what to do. He would go down
to the Blake's cottage again and see what
Mrs Blake had to say.

She listened to him in silence sitting in her
chair with her hands folded in her lap. Then
she left him in the kitchen while she fetched
pen and paper. 'A short letter this time,' she
advised, 'and don't leave it in the dairy, take
it to church and put in into her hands. I will
tell you what to write.'

He delivered his letter next Sunday,
offering it to Betsy as she left the church but
saying nothing. And she took it and tucked
it into her pocket and gave him a bleak
smile. Then there was nothing he could do
but wait.

'I see he still writes to 'ee,' her mother
said, when they were back in her cottage.

''Twon't do him no good,' her daughter
said sadly. ''Twas boy an' girl nonsense, an'
now 'tis over an' done.' But she read the
letter, because it was short and didn't say
much. *'Go and see Mrs Blake. She will help
you.'*

'Well, here's a thing,' her mother said. 'Shall you go?'

'Yes,' Betsy decided, 'I think I might.' It would be a comfort to have someone she could talk to freely, someone who would understand what had happened to her and why it had happened. She'd kept her misery to herself for so long it was making her chest ache.

She went that afternoon as soon as she'd finished her dinner. The dairyman could wait. After all, it *was* Sunday, and none of the other dairymaids ever got back early. They were all too glad of the rest. As it turned out he had to wait rather a long time and was none too pleased when she finally *did* return to her duties. But the visit had been just what she needed.

She talked for nearly an hour. Mr Blake was out on one of his walks and wouldn't be hindered by anything she said, even if she were to cry, which she did, for a very long time. It was a terrible outpouring of guilt and anger and loss. 'It weren't a sin,' she grieved, ''twas natural an' lovin'. Everythin' we done was natural an' lovin'. *You* know that, don't you, Mrs Blake?'

She did indeed.

'Mrs Beke said I was a wicked sinner an' a common slut, an' I ought to be ashamed of mesself an' I'd get a reputation an' I don't know what-all. I couldn't stay there after

254

that, could I?'

She could not.

'An' now I'm working so hard in the dairy there's barely time to sleep and 'tis all over 'atween us an' I'm so unhappy you wouldn't believe.

That was clear from her face and her tears.

'Why are they so cruel?' Betsy wept. 'I don't understand it. Why can't they leave us be? We shouldn't ha' been in the stables, that I'll grant, but we wasn't hurtin' no one.'

'There is much that is wrong in the world,' Catherine told her. 'We struggle against it endlessly, William and I, the cruelty of it. Dry your eyes, for he will be home presently, and I will find you a poem about it, that might be of some comfort.'

It was a long poem and had a difficult title, which Betsy couldn't read, so Catherine read it for her, 'Auguries of Innocence'. It didn't make much sense to her even then, because she didn't know what the first word meant. Johnnie would have known if he'd been there and he'd have told her. But there was nothing to be gained in thinking about that now. She stood with the paper in her hand and began to read it.

'We are printing off several copies for sale,' Catherine said, 'which is why I could find this one so readily. You do not have to read it now. You may have it to keep. Dip into it from time to time, that's my advice to 'ee, take it in sips. There's a deal of rage in it. When you've read it, come and see me again. Take heart. There *is* kindness in the world. Not everybody is cruel.'

The words on the printed sheet danced before Betsy's eyes, bright as jewels. She was touched by such kindness – and honoured. Oh very, very honoured. 'Thank 'ee, ma'am,' she said. 'Thank 'ee kindly.' And on a sudden grateful impulse, dropped a curtsey. It seemed the proper thing to do.

She sped back to her mother's cottage clutching the gift to her chest, her cheeks pink for the first time in weeks, as her mother was quick to notice.

''Twas a good visit seemingly,' she said.

'She gave me a poem, Ma,' Betsy said, showing her mother the paper.

Mrs Haynes wasn't impressed. What the child needed was food in her belly and somewhere warm to sleep, not fancy stuff like poetry, but she said it was a kind thought.

'The thing is,' Betsy said, looking at her gift, 'I can't take it back to the dairy. It'ud get trod in the muck in no time an' I'm not havin' that. Do you think I could leave it here. I could read it when I come home of a Sunday.'

And be fed at the same time, Mrs Haynes thought. It was a sensible arrangement and made a deal more sense than a line of words on a paper. So the poem was nailed to the wall above the dresser and left there as a Sunday treat, and Betsy walked back to the dairy, feeling cheered even though she knew she'd be scolded for being late.

From then on her life settled into an easier pattern. Life in the dairy was still hard and the food still poor but now that she had something to occupy her mind it didn't seem so bad. She thought of the poem at odd moments of the day, remembering the words as she ate her bread and cheese with the others, or stood to churn the butter, or sat on the milking stool with her forehead pressed against the flank of the cow and her chapped hands working automatically. *'A Robin Red breast in a Cage / Puts all Heaven in a Rage.' 'A Horse misus'd upon the Road / Calls to Heaven for Human blood.'* There is so much cruelty in the world, she thought, but there is justice, too, or the hope of it.

Sunday dinners were changed by the poem, too, for she read a little more of it before they sat down to eat and chose something particular to read aloud to her parents as the meal progressed. They were impressed despite themselves.

'He's a man a' compassion, I'll give him that,' her mother said. 'He don't like to see hanimals tormented.'

Her father was taken by the couplet about the hunted hare. 'I never did like the screams they give when the dogs tear at

257

'em,' he said. 'I've heard it many's the time an' never liked it. Read it again.'

And Betsy read, *'Each outcry of the hunted Hare / A fibre from the Brain does tear.'*

'Can't see anyone stoppin' it, mind,' her father said. 'Hare coursin'. Not when the gentry enjoys it so much.'

Each Sunday brought a new idea to challenge them. *'The Lamb misus'd breeds public strife / And yet forgives the Butchers Knife.'* 'Well, there's a thing,' her father said. 'I've never thought how the lamb feels about it. Never occurred to me.' *'A truth that's told with bad intent / Beats all the Lies you can invent.'* 'He's a learned man, your Mr Blake, I'll say that for him. For tha's as true as anythin' I ever heard.' And Betsy was pleased to think that she could almost claim this learned man as a friend. His wife was certainly a friend or she wouldn't have given her this precious poem nor listened to her with such patience.

But the loss and sadness at the centre of her life still remained and hurt like a wound. She knew she had to endure it and that there was nothing she could do about it but that didn't diminish the pain. She'd known both those things from the moment she ran out of the kitchen, hot with shame and anger and frantic to get away. She'd known it all through that first dreadful night, as she lay on her frowsy straw mattress among her

258

snoring companions and tried to weep without making a noise. And when the morning finally came and she had to get up before dawn and put on her sacking apron to go to her first milking, breathing in air so cold it hurt her lungs and striding cold-footed over ridged mud that crackled with frost, she felt as if her life had been frozen to a stop within her. She saw her breath streaming before her like smoke and rubbed her hands in a vain attempt to warm them and thought of the fire in the kitchen at Turret House and the good food that would be on the table there and she knew she'd thrown away all hope of a better life. But what else could she have done, after all the terrible things that had been said to her? And what else could she do now? Nothing except get on with this new existence.

She'd expected to feel unhappy when she saw Johnnie again, after walking out for so long and loving one another so much, but oddly she felt nothing at all, not even anger because he hadn't been there to protect her when she needed him. It was as if she was seeing him from a great distance, as if he was somebody she had once known and almost forgotten, as if her ability to love him or be angry with him had been frozen along with everything else. And perhaps it was just as well she felt that way, for there was no going back. She couldn't walk out with him again, even if she wanted to. That would set tongues wagging and she would be insulted all over again. Better to lie low, do the work that offered, keep away from gossip and hope it would all die down.

Mr Haynes was all for taking a stroll to Turret House and having it out with Mrs Beke 'there an' then, bein' someone should stand up for the child, which I mean to say, I don't like to see her cast down, pretty dear,' but his wife dissuaded him. Whatever the cause of the quarrel – and she had a pretty shrewd idea she knew what it was – in her opinion it was better to leave well alone.

'She'll come round in time,' she hoped. 'She's a sensible girl even if she is head-strong. Keep her fed an' healthy an' she'll come round. You'll see.'

But the weeks passed and there was no change in her. She came to church and walked home with them soberly afterwards, enjoyed her meal and read another line or two from the poem, but she was still sub-dued and too quiet for comfort. And she barely said a word to Johnnie Boniface even though he greeted her lovingly every Sun-day and everybody could see how upset he was to be treated so coldly.

The year began its tilt towards spring. The first crocuses pushed tentative buds through the dark soil, there was an occasional day of blue sky and green sea, March winds blew boisterous, the apple blossom erupted into a joyous froth.

'Our ol' daffydillys are comin' up lovely,' Mr Hosier said, as he and Johnnie worked in the vegetable garden. It worried him to see the boy so miserable. 'We done well with them this year.'

Johnnie didn't care one way or the other. They could come up lovely or fall over and die. 'Twas all one to him. He'd lost his love and spring was an irrelevance.

It was also a time for bad news. To nobody's surprise, the war with France had broken out again and Napoleon was reported to be gathering his troops ready for his long threatened invasion. After a year's grace and good earnings, there were no holiday-makers in the village and no hope of any. The Dome was shut up, the inns and their stables were empty and William the ostler had gone back to digging Mr Blake's garden for want of any other employment.

'There's times,' Mr Haynes said to his friends in The Fox, 'when I wish them danged Frenchies 'ud invade us an' have done with it. All this off an' on gets wearyin'.'

'Quite right,' Mr Cosens agreed. 'I'm sick of alarums an' invasions an' such. If they're comin', let 'em come say I. Then we can get it over an' have somethin' else to talk about.'

'Seen a rare ol' funeral this a'ternoon,'

Reuben offered, wiping his mouth with the back of his hand. 'Two black hosses, plumes an' all. Very grand affair. Young Molly was there.'

That roused more interest. Funerals were always a happy topic. 'Who's gone then?' Mr Grinder asked.

'Her aunt, seemingly,' Reuben said, 'what was cook-housekeeper to ol' Miss Pearce, what lives opposite the George an' Dragon. Very grand affair for a housekeeper. She must ha' saved up for it for years. The aunt Oi means, not young Molly. She never got two ha'pennies to rub together that one.'

'I s'ppose she'll go an' see young Betsy,' Mrs Grinder said, 'which'ud be no bad thing. Bit a' comp'ny 'ud do her good. They was allus pretty thick together.'

'She'll have a job to find her,' Mr Haynes sighed, 'stuck in that dairy all hours. We onny ever sees her a' Sundays.'

But Molly hadn't come all the way from Lavant just to go to the funeral. She had every intention of visiting her friend and, as soon as the funeral tea was done and her mother had dried her eyes and was settled, she put on her bonnet and walked straight to Turret House. She was most put out to discover that Betsy wasn't there.

'Why didn't she write an' tell me?' she said to Nan. 'I call that unkind. I might not be quite the scholar she is, but I can read a letter. So where is she?'

Nan shrugged her plump shoulders. 'Best go and ask Johnnie Boniface,' she suggested. 'He's more like to know her whereabouts than we are. All we know is she's upped an' gone, an' the rumour is she's workin' in a dairy somewhere.'

Molly stomped out into the garden at once and found Johnnie in the orchard. He was digging over the compost heap, sweating in the unaccustomed heat and pungent with the fumes that were rising all round him. 'Yes,' he agreed, ''twas a bit sudden like. She had words with Mrs Beke.'

Molly was intrigued. 'What about?'

'That I couldn't say,' Johnnie told her diplomatically and truthfully – for it would have been disloyal to explain – and unwise. There were some things it was best to keep hid. 'You'll find her in the dairy up Middleton way.'

'You means the farmhouse, surely,' she said. 'She's not workin' as a milkmaid. That I won't believe.'

Johnnie rested on his fork, took off his cap and wiped his forehead with it. 'Tha's what she said,' he told her. 'Milkin' cows. I heard her with my own ears.'

'Well I never heard the like,' Molly said, trenchantly. 'She's much too good to be a dairymaid. I don't know what she's thinkin' of. I shall go straight there an' tell her so.'

'Won't do you no good,' Johnnie warned. 'She's set her mind on it.'

Molly straightened her bonnet. 'We'll see about that,' she said. 'I got a mind an' all.'

Johnnie watched her go and sighed, feeling miserably worldly wise. All these months, he thought, an' love letters she don't read, an' visits to Mrs Blake she don't take no notice of, you don't know how stubborn she can be. Then, since there was nothing else he could do, he got on with his work.

Chapter Fourteen

Betsy was sitting on a pile of dirty straw with her aching back against the byre, taking in the spring sunshine. It was the first time it had been warm enough to rest outside and she and her three workmates were making the most of it. The others were gossiping, as they usually did, but Betsy sat with her eyes shut and her red hands idle in her lap, and simply drank in the warmth.

Molly was shocked by the sight of her. She looked so dirty, her skirts swathed in a sacking apron, her boots thick with mud and muck, her face smeared and her once pretty hair uncombed and frowsy and tied up in a piece of tattered cloth.

'Land sakes, Betsy Haynes,' she said, as she walked across the yard. 'What *have* you done to yourself?'

To her horror, Betsy opened her eyes and burst into tears.

Molly was a sensible young woman and, being one of a large family, she was quick to respond to distress. She skimmed across the yard and was down on her knees beside her friend before the other milkmaids were aware of what was happening. 'Hush now,' she said, putting an arm round Betsy's shoulders as if she were one of her siblings. 'Don' 'ee fret. Molly's here.'

But Betsy fretted for a long time. 'What's to become of me?' she wept. 'Oh, Molly, what's to become of me?'

Molly wasn't just sensible, she was practical too. 'You're to wash your face and put on a clean cap and get rid of that horrid apron and come for a walk,' she said.

And although Betsy protested that she had to be back for the milking, she did as she was told. They walked arm in arm towards the village, as the spring sun warmed the fields and dappled their path with shadows. And bit by bit, Betsy told her story, with suitable embellishments to show how intolerably unkind Mrs Beke had been, and a few necessary omissions to keep her own part in the tale as respectable as she could.

'I thought you an' Johnnie was walkin' out,' Molly said. 'I thought you'd be wed by now. I been waitin' for the invite.'

'No chance a' that now,' Betsy sighed. 'He don't feel nothin' for me or he'd ha' come into the kitchen an' stood up for me when Mrs Beke was givin' me what-for, which he never. An' I don't feel nothin' for him. 'Tis all changed. Walkin' out's a fool's game. You gets called a common slut if you walks out.'

'But you didn't have to come out here an' work as a milkmaid,' Molly said. 'There must ha' been better jobs for 'ee.'

'I tried for 'em,' Betsy told her. 'I knocked on every door, all that day, mornin' an' afternoon, every single door, and no one needed a servant of any kind. I didn't come here by choice.'

'Pity my aunt couldn't ha' died back then,' Molly said. 'You could've had *her* job if she had. Which come to think of it, why don't you ask for it now. Miss Pearce is high an' dry. She's onny got ol' Mrs Mumford to wait on her now an' she's no use to man nor beast on account of she can't see what she's about. She must be looking for someone.'

'She won't want me,' Betsy said gloomily.

'If she don't, she don't,' Molly said. 'There'd be no harm trying. Least you got a clean face an' you've combed your hair an' took off that horrible apron. She wouldn't have took you the state you were in when I found you. We're nearly in the village look. I can see the mills. What do 'ee think?'

There was a robin singing lucidly in the hedgerow, the sun was blessedly warm, Molly's face was encouraging, even the dust of the path smelled sweeter. There was no harm in trying. If she don't, she don't.

Miss Pearce lived in a small cottage just up the road from the smithy. She was a skinny old lady, with a fluff of sparse white hair, faded brown eyes, six teeth the colour of weak tea and long gaunt cheeks powdered pale. At first sight she seemed frail and unassuming but her appearance was deceptive. Underneath that cloud of hair and the feminine lace of her cap, she was a martinet, her spirit as strong and her determination as rigid as the whalebone in her stays. She dressed in the style that had been fashionable when she was a young woman, with an embroidered stomacher to restrain the bodice of her gown and keep her upright, and a fine lace apron to cover her skirts with modesty. She had a variety of spectacular caps, all of them made of lace and trailing long lappets, her hands were decently covered with matching lace mittens, her boots strictly buttoned. Thanks to her father's skill in the City, she had always been comfortably off, so her house was well furnished and immaculately clean, for she ran two servants and always kept them under tight control. Her voice might be soft but her commands were absolute.

'I keep an orderly establishment,' she said to the two girls, when Mrs Mumford had hobbled them into her presence. 'I wish that to be understood directly, or we shall not proceed.'

It was understood. Solemnly.

Miss Pearce nodded. 'I've seen you in church, I believe,' she said, holding up her lorgnette to take a close look at her applicant. 'Wearing a red cardinal. Do I know your parents?'

Betsy explained who they were and was nodded at again.

'I will tell you what I require in a cook-housekeeper,' Miss Pearce said. 'I believe in complete honesty. You will cook my meals and shop for such foods and delicacies as I require, you will bake my bread – I presume you can do that – you will wait at table, you will wash and iron the more delicate items of my apparel, with particular attention to the lace – we have a wash-house in the garden – you will dust and clean and you will open the door. Mumford will wash the heavier items and keep the floors scrubbed and empty slops and so forth. I will provide board and lodging and such clothing as you require for service when I have company and you will have one afternoon a week when you will be free for your own devices – although understand that I do not allow followers. As to remuneration, I will pay you £4 per annum, sums to be received quarterly.'

Betsy stood before her, thinking hard. It was a good offer, less than she'd received at Turret House but a great deal more than she was earning as a milkmaid and she knew she could do the work and do it well. She was aware that Molly was pinching her arm to make her reply but Miss Pearce was peering at her through that lorgnette again.

'Can you read?' she asked.

'Yes, ma'am.'

'Then I shall require you to read to me sometimes of an evening,' the lady said. 'My sight is not what it was, I fear. Would that be agreeable?'

It would.

'Very well, then,' the lady said. 'I think we have covered all the salient points.' She smoothed her apron with a mittened hand and looked up to make her final pronouncement. 'I shall require a reference, as you would expect. Could you provide one? Who was your previous employer?'

Betsy's heart shrivelled. Just at the very moment when she was thinking that this was a job she could do and that she wanted to come back to Felpham and do it, all hope of it was being swept away. But she offered Mrs Beke's name. How could she do anything else?

'Return tomorrow at the same time,' Miss Pearce instructed, 'and I will tell you my decision. That will be all.'

'She'll say no, sure as eggs is eggs,' Betsy said as they walked away from the cottage. 'Old Ma Beke'll tell her I'm no better than a trollop and that'll be that.'

Molly tried to encourage her. 'You don't know that,' she said valiantly.

They'd reached the church and the footpath to Molly's home. 'I've got to go,' she said. 'Pa'll have the cart ready for me an' he hates bein' kept waitin'. Write to me an' tell me what happens.' And she kissed her friend and ran off along the path.

Betsy walked back to the farm as slowly as she dared and very miserably. There was no hope for her. It *was* all over.

But she was wrong. Mrs Beke had a sharp tongue but she wasn't vindictive. The letter she wrote in answer to Miss Pearce's query was honest but certainly not damning. She had employed Betsy Haynes for the last six years, she said, ever since she joined the household as a girl of twelve. She was a hard worker and willing, was an adequate cook, baked an excellent loaf and was fast becoming a skilled needlewoman. If there was a drawback to her character it was that she had a tendency to be a trifle headstrong and would therefore need firm handling. 'However that would present no problems to such as yourself. I trust you are in good health. I remain yr obedt servant, Margaret Beke.'

The job was offered to Betsy that afternoon and was taken with such obvious relief that Miss Pearce made use of her lorgnette again and decided to re-emphasise her most important restriction. 'I don't tolerate followers,' she said. 'Not under any circumstances. I hope you understand that.'

'Yes, ma'am,' Betsy said, drawing herself up tall to emphasise her understanding. 'There's no likelihood of any followers, ma'am. No likelihood at all. When would you wish me to start work?'

It was arranged that she should join the household early next morning so as to be in time to cook breakfast. By midday, news of her return was all round the village, because her mother had met her when she was buying meat at the butcher's and old Mrs Taylor had seen her when she came down to the brew house for yeast. By the time the regulars gathered in The Fox that evening, even her follower knew about it, and it was generally agreed to be 'a danged good thing'.

I shall see her Sunday, Johnnie thought, and we can walk out again. The weather's fine an' she's back an' everybody walks out after Sunday service. Everybody, but not Betsy. Apparently she had to stay in the house and cook dinner while her mistress attended church. It was a miserable disappointment to him and an annoyance to her father.

'I don't see why she won't let the girl come to church,' he complained. 'Tha's not Christian, keepin' her at home. She could cook the meal afterwards same as you do.'

'Not to fret,' Mrs Haynes said. 'We shall see her on her afternoon off, an' I shall make a point of meetin' her when she's out a-marketing, which she will be most days so she tells me. The great thing is she's in the village an' she'll have good food to put in her belly an' we knows where she is.'

But that didn't help Johnnie Boniface. After being parted for so long and cast into such misery, his need to see her again was more urgent than it had ever been. He took to drifting out of the grounds at odd times of the day and wandering about the village in the hope of meeting her, even though he knew he was neglecting his work and that Mr Hosier didn't approve. And eventually he discovered that she walked down the road to the George and Dragon as soon as she got up in the morning, to buy the small beer for Miss Pearce's breakfast. It was all the knowledge he needed. The next morning he was in the jug and bottle before she was and ready to open the door for her as soon as she appeared.

He was so happy to see her again he was smiling like an idiot. He wanted to dance and jump in the air, to sing and shout, to pull her into his arms and kiss her. But with so many people watching them he managed to be circumspect. 'Welcome back,' he said.

The smile she gave him seemed shy, as if they were being introduced to one another, and although she said good morning in a neighbourly way, there was a distance about her that was even more disquieting than her smile.

'I heard you were back,' he said, 'workin' for ol' Miss Pearce.'

She was holding up her jug for the small beer, but she turned to agree with him and smile at him again. 'Yes.'

The full jug was helpfully heavy. 'You got a load on there,' he said. 'I'll carry it for 'ee.'

She settled the jug on her hip. 'Best not,' she said. 'Miss Pearce don't like followers. She told me most partic'lar.'

'I shan't be followin',' he said, trying to joke her into a better humour. 'I'll be walkin' alongside of 'ee.'

'You knows what I means Johnnie. It aren't a bit a' good you sayin'.'

'I tell 'ee what,' he said, as she walked out of the inn. 'Why don't you come to The Fox of a mornin'? You could buy her small beer there as well as anywhere an' we could meet an' maybe have a drink together. I goes down about noon, reg'lar as clockwork, for to get Mr Hosier his afternoon ale. Partic'ly if 'tis warmish. That wouldn't be followin' now would it?' It was part question and part hopeful plea.

She pondered before she set off along the road. 'Well,' she said, 'we'll see.'

'Tomorrow?' he hoped.

And tomorrow it was. But it wasn't a success. She was so formal with him, aware that people were watching them, sitting as far away from him as the settle would allow, careful not to allow any touch of any kind. And as his senses were in a state of aching alert, he was uncomfortable and ill at ease. When they'd finished their beer, he walked back to the house with her, as far as he dared, and carried her jug and offered his arm to her – and tried not to let her see how crushed he was when she didn't take it. But as he strode back to The Fox to buy Mr Hosier's ale, he felt cast down and dispirited. Winning her back was going to be a long slow job.

From then on, he made sure he was in The Fox at noon every day, whether or not she was likely to be there. Sometimes she arrived with her jug and stayed with him for a few minutes and sometimes she didn't. After a week he asked her whether they might meet on her afternoon off, but she told him she was pledged to spend it with her mother, 'least for the time bein', on account of Miss Pearce'll be watchin'.' He tried to persuade himself that she was being sensible, and told himself that time was a great healer, that love conquers all, that faint heart never won fair lady. But country saws were no comfort to him and there were days when his heart felt faint as a shadow. And to make everything worse, he was being plagued by the local militiamen to join the Volunteers.

There were thirteen in the company already, mostly young men and boys, and mostly farm labourers, and they were putting pressure on everyone likely. 'You got a spade 'aven't you Johnnie?' they said. 'Spade, shovel, saw, strong pair a' hands. Tha's all you need. You can dig trenches an' fell trees, can't you? You must have a fellin' axe, workin' for ol' man Hayley. Very well, then.'

At first Johnnie had mocked that a spade wouldn't be much use against a soldier with a musket but they soon dealt with an excuse as feeble as that.

'We aren't s'pposed to be fightin' men,' they said. 'Oh, no. We aren't required for to fight the beggars. What we're a-goin' to do is harass 'em, so's they can't jest go a-marchin' across the country wherever they thinks fit, on account of we'll have blocked the roads and the bridges and dug up trenches to stop their hosses. We got all sorts a' tricks up our sleeves. You join us, you'll see.'

'I got too much work in the garden,' he told them. It was an excuse and a very transparent one and they all knew it. What he really wanted was to stay where he was and look after Betsy. That was the important thing. He had to make sure she got away to a safe place. He wasn't sure where, although he'd been thinking about it ever since she came back to Felpham. Slindon Woods probably. They'd hardly want to fight their way through that. If he was any judge of what was likely, they'd head off for Chichester and the road to London.

'If them Frenchies come, you won't have a garden,' they warned. 'You wait till the next high tide. Be a different story then.'

It was a different story for everyone in the village, for this time it really did look as though the invasion fleet was coming. The barracks north of Chichester were built and occupied and Chichester was loud with redcoats; the farmers had made plans to move out all their livestock; the millers had prepared carts to carry the corn into hiding; the wagons to evacuate the women and children were cleaned and ready, and all the draught horses in the village had been commandeered to pull one vehicle or another. Every high tide brought a flurry of anxious activity and when the immediate danger had passed, the villagers were bad tempered with the worry and fatigue of yet another alert.

'Oi can't be doin' with all this taradiddle,' Reuben complained. 'Evasion, evasion, tha's all we ever hear. Oi tell 'ee straight, tha's gettin' roight on my wick. If they're a-comin', let 'em come says Oi. We had enough a' talk.'

It was a warm spring evening and the doors and windows of the inn were open to allow the regulars to enjoy the air. In ordinary times they would have been talking about the growing harvest and predicting a good one.

'Quite right, Reuben,' Mr Cosens said. 'I've had my sacks on an' off the wagons these last weeks more times than I've had hot dinners. It's really getting me down.'

'We're all down,' Mrs Grinder sympathised. 'What we needs is somethin' to gee us up a bit.'

And as if in answer to her prayer there was a sudden confused noise in the street outside, a thud and crunch of hooves, a man's voice shouting orders, much clinking and rattling, and the steaming rump of a huge bay horse appeared in front of the windows, followed by another and another. Within seconds the inn was empty as the regulars ran out of all three doors, tankards in hand, agog to see what was going on.

Their quiet village street was full of cavalry

and more were arriving as they watched. Ten, twenty, and still they came, filling the space before the inn with noise and movement and pulsing colour and the strong smell of horses. They looked like giants, sitting so high on their red and blue saddles with their long blue-clad legs commandingly astride, and their uniforms were a wonder to behold, their scarlet jackets dazzling against the grey browns of the flint walls behind them, their great tricorne hats richly plumed and heavily black against the unassuming thatch. And what accoutrements they had. Sabres and sabretaches swung from their waists, formidably to hand, and their jackets were sashed and braided and beribboned as if they had ridden straight from the king's court at St James's Palace.

Their officer was the most splendid of them all and had the most impressive manner. 'Mr Grinder!' he called. And when that gentlemen stepped forward to acknowledge his name, 'You have stabling for nine horses, I believe, sir. Very well. You are prepared to take nine troopers are you not? Cock! Smithson! Scolfield!'

The military had arrived.

Chapter Fifteen

*The offices of the Sussex Advertiser, Chichester.
Friday April 23rd 1852*

My very dearest Annie.

*This to you in some haste for I have much
work to do and a mere five minutes before I have
to catch the postman. This office is a treasure
house, where I believe I have found the material
evidence I have been seeking all week not hear-
say or gossip this time but written records. There
are two reporters here who have offered to help
me – uncle and nephew and both knowledgeable
– and I have already seen a list of the jurymen
who served at Blake's trial and – which is even
better – discovered the names of the villagers
who gave evidence on his behalf, and there are
more papers to come. By the end of the day I feel
sure I shall have reached the truth about this
trial and possibly solved my mystery into the
bargain.*

*I intend to travel home tomorrow on the
morning coach and shall be with you by
evening, when I will tell you everything I have
discovered. No time for more now, the postman
is walking through the door.*

Your most loving husband. AG

Summer 1803

Life in Felpham was revolutionised by the arrival of the 1st Royal Dragoons. Within twenty-four hours the troopers had taken over the village, swaggering about in their red jackets, flirting with every female in sight, or galloping off to some manoeuvre or other, in a thunder of well-shod hooves and a clatter of accoutrements.

On their third day in residence they gathered on the beach at low tide and staged a full cavalry charge. Half the village went down to the beach to watch and very exciting it was for a trooper's horse is an extraordinary and mettlesome animal, capable of breathtaking speed, able to stop dead at full gallop, and to wheel or fall to its knees on command. Their exploits made the village draught horses look like mules and the panache of their riders took the village maidens by storm. 'Fancy ridin' a hoss loike that,' they said to one another. 'Moi stars! Aren't that a soight for sore oiyes.'

Even Mrs Haynes was impressed. 'I wouldn't like to be on a battle field on the receiving end of that lot,' she said to her daughter.

And Betsy, who should by rights have been busy in the village doing Miss Pearce's shopping, looked at Johnnie, who had contrived to stroll down to The Fox at just the right minute to meet her and was now standing beside her on the sand, and said they frightened her half to death. Which was true, for in her present too-tender state, the arrival of so many eligible and attentive young men made her feel vulnerable, as if she was about to be besieged. She was being very careful not to give Miss Pearce any cause to rebuke her, had been so guarded with Johnnie and so distant to every other young man, that it alarmed her that these gaudy newcomers could spoil it all with their swagger and the way they would keep talking to everybody. Well, let 'em try, she thought, I shall be more than equal to them.

Within a week she was the only girl in the village who hadn't acquired a military admirer. Plenty had offered, as she'd feared – for even in her present excessively sober mood she was much too pretty to be ignored – but her answer was always the same.

'I got my livin' to earn,' she told them, when they stopped her in the street and tried to pass the time of day. ''Tis all very well for the likes a' you. You may talk to anyone you please, you got a job so long as you wants it, an' come the winter you'll be off an' away again, but if I was to be seen so much as sayin' "good morning" to a young man, I should be out on my ear wi' no job an' no earnin's. My missus is most par-tic'lar. We aren't allowed to have followers an' tha's all there is to that. So good morn-ing to 'ee an I'll trouble you not to stop me no more.'

Her severity rapidly made her one of the most attractive girls in the village. 'I been talking to the Ice Maiden,' hopefuls would report. 'Dashed pretty gel.' And their older companions would mock them, 'You been trying more like. Bet you never got no answer. I'd try elsewhere if I was you, you won't get no joy there.'

There was plenty of joy elsewhere. Betsy's old companions at Turret House strolled about the village sporting cherry red rib-bons in their caps and making eyes at every soldier they passed and it wasn't long before they had two admirers apiece. Mrs Beke was *not* pleased.

'There is nothing to be gained by spend-ing time with a soldier,' she warned them. 'Soldiers are all the same, here today and gone tomorrow, with no more responsibility than a gadfly. And when they go they leave you with a reputation and ruined into the bargain, as like as not. You would be well to steer clear of them. You don't want to end up like Betsy Haynes.'

The two maids exchanged looks and couldn't wait to report what they'd been told to Betsy herself. Which they did the very next morning when they were out in Limmer Lane, taking the air for a few minutes in the hope that their beaux would come along and meet them.

'She says you got a reputation,' Nan said. 'What d'you think a' that?' She was feeling quite pleased with herself to be scoring such an easy victory but then Betsy turned to glare at her with eyes as fierce as an owl's and she was alarmed and hastened to change tack. 'Tha's not what we says, mind. 'Tis what ol' Ma Beke says. We jest thought you ought to know.'

Betsy drew herself up to her full height. Wasn't this just exactly what she'd been afraid of? Wasn't this why she'd been so careful not to talk to anyone? Wasn't this why she'd even kept poor Johnnie at arm's length? And hadn't she been right? 'Well you can jest go straight back to your Mrs Beke,' she said, 'an' tell her I got no followers of any description. Not a single blamed one, nor likely to have. I don't talk to soldiers an' I don't talk to any a' the young men in the village neither. I keeps mesself to mesself, always, an' if I got a reputation that's what 'tis for.'

'But you talks to Johnnie Boniface, surely,' Susie said and it was only just a question.

'No,' Betsy said firmly. 'I partic'ly don't talk to Johnnie Boniface. An' I aren't walkin' out with him neither, to save you askin'.

Tha's all over an' done with, thanks to her cruelty t'wards me. You tell her that. If you walk out you gets called names, like slut an' trollop an' I don't know what-all, an' *nobody's* a-goin' to call me names like that *ever again*. Now you'll excuse me. I got work to do if you haven't.' And she left them, walking with great dignity and her head held high.

'Shall you tell her?' Nan asked her friend.

'Who?'

'Ol' Ma Beke.'

'No fear,' Nan said. 'She's tetchy enough without that. I shall leave well alone, that's what I'll do. Oh, look, there's my Frederick a-comin'. Coo-ee Frederick!'

There was considerable tetchiness at Turret House that summer. Demoralised by all the dashing young men who were now overrunning their village, the stable lad and Bob the boot boy had joined the pioneers by way of boosting their morale. It didn't do much for them because nobody took any notice except the butler who was annoyed to be told that they had to spend two nights a week away from the house, learning how to block roads and bridges in Slindon Woods.

'And what good that will do I cannot imagine,' he said to Mrs Beke, 'for I never saw a more gormless pair in all my life. Pioneers indeed!'

Mr Hayley took all these difficulties personally. 'I see no reason why the proper running of my household should have to be disrupted,' he complained to Mrs Beke, 'just because Napoleon Bonaparte is threatening to invade, which he won't do, you mark my words, Lord Nelson will see to that, nor why we should be overrun by the military. 'Tis insupportable, indeed it is. And while we're on the subject, why do you send that silly clumsy creature with my coffee night after night? Why doesn't young Betsy bring it?'

Mrs Beke explained, briefly and mildly, that young Betsy had taken a position with Miss Pearce.

That didn't please her master at all. ''Tis all so unnecessary,' he said. 'Constant change is bad for the constitution – as is well known and understood – in exactly the same way as an excess of scarlet is harmful to the eyes. If this goes on much longer, we shall all be irreparably damaged.'

'Your prints have come,' Mrs Beke told him, endeavouring to change the subject, that being one change she felt he could handle. 'Mrs Blake brought them up half an hour ago.'

He was still tetchy, even about that. 'Then pray have 'em sent to me,' he said. 'Why do you delay? You know how I wish to see them. They should be on my table already.'

Fortunately he was very pleased by all

three prints and ten minutes later rang for Mrs Beke again to tell her that he thought he might stroll down to Mr Blake's cottage to tell him how much his work was appreciated. 'We have been distant long enough, in all conscience,' he said. 'With the threat of war daily in our ears and the entire village overwhelmed by the military, I feel it is time we artists made peace.'

So he took his gold-topped cane in hand, donned his new cloth hat and limped down the village street in the strong sunshine towards the cottage. He was impressed, despite himself, to find that the soldiers who thronged the little street stood aside to make way for him and that many saluted him.

If William Blake was surprised to see him he didn't show it. He and Catherine invited him into the cottage and said how glad they were that the prints were agreeable, and William showed him the painting he was working on. It had been commissioned by a local magistrate called Mr Poynz and should have been finished long since. And Hayley said he'd heard of the gentleman and believed him to be a man of honour and one who would understand that a work of art should not be rushed.

'I myself work slowly nowadays,' he confessed. 'The new biography progresses but at its own pace. I am burdened by all this needless change. I was telling Paulina so, only the other morning. She was asking after you, by the way. She wished to know how your epic was progressing. I told her what I could, of course, but 'twould come better from you. I wonder you don't come visiting with me again. Why don't you? She would be delighted to see you.'

So, although Blake hadn't expected it, the Lavant rides were resumed and enjoyed and Miss Poole *was* delighted to see him. And on their return journey he and Mr Hayley spoke to one another like old companions and agreed that it was a pleasure to be out in the countryside and away from all the noise and nonsense of those dratted soldiers.

Village opinion about their enforced occupation swung from approval to annoyance all through the summer, following the tides. When the high tide made invasion more likely, and rumours of troop movements on the other side of the Channel were being reported daily and the farmers were rounding up their livestock and the millers loading up their corn ready for evacuation, the soldiers were welcomed and made much of, and particularly when they'd been down on the beach fighting mock battles up to their waists in sea water or when they'd ridden down to the empty sands to practise yet another dramatic charge. But once the immediate danger had passed, everybody relaxed and the 1st Royal Dragoons were seen warts and all. And none of them more clearly or with more disparagement than Private Scolfield.

He was a disagreeable man, tall and thin with a dark, sour, discontented face, renowned as an unrelenting fighter but given to mockery and practical jokes when he was sober, and belligerent and abusive when he was drunk. The story was that he'd once been a sergeant and had been demoted on account of being drunk and disorderly, and that was why he was so sour and hard-done-by and so quick to take umbrage. He'd quarrelled with old Reuben Jones on his very first evening in the inn.

Reuben had come strolling in to the bar with two of his workmates and they were so deep in conversation that at first he didn't notice that there was a trooper sitting in his seat in the chimney corner, with his long blue-clad legs sprawled in front of the fire taking all the heat. It didn't worry him unduly. Strangers had been known to occupy that seat from time to time but they always vacated it when the position was explained to them. He bought his pint of porter and, tankard in hand, ambled across to put the soldier right.

'Evenin' to 'ee,' he said and tried a gentle joke. 'Oi see you're a-keepin' moi seat warm for me.'

The soldier sneered. 'Your seat?' he said. 'Since when has it been the practice for an old man to own a seat in a public inn?'

Reuben was taken aback by such rudeness but he answered kindly. 'Oi don't know nothin' about practices,' he said, 'but that there's moi seat. Has been ever since Oi first sat in it. An' 'twas my father's afore me, an' his father's afore him. Toime immemorial, so to speak. You ask anyone.' He looked round at his companions who nodded to show support.

'Well, now you've lost it, aintcher,' Private Scolfield said. 'For I'm sittin' in it this evenin' and it's mine by virtue of I'm sittin' in it.'

'Oi don't think you quite got moi drift, young man,' Reuben said patiently. 'You're in moi seat. Tha's allus been moi seat an' you got no roight to sit in it.'

'Now look 'ee here *old man*,' Private Scolfield said. 'I'll tell you what. You're beginning to get on my wick. Be off with you and find somewhere else for your scraggy ol' bones. You'll not have me out of this chair and there's an end of it. Unless you want to fight me for it.'

At which point half a dozen of his comrades wandered out of the shadows and stood in a menacing circle around them, tall and muscular, their coats blood red in the candlelight. Reuben was caught between fury

289

at being treated so rudely and fear of what they might do to him if he protested. Eventually fear won and he retreated to the settles on the other side of the room, growling and making alarming faces. 'Oi'd ha' fought him fair an' square if it hadn't ha' been for all them others,' he told his friends, 'but Oi'll have him tomorrow, you see if Oi don't.'

The next evening he was the first man in the inn and had settled into his chair with his tankard on the table in front of him before the soldiers came strolling in.

'Hop it, old man,' Private Scolfield said. 'You're in my chair.'

Reuben chewed his teeth for a few minutes while he savoured what he was going to say. 'Seems to me,' he said, winking at his neighbours to signal that what was to come would be worth their attention, 'seems to me Oi heard somethin' about chairs in this here bar onny yes'day evenin'. Yes, Oi'm sure 'twas yes'day evenin'. 'Parently, if you're a-sittin' in a chair, then 'tis yours on account of you're a-sittin' in it. That was the gist of it. If you're a sittin' in it, 'tis yours. Or was Oi mistook?'

He got a round of applause and tankards were raised in his direction from every corner. 'Well said, Rueben!' his friends called. 'Tha's the size of it roight 'nough!' 'He's a sittin' in it, so 'tis his. You can't argue with that.'

Private Scolfield's face twisted with anger. 'You're a stupid old man,' he said, 'an' a fool to set yourself up against a member of the 1st Royal Dragoons. It won't do you no good. As you'll find out.' Then he kicked out of the bar.

'Moi stars!' Hiram Boniface said. 'You've riled him now, Reuben. He won't forget that in a hurry.'

'No more will Oi, Hiram,' Reuben said. 'No more will Oi. Ho no! He needn't think he can go a-takin' moi chair an' get away with it. Saucy beggar!'

From then on the battle was fought on every single evening. Whichever of the two was first to arrive took possession of the chair and sat in it, smirking, until Mr Grinder called closing time. Even when it was too warm for a fire and the chimney corner grew dark as the evening progressed, the coveted position was still occupied. At first Mr Grinder thought it was a bit of a joke and decided to ignore it, then he grew worried in case it led to fisticuffs and wondered whether he ought to remove the chair and have done with it, then he realised that it was good for trade, for it brought in more troopers as witnesses, and many more locals to cheer their hero on.

'Although what good it'll do in the long run,' he said to his wife as they closed the bar after one particularly lively evening, 'I cannot imagine.'

'They're like cocks on a dunghill,' Mrs Grinder said. 'They needs a good slapping, the pair of 'em. I'm sick an' tired a' their silly nonsense. You ask me, we could do with a rest from it.'

At the beginning of August she got her wish. The 1st Royal Dragoons were sent off to the downs for lengthy manoeuvres and the village sank back into its usual plodding pace for a few days. Betsy made it her business to tell Miss Pearce as soon as she heard the news and to let her know how very pleased she was to see the back of them. 'I've had a hard time persuadin' 'em I don't have followers an' I don't talk to no one.' And Miss Pearce said, rather ambiguously, that she was glad to hear it. Nan and Susie put away their caps with the cherry red ribbons and went back to wearing serviceable white, the pioneers began to brag of their exploits, there being no opposition, Reuben left his protected seat and hobbled about The Fox, Mr Hayley told his dear friend Mr Blake that he was very much relieved.

''Twill be an interlude, no more,' he confided as they rode to Lavant. 'They will return, I fear, and as noisy as ever, I have no doubt. We must make the most of such peace as offers.'

Noise and difficulty returned the very next

Friday and in a way that nobody could have predicted.

It was a sultry day, the sea oily smooth, the air hot, still and enervating, and a slight haze turning the horizon to a smudge of mauve. Even the short walk from Miss Pearce's house to her mother's cottage left Betsy feeling hot and sweaty. She was glad to go out into the garden and wash her sticky hands at the pump.

'Tha's better,' she said to her mother as she returned to the living room refreshed and tidied. 'Bit a' cold water works wonders. Tha's too hot to breathe outside.'

'Tha's too hot for anything,' her mother agreed. 'I just wants to sit in the shade an' do nothin'.'

But not too hot for shouting apparently, for at that moment the quiet was suddenly broken by the noise of somebody roaring and swearing. The two women forgot the heat and ran out at once to see what was happening.

The dusty square in front of The Fox was full of running figures, Mr Grinder in his blue apron, with his wife close behind him, her skirts swinging as she ran, Mr Hosier with a tankard still in his hand, grinning cheerfully, Reuben Jones, peering and grimacing, with his right arm in a sling and his hat on sideways, Mr Cosens massive and disapproving, Mrs Taylor hobbling down the road as fast as she could on her bandy legs and agog for excitement, and Johnnie running light-foot ahead of them all, his fair hair haloed by sunshine. And in the excitement and muddle of all that movement and sudden excitement there were two figures struggling and shouting: Private Scolfield, which was no surprise to anybody, and their nice quiet poet, Mr Blake, in his shirtsleeves and printer's apron, looking very dishevelled and red in the face. Their shouts rose into the general hubbub.

'I don't allow it,' Blake's voice yelled. 'You are not welcome...' The trooper was swinging punches. '... I've the right to go where I please, damn you,' he roared.

'You do not, sir. You...'

'...can't tell me what to do. Damn you for a knave. I'm a soldier of the line.'

'You're a slave, sir, like all working men. A slave and you'd be...'

Then although he was a head and shoulders shorter than the soldier, Blake suddenly grabbed him by the arms, twisted them behind his back and held them there. Scolfield wriggled and heaved and laid his tongue to every oath he knew but he was caught and held and now Blake was pushing him forward, yelling at him to 'Move damn you!' The trooper yelled back, threatening to punch Mr Blake's damned eyes out or push his damned teeth down his stinking throat, and struggling to wrench his arms free or to land a backward kick on his opponent's legs but he had to walk whether he would or no. It was wonderfully entertaining. Better than a dog fight.

'Well, here's a thing,' Mrs Haynes said as she ran towards them. 'What's brought this about?'

The fighters had reached the entrance to the stables and were surrounded by on-lookers, who swirled about them, some avoiding blows, some ready to intervene if need be, more arriving by the second. Having dragged his adversary to the doors of his billet, Blake relaxed his hold on the trooper's arms and stood back to recover his breath. It was a mistake, for Scolfield immediately took up a stance like a prize-fighter, clenched fists at the ready, and began to swing punches again, daring him to 'fight like a man, damme.'

There were several seconds of confusion, as Reuben fled into the safety of the inn, the crowd pressed closer and Mr Grinder, Mr Hosier and Mr Cosens waded into the fray to restore order, grabbing at the trooper's flying fists and the tails of his red coat and any other part of his uniform that offered them purchase. Then Private Cock came sloping out of the inn to join in and Johnnie took action to restrain *him*, yelling at him that his comrade was drunk and he'd do well to keep out of it, and the scene was a hot blur of flailing arms and kicking boots. And at last it was all over and the two soldiers went grumbling off to the stables, swearing to be revenged, and Blake, having thanked Mr Grinder and Mr Hosier and Mr Cosens, ''Twas good of 'ee sirs,' walked back to his cottage, combing his tousled hair with his fingers.

'Well, who'd ha' thought it,' Mrs Taylor said. 'Fancy our noice engraver feller goin' on loike that.'

''Tis the heat,' Mrs Haynes said. 'Dog days, you see.'

Betsy was still gazing at her retreating poet, surprised to have seen him show such physical strength. 'An' I allus thought he was such a gentle man,' she said to Johnnie, who'd come over to stand beside her.

''Tis mortal hot,' Johnnie said. 'Let's take a stroll on the beach. 'Twould be cooler there.'

She smiled at him in the old affectionate way. ''Aven't you got work to do?'

''Tis all done for the day,' he told her happily. 'Mr Hosier said 'twas too hot an' we'd finish up this evening. Tha's why we come down. To get a bit a' breeze.'

'Good job you did, or that soldier 'ud be fighting still.'

'So shall we?'

It was too much of a temptation and there

was no Miss Pearce to rebuke her and her mother said she didn't mind, so she agreed.

They walked for nearly a mile along the empty sands towards Middleton and took off their shoes and stockings so that they could cool their feet by paddling in the sea and tried to catch the little brown shrimps in the rock pools as if they were children out to play.

'I don't know what ol' Miss Pearce would say if she could see me,' Betsy said as they walked back hand in hand.

'Just as well she aren't here, then,' Johnnie said, wondering if he could kiss her. 'I do love you, Betsy.'

Out there in the clear light with the sea lapping their feet and the sun warming their faces, love began to stir in her again, gently and tenderly, like a leaf uncurling. I've kept away from him for so long, she thought, and that aren't right nor kind. She put a sandy hand on his chest, partly because she needed to touch him and partly to beg him not to rush her. 'But not yet Johnnie. Not yet.'

'I can't wait for ever,' he said. 'I done enough a' that before.'

'I know,' she said and looked so woe-begone he kissed her anyway, permitted or not. And was kissed back, so sweetly it made him feel weak.

'Shall we walk again next week?' he hoped,

as he left her at her mother's gate.

'I don't s'ppose there'll be any more fights for us to watch,' she said, 'so we might as well.' She looked so like her old self, he had to kiss her again. What a blessing that fight was, he thought. She'd never have walked out with me if it hadn't been for all that excitement. Two men slogging it out, toe to toe, do clear the old air.

But he was wrong. Down in the stables of The Fox inn, the air was curdling into a most unhealthy plot.

Chapter Sixteen

There was no sign of the two troopers in The Fox that Friday evening, which was quite a disappointment to some of the regulars who'd been looking forward to a spot of happy mockery and the chance to feel superior for once.

'Gone to the George and Dragon, I shouldn't wonder,' Mr Grinder said. 'An' good riddance. We had quite enough of them this afternoon. 'What'll it be, Mr Haynes?'

Reuben Jones was triumphant, grinning and nodding as the story of the fight was told and retold. 'We seen 'em off, that's what we done,' he said. 'See 'em roight off.'

His neighbours turned to mock him. 'We?' they said. 'Who's this "we"? Didn't see you doin' much. You was off the first sign a' trouble.'

'Tha's on account of Oi injured moi hand,' Reuben explained, waving his sling at them. It was extremely dirty, having been trailed in the pigsty all afternoon. 'You can't aspect me to foight with onny the one hand.'

That provoked a hoot of laughter and there was much clowning and mock fighting – all one-handed naturally. After such an exciting day it was a cheerful evening, and the good humour continued as Saturday and Sunday passed without sign or sound of their two troublemakers. It was almost as if they were keeping out of the way, although Will Smith said he'd seen them in the tack room early on Sunday morning, talking to one another, 'all very serious.' 'You ask me,' he said, 'they're up to somethin'.'

'Well, just so long as it don't lead to fisticuffs, they may do as they please,' Mr Grinder said. 'That's my opinion of it. Talk don't break skulls.'

On Monday morning, the two soldiers saddled up and galloped out of the village towards Chichester. They rode so fast they kicked up a dust and their faces were hard and determined as if they were off to battle. They were gone all day and when they returned for their supper they looked so smug there was no doubt that the ostler had been right. They *had* been up to something.

There was much speculation among Mr Grinder's regulars as to what it might be and they didn't have to wait long to find out. On Tuesday morning Blake went to Lavant with Mr Hayley to take breakfast with Miss Poole and bask in the warmth of her approval and the strong sunshine that flooded her elegant room. He returned home to find an official letter waiting for him, signed and sealed and horribly alarming. Within minutes of reading it he was in The Fox and talking to Mr Grinder, ashen-faced but in tight control of himself although emanations of hellfire and torment swirled in his brain and the letter trembled in his hand.

'I am sent for to attend a solicitor in Chichester,' he said. 'Private Scolfield has sworn a deposition against me before a Justice of the Peace to accuse me of sedition.'

His words caused an uproar. Within seconds he was the centre of a group of anxious neighbours, all eager to know more. Sedition was a serious charge and especially when the French were expected to invade at every high tide. The punishment for it was five years in jail or, even worse, five years deportation. There'd been a feller up Portsmouth way only a few years back who'd been tried and found guilty and died in prison before he could serve his term.

300

'What did he say?' they asked.

Blake couldn't tell them. 'I know no more than I've told you,' he said. 'I am to go to Chichester today to read the charge and answer it. I have asked Will if he will accompany me, if that is agreeable to you, Mr Grinder. He was in the garden when this began and would be my best witness as to what was said.'

Of course he must go, Mr Grinder said. That went without saying. Would they need a carriage or did Mr Blake propose to ride? Did Mr Hayley know of it? What *was* the world coming to?

Those were Mr Hayley's sentiments when Blake appeared in his library to tell him the news. He took supportive action at once. He would accompany the two men to Chichester. 'Do not thank me, my dear, dear friend. 'Tis the least I can do.' They would take the carriage and travel in comfort. 'I cannot believe the treachery of this creature to accuse you so. What times we do live in, to be sure.'

So the little party set out, Mr Hayley wearing his new hat and warm with righteous indignation, the ostler nervous at the thought that he might have to give evidence in a court of law, Blake silent with suppressed anxiety. The summer sizzled all around them, as they drove through cornfields burgeoning towards harvest and larks sprang into the air and spiralled upwards singing as they rose, passed between hedges dusty with heat and trundled through pastures where the sheep browsed peacefully and rabbits jumped away from their wheels and bounded into the fields, white scuts flashing a warning. Oh, how could this monstrous charge be possible in such a green and pleasant land?

The solicitor's quiet offices were easily found and, as soon as the clerk had ascertained who they were, he ushered them into an inner office where the charges would be read. It was a dark cold room and the chill of it made Blake shiver, as if he'd already been found guilty and sentenced. They sat themselves down as directed and waited while the clerk found the deposition and the solicitor made his entry and enquired whether they wished him to read the indictment aloud so that they might all hear it at one and the same time.

It had been written at considerable length and was extremely alarming. It was called, 'The Information and Complaint of John Scolfield, a private Soldier in His Majesty's First Regiment of Dragoons, taken upon oath this 15th day of August 1803 before me, John Quantock, one of His Majesty's Justices of the peace... Who saith... One Blake, a miniature painter ... did utter the following seditious expressions viz: That we (meaning the people of England) were like a parcel of Children, that would play with themselves till they would get scalded and burnt: that the French knew our strength very well and if Bonaparte should come he would be master of Europe in an hour's time... That every Englishman would be put to the choice whether to have his throat cut or to join the French... That he damned the King of England – his country and his Subjects – that his soldiers were all bound for slaves & the poor people in general.'

'Preposterous!' Mr Hayley said, when the solicitor paused for breath.

'There is more, sir,' the solicitor told him. 'Private Scolfield included a complaint against Mrs Blake, too. Perhaps you should hear it all before you comment upon it.'

So the torment continued and for Blake it was even more terrible to hear what Catherine was accused of saying than it had been to be accused himself. He listened as the solicitor's dry voice read out the rest of the indictment and his heart jumped in his chest with the panic of a caged bird. '...his wife then came up & said to him ... that the king of England would run himself so far into the fire that he might not get himself out again & although she was a woman she would fight as long as she had a drop of blood in her – to which the said Blake said, my Dear you would not fight against France – she replied, no, I would fight for

Bonaparte as long as I am able.'

'This is insupportable,' Blake said. 'It is bad enough in all conscience to hear myself maligned in this way but to attack my wife is cowardice, sir. Sheer cowardice.'

The solicitor smiled bleakly. 'I will read to the end of the indictment,' he said, 'and then I will give you such advice as I may. "...the said Blake pushed this Informant out of the garden & twice took this Informant by the Collar without this Informant's making any resistance and at the same time the said Blake damned the King & said the soldiers were all slaves. Sworn before me John Quantock."'

'Lies!' Blake said fiercely. 'A pack of lies, as those who witnessed it would attest.'

'This copy of the complaint is for you,' the solicitor said, folding it in half and handing it to Blake, 'since I presume you would wish to write a memorandum to refute it.'

Indeed he would. 'I will talk to the witnesses and write it as soon as may be.'

'Quite,' the solicitor said but he seemed to have lost interest in the complaint now that he had handed it over and was sending an eye signal to his clerk, who stood up at once and left the room. Blake and his companions waited, as there was obviously more to come, and after a few seconds the clerk returned with three more people, three red-coated, aggressive people, Privates Scolfield and Cock and a Lieutenant whom neither of them had seen before.

'You should know, Private Scolfield, that Mr Blake intends to write a memorandum to refute the complaint you have made,' the solicitor told them.

'That is perfectly understood,' the lieutenant said smoothly. 'We shall expect to receive a copy of anything that is written, naturally.'

'Of course.'

'Private Cock wishes to make a deposition of his own.'

'My clerk will take it down.'

So three more chairs were produced and the six men sat in a semicircle of simmering hatred while Private Cock added his voice to that of his comrade. He had heard all that Mr Blake said and was prepared to swear to it. It took all Blake's self-control not to shout him down as he spoke.

But his deposition was written and signed and the soldiers took their leave. Then all that remained to be done was to bind over the said William Blake in the sum of £250 to appear at the next quarter sessions, which would be in Petworth in October. The said William Blake was hard put to it to pay even a hundred of those pounds but Mr Hayley came to his rescue and said that he would be happy to put up another hundred and he was sure Mr Seagrave the printer would stand surety too, and that between them they could make up the full amount, so the matter was concluded and Blake was free to go home.

By the time the carriage began its journey back to Turret House, news of the accusation had spread round the village like a gunpowder trail. Betsy heard it when she walked into The Fox with her jug.

'Poor old Mr Blake,' Reuben said. 'They been in an' out all mornin', bragging what they're a-goin' to do to him. That Scolfield he reckons 'tis treason an' he'll see the poor feller hanged. Oi don't reckon to that mesself. Oi means to say they can't hang you just fer a bit a' shoutin'.'

'Don't you believe it,' Mr Grinder said. 'They can hang you for breathin' these days. There was a feller in the papers only the other week. A Colonel something-or-other. Despard, I think. Anyway he was tried for treason and hung up straight away. Oh, they can hang you right enough.'

'Then we must stand up for him,' Betsy said, fiercely, 'an' say he never said nothin' the least bit treasonable, which I'm sure he never did nor would.' Standing there in the quiet of the taproom with Johnnie beside her and her jug on her hip, she wasn't sure she could remember what *had* been said. There'd been a lot of shouting but she couldn't swear to what it was all about. But that was of no consequence. If Mr Blake needed her support, she was ready to give it. He was a good, kind, truthful man who spoke his mind and stood up for tormented creatures and nobody was going to put him in prison if she could help it. 'We'll make a list of all the people who were here and saw it,' she decided. 'Some a' these trooper fellers are a bit too full of themselves. Well, they needn't think they can get away with this. You were there for a start, weren't you, Mr Grinder and so was Mr Cosens. You had to drag that Scolfield away, when he was roarin' an' shoutin' and tryin' to kick people. An' Johnnie said he was drunk. I remember that. I shall bring a pencil an' paper with me tomorrow an' set about it.'

But Private Scolfield was ahead of her. He and Private Cock had already visited Mrs Taylor and the miller and that afternoon they moved on to her mother and tried to put pressure on her too. 'We need witnesses to bring this man to justice,' they said, 'as he rightly should be, and you were there and heard it all, so it's beholden on you to give us assistance.'

Mrs Haynes was annoyed to be pestered and said so. ''Tis no concern of mine,' she told them. 'If you wants to complain against the poor man, which it seems you done al-a-ready, that's your affair, but don't go aspecting me to help you with it.'

'I wonder you take his part,' Private Scolfield said, 'when he's a proven spy and everybody knows it. A military painter.' And when she looked surprised he sneered at her, 'You didn't know that, did you? A military painter and a spy, that's what he is, making plans of the countryside to sell to the enemy. You should have his house searched, that's what you should do, ma'am, instead of obstructing the course of justice.'

At which she lost her temper and found her broom and proceeded to sweep them off the doorstep, saying that if there was any obstructing going on they were a-doin' of it.

'You'll regret this, ma'am,' Private Scolfield said furiously, as the broom hit his ankles. 'You should show more loyalty to your king and country, not scorn its defenders. We was sent here to defend the likes of you, don't forget. To risk our lives for king and country. You should be mindful of your safety.'

The threat was unmistakeable and worrying but she faced him out. 'Be off with you an' don't talk nonsense,' she said. 'I've better things to do with my time than stand here bandyin' words.'

'The woman's a fool,' the trooper said as he walked away. 'I could arraign her for sedition, too, if I'd a mind to. Saying such things.'

'But there's more money in the engraver

308

feller,' Private Cock pointed out. A successful prosecution for treason or sedition, especially if it was brought against a known agitator, could earn a handsome bounty. A trooper at Horsham had earned himself £70 that way.

'I shall talk to that old fool Reuben next,' Private Scolfield said. 'High time we made him jump about a bit.'

But Reuben Jones was much too wily to be caught by a pair of troopers. 'Never heard a thing,' he told them, 'on account of Oi was indoors a-sittin' in moi seat, which if Oi don't, some other beggar'll take it from me.'

'You're a lying hound,' Private Cock said. 'You was out in the street the whole time. I seen you.'

'Ho no,' Reuben said. 'Must ha' been someone else. Oi was inside loike Oi said. Never heard hoide nor hair of anythin'.'

And even though they bullied him for another ten minutes he sat tight in his chair and refused to budge. In the end they had to leave him where he was and go off and find another one of their witnesses. 'There must be someone,' Scolfield said. 'They can't all be deaf and blind. This is a matter a' law an' if the law says they're to testify they'll have to turn out and do it. Bloody old mules!'

But the bloody old mules were adamant and the more they were bullied the more they refused to give evidence. 'Be a different matter if 'twas ol' Mr Blake what come askin',' Will Smith said, 'but I aren't a-swearin' black's white to please a couple a' drunken soldiers an' that's flat, 'specially when they threatens to knock my eyes out. All this carry-on about how they're our defenders. We never asked 'em to come here.'

Old Mr Blake was keeping out of everybody's way, too anxious and depressed to move from his workroom. He was caught in the coils of the law and the law was more terrifying to him than any other institution. He'd always known it for the monstrous oppression it was, a tangle of unanswerable enforcements designed to keep the poor in their place and protect the wealth and property of the rich. And now that he was caught up in it himself, he recognised with the most dreadful certainty that innocence was no protection against it.

'I am lost,' he said to Catherine. 'If I am to appear in a court of law, as seems entirely likely, I shall be found guilty no matter what I say. They will discover what friends I have in London, if they do not know already. I shall be judged as a companion to Thomas Paine and Mary Wollstonecraft, to Joseph Johnson and Henry Fuseli and William Goodwin, and a member of the London Corresponding Society, what's more, revolutionaries all. What judge will believe a word I say?'

Catherine tried to comfort him but he had

sunk too far into nervous fear to be reached. He felt himself gripped by talons of repression and authority, saw the dread emanations of punishment, banishment and death rising on every side. 'I am lost.'

'Write to Mr Butts,' Catherine suggested. 'He might know something about your accuser. After all he does work in the office of the Muster-master General and if there is army gossip to be found he would be the man to find it.'

So a letter was composed and because it would hardly be possible to ask for gossip about the army unless there was very good cause, he wrote a full account of what had happened, saying he was 'in a bustle to defend himself' and finishing with the hope that Mr Butts might be in a position to 'learn somewhat' about Private Scolfield. At this point he remembered that in his last letter to his old friend he had said some extremely uncharitable things about Mr Hayley, and now he was ashamed to have done such a thing, and begged 'burn what I have peevishly written about any friend' adding 'I have been very much degraded & injuriously treated, but if it all arise from my own fault, I ought to blame myself.

Oh why was I born with a different face?
Why was I not born like the rest of my race?
When I look each one starts! When I speak, I
  offend;

*Then I'm silent & passive & lose every
   friend.*

When the letter was written he took it
through into the kitchen so that Catherine
could see it. But to his distress she was
sitting beside the grate, white-faced and
weeping. She had found Private Scolfield's
deposition and knew that she was being
accused too. 'What are we to do?' she cried.
'They will hang us both.'

Now it was his turn to try to comfort and
his turn to fail. She wept for a very long
time. They'd had nothing but ill fortune ever
since they came to this place. 'You cannot
deny it.' He'd been given work to do that
was an insult to his talents. He'd had no
time for his own work, which was better in
every way than the poetry he was required
to illustrate. His great epic was unwritten.
He'd laboured day and night and all for
what? She wished they'd never come, she
did indeed. The cottage was damp, even in
the summer. It had made them both ill.

'The lease is up in three weeks' time,'
Blake pointed out, 'and then we will go back
to London, as we intended, and you will
have better health.'

But she was stuck fast in her fears like a
bird in lime. 'What if they put us in prison?'
she wept. 'We could die there and never see
one another again. Oh, my dear William,
what are we to do?'

'We will fight,' he said. Her weakness had made fighting not just possible but imperative. 'We will fight and we will win. I will write my memorandum and refute all these charges with all my strength. I will not allow them to send you to prison. I will send my letter and then I will go to The Fox and see Mr Grinder and make a list of all the people who saw what happened and then I will visit them all and ask them to witness for us. You must not despair.'

Mr Grinder was busy but helpful. 'Betsy Haynes is the one you want,' he said. 'She's been makin' a list. Could be just what you want. I'll send her across to you as soon as she comes in.'

She and Johnnie arrived the next morning, she with an empty jug in her hand, he with a list of all the witnesses. Blake was touched by how many there were and how clearly they had made their feelings known.

'You see what good neighbours we have, my love,' he said to Catherine. 'They do not desert us in our hour of need. I will name them all in my memorandum and then the judges will understand that the charge has been trumped up and should be dismissed out of hand.'

He took great pains with his statement, making sure that he named all the people on the list 'so that we may not have any witnesses brought against us that were not there' and offering all the relevant facts. 'The soldier's Comrade swore before the magistrate, while I was present,' he wrote, 'that he heard me utter seditious words, at the Stable Door, and in particular Said that he heard me D–n the K–g. Now I have all the persons who were present at the Stable Door to witness that no Word relating to Seditious Subjects was uttered, either by one party or the other, and they are ready, on their Oaths, to Say that I did not utter such words.' And he finished with a flourish, 'If such a perjury as this can take effect, any Villain in future may come & drag me and my Wife out of our Home & beat us in the Garden, or use us as he pleases, or is able, & afterwards go and Swear our Lives away.'

Two weeks later the chaise arrived to be loaded with their printing press and their sixteen heavy boxes and carry them back to London. They had arrived by moonlight with only Mr Grinder, Will Smith and the potboys to welcome them, they left in sunlight with half the village gathered at their door to wave them goodbye. 'Write and let us know how you get on,' Betsy said to Catherine, 'and when you're to appear in Petworth.' And added, with sober truth, 'I shall miss you.'

Chapter Seventeen

Felpham village seemed oddly empty after the Blakes had gone, closed down and denuded of colour as though winter had arrived prematurely. To Betsy's clear eyes, the cottage seemed to have shrunk and grown cold without them. She missed the sound of their voices, the wood-smoke rising from the chimneys, the yellow light shining from that familiar western window. Now the windows were empty and the thatch forlorn and a film of dust dulled the doorstep.

Three weeks after the Blakes left, the troopers were recalled to Chichester. The last high tide had passed without invasion, autumn was well and obviously on the way and there was no likelihood of another attempt until the spring. In the emptied streets and quiet farms, the villagers went about their now wintry business in their age-old way. Thatchers patched as many roofs as needed their attention, barns were checked and mended, fodder laid in, vegetable gardens dug over, the last apples and quinces picked and stored, pigs slaughtered and non-laying hens killed for the pot, firewood stacked high in the outhouses and sea-coal delivered by the ton to those who could afford its luxury. The village air prickled with the scent of many bonfires, wild geese honked their V-shaped formations towards the salt flats in Pagham, a grey sea rolled inexorably into shore and the beach was scattered with the debris of the autumn tides, lengths of frayed rope, torn nets and driftwood, the white bones of dead cuttlefish and the black shreds of dead seaweed. It was a time for tidying up and winding down. A melancholy time. And nobody felt the melancholy more acutely than Johnnie Boniface.

While he and Betsy had been busy collecting names for their list and visiting their neighbours to persuade them to give evidence, he had been so happily occupied that he'd given little thought to the fact that his love affair was still in abeyance and showed no signs of being resumed. Now with only digging and repairs to keep him busy, his mind returned to its summer time frustration. He still contrived to be in The Fox when Betsy arrived with Miss Pearce's jug and sometimes she allowed him to carry it back to the house for her, and on rare, rare occasions she even allowed a kiss or two, and he still made a point of strolling down to her mother's house on her afternoon off to talk to her there, but nothing he said or did could persuade her that they should be lovers again.

There was a weary sadness about her that hurt him more than a quarrel would have done. 'If we starts that up,' she said, ''twill onny lead to trouble. We'll want to be on our own together, you know we will, an' where would we go? Tha's nearly winter an' there's no stable for us now nor like to be.'

'We could ha' been on our own together all summer,' he said, rather crossly. 'There was plenty a' places then onny you wouldn't.' Her refusal had made no sense to him at the time and it made even less now. It was silly and it felt like a rejection.

'We couldn't Johnnie,' she said, wearily. 'I told you. I got a reputation to think about. Someone would've seen us, an' they'd ha' called me names. 'Tis all very well for you, men don't get called names. 'Tis all sowin' wild oats for you an' what a lad you are an' ha-ha-ha.'

That was true but it wasn't his fault. 'Well then, we should get wed,' he urged. The more he thought about it the more it seemed the only solution. 'If we was married we could be on our own together whenever we wanted. What's to stop us?'

'I'll tell 'ee what's to stop us,' she said, bitterly. 'Bein' called names. Tha's what's to stop us. They'd say you were makin' an honest woman of me an' that'ud start 'em up again. It'ud be how I was a slut an' a trollop all over again an' I couldn't bear it.'

He tried to argue against such pessimism. 'No they wouldn't.'

But she knew better. 'Yes they would. That's how they goes on. Besides, what would we live on?'

It was a crushing question because there was no answer to it and it had been asked and unanswered for so long. It was a thorn embedded and growing into his flesh and the irritation of it was perpetual.

'Let's wait till the spring,' she said. 'It might be better then.'

He sighed. 'Tha's years off!'

That provoked a sad smile. 'Well, till our Mr Blake's had his trial then,' she said. 'Tha's onny a week or two. We'll all feel better when that's over.'

'If he gets off.'

Something of her old fire flickered in her. 'He will,' she said. 'He must. I've set my heart on it.'

The trial was the main, and sometimes the only, topic of conversation at every gathering place in the village. It was the one thing Johnnie really enjoyed in those depressing days, for he and Mr Hosier were the bearers of the latest news from Turret House and there was excitement in being a messenger. They reported when Mr Blake's first letter arrived to say that he and Catherine were back in London safe and sound and were living in Broad Street with his brother. They spread the news that Mrs Blake was sick with worry. 'Is it any wonder, poor woman, with that sort a' thing hangin' over her head?' And they delivered the date of the trial as soon as Mr Hayley knew it himself.

It was a surprise to his neighbours that Blake proposed to attend the court on his own. Some said it was a sign of confidence, 'He knows they'll let him off, tha's the size of it,' others that it was a mark of folly. 'What if they was to ask for evidence an' he couldn't give it?' and some were annoyed to have had their offer of help ignored. 'What's the point of us puttin' our names to Betsy's list if he aren't a-goin' to take no notice of it?'

But when the day arrived, most of them were anxious on his behalf and impatient to hear the outcome. There was an outcry of disbelief when it came.

''Tis a civil case seemingly,' Mr Hosier explained. 'They found a bill of indictment against him.'

His listeners were baffled by such terms. 'What's that when it's at home? Was he found guilty or not?'

'That I couldn't say,' Mr Hosier confessed. 'All I knows is they found a bill of indictment against him an' now 'tis a civil case, seemingly, an' he's to appear at the next quarter sessions here in Chichester an' be tried by a jury.'

'Which means he'll have to engage a counsellor to defend him,' Johnnie told them,
'though how he'll pay for that I can't
imagine, for they costs the earth. And he'll
have to call witnesses, so you'll get to see the
trial after all. Mr Hayley's gone to Lavant
this very morning to tell Miss Poole.'

'Samuel Rose,' Miss Poole said. 'If anyone
could prevail against the military establishment, he would be the man. You must write
to him this very afternoon and acquaint him
with the matter. We cannot have our Mr
Blake sent to prison, that would be intolerable, for not only is he totally innocent
of the crime imputed to him but he is also a
man of exquisite sensibilities and has too
tender a constitution for harsh treatment.
'Twould be the ruin of him.'

The two of them were sitting in the delicate sunshine in her delicate drawing room,
drinking her delicate tea, and the mere
thought of incarceration was making her
shiver.

Mr Hayley had ridden to Lavant in a fury,
enraged to think that his dear friend should
be put to the misery of another three
months' anxiety before this ridiculous
matter could be resolved. Now, under her
gentle influence he was eased and reassured.
'I entirely agree,' he told her. 'Entirely.' It

went without saying that he would cover the costs. 'Your advice is admirable as always, my dear Paulina. Quite admirable. I do not forget how superbly he handled the case of the Reverend Boaz, and, of course, my dear friend Cowper thought most highly of him. Oh, most highly. I will write to him at once and the letter can be dispatched post haste.'

Ten days later, the regulars in The Fox were excited to hear that a famous barrister had been hired to defend their old neighbour, had gone to meet him up in London, and was coming down to Felpham in a week or two to stay with Mr Hayley so that he could talk to the witnesses.

Betsy and Johnnie and Mr Hosier were interviewed in Mr Hayley's library. They were very impressed by their new ally for he wasn't at all the sort of figure they'd imagined a barrister would be. For a start he was a young man and very slender and they'd expected somebody old and stout, then he had a pale face and dark eyes which made him look more like a poet than a man of law, but he was obviously a gentleman, for he wore fine clothes and spoke gently in an accent that none of them recognised, but that Johnnie discovered afterwards was Scottish.

'Tell me,' he said, 'exactly what you can remember. Omit nothing. I will be the judge of those things that should be stressed come the time.'

So they told him what they could remember and left out everything they didn't want him or anybody else to know. 'A lot of hollerin' an' shoutin',' Mr Hosier said, 'same as there allus is when there's a fight. Scolfield was threatenin' to knock Mr Blake's eyes out, I remember.'

'Did he often offer such threats?'

'When he was drunk, yes he did.'

'Was he drunk on that occasion?'

'He was drunk on most occasions,' Mr Hosier said. 'Famous for it, you might say. Accordin' to the rumour that's why he was demoted. Used to be a sergeant, seemingly, an' they demoted him.'

'Thank you, Mr Hosier,' the counsellor said. 'You've been extremely helpful.'

'A good man,' Betsy said when they'd all been interviewed. 'If anyone can get him off he will. Now I'd best be gettin' back to the house or Miss Pearce'll have somethin' to say.'

Miss Pearce *did* have something to say and called Betsy to her presence so that she could say it as soon as the girl was back in her kitchen.

'What's all this nonsense I hear about you giving evidence at Mr Blake's trial?' she said. She sat ramrod straight behind her heavy stays and her powdered nose was pinched with displeasure.

'Tha's quite true, ma'am,' Betsy said. 'I

been asked to give evidence, bein' I was there at the time, an' I've said I will.'

'Total folly!' her employer said. 'You'll regret it, you mark my words. No possible good will come of it. There's a deal more to this business than meets the eye. The man is an agitator. That much is plain or the military would not be pursuing him.'

Betsy couldn't let such an insult pass, even if Miss Pearce *was* her employer and could hire or fire her as she pleased. 'He's a good honest man, Miss Pearce,' she said. 'An' I'm proud to be givin' evidence for him.'

Miss Pearce snorted. 'Then you've got less sense than I gave you credit for. Why do you imagine the military are spending money and time to bring him to court, you foolish child? Because he's been up to no good, spying or some such or sending messages to the enemy, and they know it. There's no smoke without fire, as you will discover and you would be well advised to keep out of it. Did you get the herring?'

Her poor opinion of William Blake was shared by the formidable Lady Hesketh. At the end of November, when Counsellor Rose had gathered all the information he needed and returned to his chambers in London, she wrote fiercely to 'her dear friend Mr Hayley' to warn him that his championship of Mr Blake could be misplaced.

'I have never taken up the subject you

323

mention'd to me concerning Mr Blake,' she wrote, 'and this, because I had at the time great reason to fear that your kind unsuspecting *Friendship* was drawing you into a *Scrape*, for one *who did not merit* that you should incur blame on his account. If I may give credit to some reports which reached me at the time, Mr B was more *Seriously* to blame than you were at all aware of. But I will only add on this subject that *if he was* I sincerely hope that you are no stranger to it.'

For once, her heavy emphasis only increased Mr Hayley's determination to do exactly the reverse of what she wanted. He would, he told Mrs Beke, do everything in his power to see his dear friend William Blake acquitted.

That was the general feeling in the village too, as the long empty winter crouched towards January. 'We'll see him right,' they said in The Fox, as they huddled round the fires on those dark evenings. 'We got the measure of that Scolfield feller.' They even teased Reuben Jones about it. 'You should come with us Reuben,' they said, 'an' give your evidence alongside of us. You was there. You seen what happened.'

But Reuben wasn't going to be budged from his neutrality by anyone. 'Oi was in the tap room,' he said, 'on account of Oi'd got moi arm in a sling. Oi never heard hoide nor hair of anythin'.'

'Makes you deaf, does it,' they asked him, 'havin' yer arm in a sling? Blocks yer ears?'

'There's toimes to hear an' toimes not to hear,' he told them. As you'll foind out. 'Tis no good argyfyin' with me. Oi knows what's what.'

And then with the suddenness of a sea storm, everything changed. Towards the end of December, Mr Hayley and the other witnesses received notification of the date of the trial. It was to be on Tuesday January 10th 1804, in the Guildhall in Chichester, which was where they expected it to be. What they didn't expect, and were alarmed to discover, was that it would be presided over by the Duke of Richmond. Mr Hayley was most upset.

'He has a poor opinion of me and I of him,' he said to Mrs Beke, 'and always has done, as I'm sure you know. 'Tis a black day to see him in this particular seat of judgement, an unconscionable black day. I fear he will have a poor view of Mr Blake in consequence of our friendship.'

The reaction of the villagers was immediate and fearful too, for the duke was the biggest landlord in the area and owned the farmland they worked on, which was bad enough, and the tied cottages they lived in, which was worse. Even Mr Grinder, who besides being landlord of The Fox and the cottage, also owned a hotel in the fishing village of Bognor a few miles along the coast and was well on his way to being a man of consequence, could see what a quandary they were all in. You simply didn't argue with men as powerful as the duke. Nobody ever had or ever would. It would be asking for trouble.

'If we says somethin' he don't like, he'll have us out the minute we so much as opens our mouths,' Mrs Haynes said to her daughter, 'an' we can't say what he wants us to say if we don't know what it is. No, no, we can't do it Betsy. 'Tis too much of a risk.'

'You can't let Mr Blake stand up in that court without a soul to speak up for him,' Betsy urged. ''Twould be downright wickedness.'

'Better downright wickedness than downright folly,' her mother said. 'We needs a roof over our heads. I 'aven't forgot that family in Bersted. They had them out that cottage so quick you wouldn't believe. An' she with a babe-in-arms. An' I knows that wasn't the Duke a' Richmond but landlords are all the same. Let Mr Hayley do it. He can afford to. He's a rich man.'

'Mr Hayley wasn't there,' her daughter argued. 'He never saw what went on. We're the ones what did an' we're the ones what has to speak out.'

But she was wasting her breath. 'What are

we to do?' she asked Johnnie as he was escorting her back from The Fox the next morning. 'I never see such cowardice in all my life. Even Ma says she won't do it, an' I never thought to see her let anyone down. Ever. Not once she'd given her word. Poor Mr Blake. We can't let him stand up in that awful court an' no one there to say a word for him.'

'Except us,' he pointed out.

'We wouldn't be enough,' she said seriously. 'Not if 'tis trial by jury. If no one else is prepared to speak they'll wonder why not and come to the wrong conclusion. 'Tis all or none. Can't you persuade 'em?'

'I *have* tried.'

'Well you must try again,' she said, taking the jug from him as they'd reached the George and Dragon. 'We must both try. They can't desert him now.'

During the next few days they went out of their way to talk to all the witnesses one after the other – and got nowhere. 'They're afraid,' Johnnie said. 'Tha's what, an' all the talk in the world won't change 'em. They all say the same. Upset the duke an' we shall be out on our ears. If I've heard about the family in Bersted once, I've heard it a dozen times.'

'Maybe 'twould be better if we asked 'em to meet up together,' Betsy decided. 'There's

327

safety in numbers if we could get 'em to see it. We could use the hall next to The Fox. Mr Grinder would let us.' Which was true enough for the single storey room alongside the inn was often used for village meetings.

Getting all their witnesses to gather there was a great deal more difficult than getting permission to use the room. 'There's no point,' they were told. 'Let it lie.' 'I 'aven't got time.' 'It's no good you keepin' all on.' But they kept all on and in the end they persuaded their neighbours 'at least to come an' listen' and their neighbours came.

It was a miserably cold night and they were glad that Mr Grinder had provided them with a fire and plenty to drink. They sat in a semicircle round the blaze on stools and benches carried in from the inn and told one another at length how foolish it would be to make a stand – Mr and Mrs Grinder, Mrs Haynes, Mr Cosens, Mr Hosier, William Smith and old Mrs Taylor, holding her hand to her ear so as not to miss what was being said.

Johnnie and Betsy sat in the middle of the circle. They were the youngest people there but over the last few days they seemed to have become the leaders of the group for want of any others, and although their elders didn't defer to them they listened when either of them had something to say. That evening it was Johnnie who did most of the talking, partly because Betsy said she was too cross to trust herself to speak but mostly because his mind was working so clearly, as if anxiety about this trial had sharpened his wits.

'Mr Cosens is quite right,' he said, when there was a pause in the long explanations of the need to avoid action. ''Tis neck or nothin'. Either we all gives evidence or none of us does.'

'Then none of us does,' Mr Cosens said. 'Sit tight an' say nothing, that's my advice. There's safety in silence.'

'Tha's true, too,' Johnnie said. 'But then again, if we says nothin' that means the trooper will win. He's got a mortal loud voice an' the regiment behind him an' he means to have his revenge. He never made no secret of it.'

'He's got the duke on his side too, don't forget,' Mr Hosier said. 'Mr Hayley was sure of it. Soon as he saw the letter he said the duke took a poor view of him an' a poor view of Mr Blake an' 'twas a bad day when he was chose to sit in the seat a' judgement. I'm for silence too in the light a' that opinion. There's no sense courtin' disaster.'

'What we got to consider,' Johnnie told them, thinking hard, 'is what will happen if we do keep quiet. An' I tell you, that what will happen is that Mr Blake will be sent to prison. If we keeps our mouths shut an' says nothin' we might just as well lock the prison door on him. Which to my way a' looking at it, would be a cowardly act. Fact, the more I think of it, the more cowardly it looks, an' foolish besides, if you considers it. The truth of it is, if we keeps our mouths shut we'll be letting that Scolfield bully us, an' I'm damned if I wants to be bullied by a drunken soldier. Why should we do his work for him? What's he ever done for us, besides get drunk an' spew in the hedges? Is that the sort a' man you wants to see get his own way? No, you don't an' no more do I, an' that's the truth of it. Whereas Mr Blake's a different kettle a' fish altogether. We knows Mr Blake. We've known him for years. He's been a good neighbour an' a fine upstandin' hardworkin' man, what never put a foot out a' line in all the years he was here, which you got to admit. Well, now we got to make a choice between 'em, whether we likes it or not. Stay silent an' give Private Scolfield what he wants and be known for a pack a' cowards, or speak up an' show our mettle, an' keep our neighbour out a' prison.'

They were rallying. He could see from the expressions on their faces that they were shifting their opinions. 'But what if we stands up for him an' the duke don't take no notice an' he gets sent to prison just the same?' Mrs Taylor wanted to know.

'He won't be,' Betsy said, finding her voice

330

at last. 'On account of 'tis trial by jury, twelve good men an' true, an' if the jury says you're innocent, tha's what you are an' the judge can't sentence you.'

Mrs Taylor was surprised and impressed. 'Is that a fact?'

'So,' Johnnie urged, 'if we all stand together an' we all says the same thing, we can prove the troopers wrong no matter how loud they shout. It'll be their word against ours and there's two of them and nine of us. Yes, the duke can pick us off one by one, or any of our other landlords can, come to that, like they done in Bersted, there's no arguin' with that, but not all of us and not all at once. There's nine of us here and nine's a fair number. Enough to be safe in.'

The nine faces looked round at one another, sensing the power of their number. And watching them, Johnnie knew that they were going to agree, despite what it might cost them, and he was full of admiration for them.

Christmas was quiet that year, for Mr Hayley only had half a dozen guests and was miserable at the thought of what might happen to his dear friend Blake and distressed to have heard how ill poor Catherine was.

'Sick with worry,' he explained to his guests. 'Brought to death's door by it. Oh, what a weary world this is.'

'Come riding,' they suggested. ''Twill cheer you.'

So they went riding every day and he told them he was obliged to them for their care of him and admitted that he felt happier on horseback than anywhere else on earth, 'even in these dark days' and when they parted from him at the end of their stay, he smiled and joked and told them he had been much improved by their kindly company. It was no surprise to anyone in the house that he decided to go for a good long invigorating ride on the day before the trial.

'All is prepared,' he said to Mrs Beke. 'The witnesses are to travel in Mr Cosen's wagon and I shall ride. Johnnie Boniface will accompany me on Bruno and then Mr Blake can have him when the trial is over. Miss Poole has agreed to have supper ready for us when all is done and we shall ride across to Lavant together. All will be well, I am sure of it.'

His horse was in a sprightly mood that Mrs Beke found rather alarming, especially as her master had that dratted umbrella slung over his arm. 'Would you not be better to wear your new hat,' she suggested. 'It is stronger than the old one and would offer you more protection – should it come on to rain.'

He allowed himself to be persuaded, not

because the hat was stronger but because it was more becoming. As he rode out of the gates, he lifted it from his head and waved it jauntily.

Half an hour later he was back, slumped over the saddle, white in the face and with blood streaming from his forehead. 'Johnnie must ride into Chichester for Doctor Guy, I fear,' he said. 'I am not well.'

Then what a coming and going there was, with the master led into the front parlour and eased into a chair by the fire where he groaned and held his head, and servants dispatched in every direction: Susie to the bedroom for the brandy bottle, Johnnie to the stables to saddle Bruno, Nan to the kitchen to fetch a bowl of warm water and towels and a length of lint to staunch the bleeding and the boot boy to the store cupboard for a roll of drugget to protect the carpet.

'Such a thing!' Mrs Beke said, as the required goods were brought into the parlour and placed before her, 'and for it to happen today of all days. I don't know what the world is coming to, indeed I don't. Hold your head quite still Mr Hayley, dear, while I get this dressing in place and then you shall have some brandy. Dearie, dearie me what a thing to have happened.'

Dr Guy was remarkably quick, following Bruno in at the gate after little more than half an hour, and once he was in the parlour he set to work at once to reassure his old friend as he examined his bleeding head.

'You must patch me up, my dear friend,' Hayley said to him, adding dramatically, 'for living or dying I must make a public appearance at the trial of my friend Blake.'

'If that is so,' the doctor smiled, reaching for a length of catgut, 'I must make speed to insert such stitches as are needful to ensure that you are delivered to the Guildhall alive.'

Chapter Eighteen

William Blake took the stagecoach to Chichester on the day before his trial so as to be in good time to attend. He booked a room in one of the cheaper hotels, spent an anxious night watching the moon describe its long parabola across the Sussex sky and rose early to prepare himself for his ordeal. But his careful planning came to nothing, for when he presented himself at the Guildhall at the appointed time, clean, newly shaved and having wound himself up to a high pitch of emotional preparedness, he discovered that the trial was to be delayed until four o'clock on the following day, which meant that he had to kick his heels in Chichester for more than twenty-four hours. He wrote to his poor Catherine to explain the delay and to hope she was feeling a little better, and then walked about the town, prowling up and down its four main streets and circling its walls, round and round and round, getting steadily more depressed and agitated, until darkness forced him to retreat to his hotel room again and to the bed in which he still couldn't sleep. By the time he finally walked across the park to his fate on the following afternoon, he was in a very poor state indeed.

The Guildhall stood in damp and disconcerting isolation under a grey sky in the middle of a grey field. In ordinary circumstances he would have enjoyed the sight of it for, having been the chancel of an ancient monastery, it was built in the Gothic style, which he'd always admired, but on that day it seemed forbidding in the extreme, its stone walls a sign of entrenched and implacable power, its stone-flagged floor and high Gothic windows cold as the punishment that was sure to come. With every single one of those windows shuttered, it was dark inside the building even with a flutter of candles on every table, and it took a minute or two for him to become accustomed to the change of light and even longer to take in all the details of the busy scene before him.

The space inside the building was divided by a wooden screen, in the centre of which was a double gate, which now stood open to admit the participants. Beyond it, and in front of what had once been the high altar, there was a dais where the judge and his six accompanying magistrates were sitting, he in his red robes and full-bottomed wig, looking larger and more powerful than anyone else at the hall, they in top coats, winter hats and stout boots, for it was as cold inside the building as it had been out in the field, and all of them talking and laughing together as if they were members of a club at some happy social gathering. The sight of them was more chilling to Blake than the cold air. Below the dais was another long table where the two counsels, also wigged and gowned, were pretending to ignore one another, while their solicitors sat beside them shuffling papers, and behind them were the benches for the witnesses. He was encouraged to see so many of his old neighbours: Mr Grinder in a huge winter coat with a triple collar like a coachman; Betsy in her scarlet cloak sitting beside her mother who was wearing a hat like the one Mary Wollstonecraft used to wear; William the ostler bundled up in waistcoats and jackets like an over-wrapped parcel; Johnnie Boniface blowing on his hands to warm them. He tried to catch their eyes but they were all too busy talking to one another or looking round them at the judge and jury, who were ranged on two long benches, to the left of the judgement seat, looking like the tradesmen and labourers they were and plainly overawed by all the pomp and importance that surrounded them. And in the middle of it all, set apart and facing the judges and lawyers, was an empty box just big enough for a single occupant, where the witnesses would take the stand. Without doubt or any possibility of avoidance, he was in a court of law.

He stood before the gate, trying to still the anxious trembling of his heart, and emanations rose ice-white and sinister to coil about his body and numb his limbs. But then his counsel looked up, saw him and strode across the stone flags to welcome him. 'Mr Blake, my dear sir, I trust I see you well.'

'I am the better for seeing you, Mr Rose,' Blake said, 'although I could have wished our meeting anywhere but here.'

'Tush man, have no fear,' the counsellor said. 'We are well prepared and will prevail.' His Scottish accent was a comfort to Blake for it showed that he was an outsider too and not a member of the club at the high table. 'However,' he went on, 'I should tell you that one of our judges is Mr Quantock who, as you probably remember, is the magistrate who took Scolfield's original deposition.'

'A bad omen,' Blake said.

'Not necessarily,' his counsellor said. 'Do not forget that you are being tried by jury and juries are unpredictable by their nature. That is their great strength.'

The two soldiers were arriving, pushing through the wooden doors as if they were storming a citadel, bright in their red jackets, blue facings rich in the candlelight, buttons polished to a gleam, epaulettes dangling gold, wearing their white doeskin trousers for the occasion with their red greatcoats slung about their shoulders and looking extremely tall and imposing under their black cocked hats. Their counsel was on his feet at once to greet them, which he did very loudly, and to lead them in military procession to the seats beside him. They were causing a stir and they knew it and enjoyed it.

Blake sat beside Counsellor Rose, as far away from his adversaries as he could get and tried to appear unconcerned. But the usher was calling the court to order, banging on the flagstones with his staff and singing 'Silence in the court!' in a very loud voice. 'The case of William Blake engraver versus Private Scolfield of His Majesty's First Regiment of Dragoons, His Honour the Duke of Richmond presiding.' His ordeal was about to begin.

It was humiliating to be named so publicly

and loudly, alarming to watch the gates being closed and to know that they were all shut in, demoralising to realise that all eyes had turned in his direction and that most seemed unfriendly. He looked along the line of judges, trying to guess which one was Mr Quantock and saw that the gentleman sitting at the end of the table was Mr Poynz, who lived in Aldwick and was an old customer of his, and that encouraged him a little. But even so the chains of torment held him shackled and his heart shook in his breast.

The formalities were gone through, the two counsels were required to identify themselves, as Counsellor Rose and Counsellor Bowen, and the charge was read. 'That on the twelfth day of August in the year of our Lord one thousand eight hundred and three, War was carrying on between the persons exercising the powers of Government in France and our said Lord the King, to wit, at the parish of Felpham in the County of Sussex, one WILLIAM BLAKE, late of the said Parish of Felpham in the said County of Sussex, being a Wicked Seditious and Evil disposed person and greatly disaffected to our said Lord the King and Wickedly and Seditiously intending to bring our said Lord the King into great Hatred Contempt and Scandal with all his liege and faithful subjects of this realm and the Soldiers of our said Lord the King to Scandalize and Vilify and intending to withdraw the fidelity and allegiance of his said Majesty's Subjects from his said Majesty and to encourage and invite as far as in him lay the enemies of our said Lord the King to invade this Realm and Unlawfully and Wickedly to seduce and encourage his Majesty's Subjects to resist and oppose our said Lord the King.'

The sonorous words and the convoluted manner of their delivery were enough to strike terror into any one, let alone an accused man, and, as if that weren't enough, Counsellor Bowen stood up at once to underline the severity of the charge and spell out its implications.

He would, he said, produce incontrovertible proof that the accused had uttered an abominable and seditious calumny upon His Majesty the King and all his subjects, that the words he had uttered were: – damn the King (meaning our said Lord the King) and Country (meaning this Realm) his Subjects (meaning the subjects of our said Lord the King) and all you Soldiers (meaning the Soldiers of our said Lord the King) are sold for slaves. 'Gentlemen,' he said, inclining his bulk towards the jury, 'this is a very uncommon accusation. It is foreign to our natures and opposite to our habits. Do you not hear every day, from the mouths of thousands in the streets, the exclamation of "God Save the King!" It is the effusion of every Englishman's heart. The charge therefore laid in the indictment is an offence of so extraordinary a nature, that evidence of the most clear, positive, and unobjectionable kind will be necessary to induce you to believe it, which I shall presently lay before you. Extraordinary vices, gentlemen, are very rare, which is all the more reason why they should be dealt with swiftly and decisively, that their malignancy – for that is what it is – should be rooted out from our loyal and God-fearing society and that any unprincipled, malignant and evil wretch, such as the man who stands here accused, should, if found guilty, as I truly believe will be the case, be punished for his seditious utterances. Truly, I wonder that a counsellor of such eminence as my esteemed colleague, Mr Rose, should undertake to defend such a wretch, when he must surely be aware of the atrocity and malignity of the crime of which he is accused.' Then, looking plumply pleased with himself, he smiled at the jurymen, bowed to the duke and sat down.

There was a flutter of interest as Mr Rose stood to make his opening statement. He began smoothly and with great courtesy. 'I perfectly agree with my learned friend,' he said, 'with regard to the atrocity and malignity of the charge now laid before you. I am also much obliged to him for having given me the credit that no justification or extenuation of such a charge would be attempted by me, supposing the charge could be proved to your satisfaction – and I must be permitted to say, that it is a credit which I deserve. If there be a man, who can be found guilty of such a transgression, he must apply to some other person to defend him. My task is to show that my client is not guilty of the words imputed to him. We stand here not merely in form, but in sincerity and truth, to declare that we are not guilty. There is no doubt that the crime which is laid to the charge of my client is a crime of the most extraordinary malignity – I chose the term malignity purposely – for if the offence be clearly proved I am willing to allow that public malignity and indelible disgrace are fixed upon my client. If on the other hand when you have heard the witnesses, which I shall call, you should be led to believe that it is a fabrication for the purpose of answering some scheme of revenge, you will have little difficulty in deciding that it is a still greater malignity on the part of the witness Scolfield.'

It was a skilled answer and Blake was cheered by it, but the chains still bit, for now Private Scolfield was being asked to take the stand. There was much neck craning on the public benches, as the soldier removed his cocked hat, put it under his arm and marched to the witness box.

He agreed to his name and rank and allowed that Mr Bowden should take him back 'to the day in question, when you were in Mr Blake's garden, were you not?'

'I was, sir.'

'Would you tell the court what took you there?'

'Well, sir, I walked across from The Fox Inn...'

'Where you were billeted.'

'Where I was billeted, yes, sir. I walked across, like I said, sir, with a message for the ostler. He was helping in the garden on account of there wasn't much work in the inn at the time.'

'Did you deliver your message?'

'I did, sir.'

'And what then?'

'Well, then, sir, Mr Blake, he come out the cottage and he sees me there and starts shouting at me.'

'Had you said anything to him to occasion such behaviour?'

'No, sir. I had not.'

'Quite. Pray continue. Can you recall the words he used when he started to shout at you?'

'I can indeed, sir, on account of they was such shameful words, seditious words, words against King and Country, sir, words what in my opinion, ought never to have been said.'

'Your opinion does you credit,' Mr Bowen approved. 'Pray continue.'

'Well, sir, he said the King should be damned and the people of England were like a parcel of children what would get burnt in the fire and they would be damned and when Bonaparte came, he would be master of Europe in an hour, and England could depend on it that when he set foot on English ground every Englishman would have a choice whether to have his throat cut or join the French. And he said he was a strong man and would certainly begin to cut throats. It will be cut throat for cut throat, he said, and the weakest will go to the wall.'

'What else?'

'Well, sir, he damned the King, and his country, and his subjects, and he said soldiers were all bound for slaves and all the poor people in general. And then his wife came out and she said she would fight as long as she had a drop of blood in her and Blake said, "my dear, you would not fight against France", and she said she would fight for Bonaparte.'

There was a hiss of indrawn breath at such a wicked utterance. The little sound tipped Blake into open fury. He sprang to his feet and roared at the soldier 'False!', his voice so loud in the echo chamber of the hall that several people jumped.

The Duke of Richmond was displeased. 'I

will have order in my court,' he boomed. 'If you cannot contain yourself, Mr Blake, I will have you ejected.'

The desire to fight back rose in Blake like a black tide but Mr Rose had a restraining hand on his arm and was gentling him back into his seat, sending him eye signals that he was to obey, and the moment passed.

'To continue, Private Scolfield,' Mr Bowen said. 'How did you reply to these seditious remarks?'

Having seen his adversary publicly rebuked the trooper puffed up like a turkey cock. 'I remonstrated with him, sir, and said he shouldn't be saying such things.'

'Quite. And what happened next?'

'Then Mrs Blake she said, "Turn him out the garden".'

'And then?'

'Mr Blake come at me, sir, to try to grab hold of me.'

'What did you do then?'

'I prepared to defend myself, sir, as an Englishman and a soldier of the line.'

'You fought him?'

'I defended myself from his attack, sir.'

'Quite. Was anything further said?'

'Yes, sir. He went on shouting and saying dreadful things all the way to The Fox Inn.'

It was an impressive performance and Blake could see that the jury was impressed. He looked at Mr Rose as he stood to cross-examine and wondered what he would say in his defence.

The counsellor gave the soldier the benefit of his gentle smile. 'You were once a sergeant, were you not?' he asked.

Private Scolfield was surprised and said he couldn't see what that had to do with it. But Mr Rose persisted.

'You were, were you not?'

It was grudgingly admitted.

'Would you kindly tell the court the reason why you were degraded.'

The private was annoyed to be brought down to such a petty level, but after a long pause he admitted that it had been on account of having been a little the worse for wear on one occasion.

'Drunk, you mean?'

'Yes, sir.'

'Drunk and disorderly?'

''Twas said.'

'Thank you, Private Scolfield. No further questions.'

There was a shift and a shuffle, as Private Scolfield stood down, and those who needed to cough, coughed, which gave Mr Rose the chance to wink at his client, and to whisper that they had made a good start. Then Mr Bowen called his second witness, Private Cock, who answered every question in exactly the same way as his comrade, like a red-coated echo. He had heard all the

346

words mentioned in the charge, every single one, he'd take his oath on it.

'Very well,' Counsellor Bowen said. 'Will you tell the court exactly what happened.'

He'd been in the stables, the trooper said, and he'd heard a row and come out to see what it was.

'And what was it?' Counsellor Bowen prompted.

'It was Mr Blake attacking Private Scolfield.'

Counsellor Rose put his hand on Blake's shoulder because he could feel him bristling. 'No,' he whispered. 'Let it ride. Leave it to me.'

'And did you hear what was being said?'

Indeed he did and could repeat it, word for word, in exactly the same way as Private Scolfield had done. 'He said, damn the king and damn his country and damn his subjects and soldiers were bound for slaves and all the poor people were slaves.'

'You heard this clearly? There is no mistake in what you heard?'

'Yes, sir, very clearly. There's no mistake. We both heard it, sir.'

This time Counsellor Bowen handed over to Counsellor Rose with a nod of triumph. Private Cock had been firm in his evidence and had not had the misfortune to be demoted.

Counsellor Rose had to pause for a few

seconds to cough into a white handkerchief, but when he spoke he was kindly and patient. 'Let us see if we can be completely clear,' he said. 'You say that you heard Mr Blake say all the words on the charge. We need not rehearse them, for I am sure everybody in the court knows what they are by now. You heard them all, is that correct?'

'I did, sir.'

'These are the words that Private Scolfield says he heard when he was in the garden, is that correct?'

'Yes, sir.'

'Then, explain to me, if you will, how it was you were able to hear them too. You were in the stables at the time they were spoken, I believe, and did not come out into the street until you heard a noise. Is that correct?'

Private Cock admitted that it was but he looked puzzled as if he knew he was being led into a trap and couldn't see how to avoid it.

'So if you were in the stables at the time, you couldn't have heard what was being said in the garden. Is that correct?'

Private Cock said he supposed it was and added that he must have heard the words when he was in the street.

'Ah! So what you are telling us is that Mr Blake spoke these incriminating words on two separate occasions, once in the garden when they were heard by Private Scolfield and once in the street when they were heard by you?'

The trooper was surly but said he supposed so.

'We must be quite sure about this,' Counsellor Rose said, after pausing to cough again. 'Either you did hear them, or you did not. Supposition is not enough.'

'I did hear them, sir. On my oath.'

'In the street?'

'Yes, sir.'

'But not in the garden.'

'No, sir.'

'You are certain about that?'

'Yes, sir.'

'But when you began your evidence for Counsellor Bowen you were certain you had heard the accused say all the words on the charge when he was in the garden, were you not?'

'I suppose so, sir.'

And now you are not so certain.'

By this point, Private Cock was so uncertain he couldn't answer.

'Your certainty,' Mr Rose observed, as he resumed his seat, 'would appear to be something of a moveable feast. No further questions, Your Grace.'

It appeared that there were no further witnesses for the prosecution either but

Counsellor Rose said he had several people he wished to call and proceeded to name them – Mr Grinder, the landlord of The Fox and his wife, Mrs Grinder, Mr Cosens, the miller, Mrs Haynes, wife to the miller's servant and her daughter, Mr Hosier, gardener to Mr Hayley and his under-gardener, William Smith, the ostler from The Fox, who was working as Mr Blake's gardener at the time, and 'if your Grace is agreeable' he would begin with Mr Hayley himself, 'a gentleman well-known to you, Your Grace.'

The duke hoisted his red robes about him. 'Are all these witnesses really necessary?' he asked.

'If they were not, Your Grace, I would not call them.'

'Oh, very well then.'

So Mr Hayley was called and stepped into the witness box, tall and imposing in his fine greatcoat with a bandage dramatic round his left temple and identified himself, with a modest smile, as William Hayley Esquire, the celebrated poet. He was a long-standing friend and colleague of the accused, he said, and knew him to be a man of singular honour, one of the foremost engravers in the land and an artist, hard working, loyal in his friendships, admirable to a degree.

'Would you say he is a quarrelsome man?' Mr Rose asked.

The answer was forthright. 'No, sir. Not in

the least. He is an artist and a man of peace.'

'Would you say he is a patriotic man?'

'Entirely so, sir. Oh, indubitably. I would not have brought him into this part of the country and given him encouragement and employed him in my house, had I conceived it possible that he could have uttered those abominable sentiments.'

Mr Bowen said he had no questions to ask the celebrated poet, so Mr William Hayley took his greatcoat and bandage back to the witness benches and was replaced by the bundle of clothes that contained William the ostler.

He was so nervous he had to clear his throat three times before he could acknowledge his name and occupation. But as Mr Rose eased him into his story he took heart and gradually spoke more confidently. He'd been working in Mr Blake's garden, he said, when Private Scolfield came in with a message. He'd invited him in 'more's the pity, for I wouldn't have, if I'd know'd then what I knows now'.

'Of course,' Mr Rose understood. 'Then Mr Blake came out into the garden. Is that right?'

'Yes, sir.'

'And what did he say?'

'He asked Private Scolfield what he was a-doing in the garden, an' Private Scolfield he said he was a soldier of the king an' could go where he pleased. He was a bit saucy like.'

'And then?'

'Mr Blake told him to get out.'

'Just that?'

'Yes, sir.'

'You didn't hear Mr Blake say anything else?'

'No, sir.'

'Not damn the King. Or damn the country. Or damn his subjects.'

'No, sir.'

'Would you kindly estimate the size of the garden for the court.'

''Tis about ten yards square, sir, give or take.'

'And was it a blustery day? Was there a wind blowing?'

'No, sir. 'Twas a fine clear day, very still.'

'So if anything else had been said by either of these men, you would have heard it?'

'Yes, sir. But I didn't, sir, on account of nothin' else *was* said.'

Counsellor Bowen took his time to stand for his cross-examination, hoisting his robes about him and fixing the ostler with the sternest look the young man had ever seen.

'Come now, Mr Smith,' he said. 'We must discover if your memory is truly as faulty as would appear.'

The ostler didn't answer.

'Do you seriously expect me to believe that not one angry word was uttered when

Mr Blake turned Private Scolfield out of the garden?'

'They was both angry, sir.'

'So there was a deal of shouting?'

'Yes, sir, there was. A great deal a' shoutin'.'

A great deal of shouting,' the counsellor repeated thoughtfully. 'Yet you maintain that you heard every word that was uttered.'

'Yes, sir, I did.'

'I put it to you, sir, that in the heat and noise of the quarrel you misheard what was said.'

William was confused and said he s'pposed 'twere possible.

'I put it to you, sir, that you have forgotten half of what was said, or chosen to forget it. It is now six months since the incident in question and memories, as we all know, have a tendency to fade.'

William s'pposed that were possible too.

'In short, you could have heard all the words of the charge, could you not, and subsequently forgotten them.'

The pain on William's face was plain for everyone to see. He knew he was being manipulated and that he ought to fight against it but the knowledge was making his brain spin and he couldn't think what to *say*. He looked across at Mr Rose, but he was coughing again and not looking at anybody. He looked at his friends and neighbours, and particularly at Johnnie, who was sitting stock still with concern, and Betsy who was biting her lip. Then he noticed that Johnnie was mouthing something and concentrated hard to see what it was. 'Say no.' Was that it? The duke turned his head to scowl in disapproval but Johnnie ignored him and signalled again. 'Say no. Say no.' And at that, William's brain unlocked itself and he could think and speak.

'No,' he said. 'No, sir, that ent the way of it. I knows what I heard right enough an' them words what he's charged with was *not* spoke, leastways not in the garden they weren't. I give 'ee my word on it. If they *had* been I'd've heard 'em.'

He was so clear and so firm about it that Counsellor Bowen decided he had no further questions. So Mr Rose called his next witness. This time it was Mrs Haynes, who adjusted her Mary Wollstonecraft hat and strode to the stand as if she was off to the wars.

She had come out of her house when she heard the noise, she said, and had seen Mr Blake propelling the trooper along the road by his arms, 'as if he was pushing a wheelbarrow'. She had watched as the two men struggled, seen them parted by Mr Grinder and Mr Cosens and seen Private Cock arrive. She had heard every word that was said and was quite certain that Mr Blake had not said any of the words he was charged with saying.

'Not a one, sir,' she said, 'an' I was as close to him an' Private Scolfield as I am to you. I've heard a lot of quarrels in my time, sir, an' 'tis my experience that when people quarrel they always charge each other with some offence, and repeat it to anyone around, over an' over, an' this time they never said a word about this offence, neither to one another nor to us, so my opinion of it is that it was all made up in the stable afterwards, as a way of gettin' revenge.'

When Mr Bowen stood to cross-examine her she squared her shoulders like a prize-fighter. 'No, sir,' she said. 'I did *not* hear any of the words you mention, an' before you asks me I'll tell you I have a very good memory and very good hearing. If they had been said, I'd've heard 'em, an' if I'd heard 'em I'd've remembered 'em.'

It was such a spirited answer that her friends on the witness benches burst into a cheer and even Mr Blake managed a smile and allowed himself the first faint hope that he might be acquitted.

The duke was very annoyed. 'You will refrain from applause,' he told them sternly. 'This is a court of law not a theatre.'

But she had made her stand and now all that was necessary was for the other witnesses to follow her lead, which they did, one after the other. Mr Grinder described how he'd pulled Private Scolfield away from Mr Blake and persuaded him to go into the inn, Mr Cosens remembered that Private Scolfield had threatened to punch Mr Blake's eyes out, Mrs Grinder said she'd thought they were in for a nasty fight and was glad when her husband intervened, Mr Hosier described the way Mr Blake had twisted the trooper's arms behind his back so that he 'couldn't punch no one and had to walk whether he would or no', Betsy volunteered that Mr Blake had never offered violence to anyone and was only trying to protect himself and Mr Hosier said he'd heard Private Scolfield vow to be revenged on Mr Blake. And none of them had heard a single word on the charge and said so forcefully.

The last man to take the stand was Johnnie Boniface, who stood in the box like an avenging angel, fiery sword in hand, his shock of fair hair bright in the candlelight.

He gave his name, said that he was the under-gardener at Turret House and told the court that, like all the others, he had come out into the street to see what all the row was about and that he hadn't heard any of the words on the charge being spoken.

'Not one?' Counsellor Rose asked, after coughing a little.

'No, sir. Not one.'

'When Private Cock arrived,' the Counsellor prompted, 'you went to speak to him, did you not.'

'I did, sir. I asked him if his comrade was drunk.'

'And was he, in your opinion?'

'He smelt drunk, sir, an' he was spoiling for a fight. He kept saying he'd punch Mr Blake's eyes out. That was really all I did hear him saying, that an' a lot a' swearing – apart from when he left us.'

'And what did he say then?'

'He said, "I'll be revenged on you, damn your eyes. You just wait an' see if I don't".' And he turned to glance at the jury to see what impact that was having on them. Oh, what power there was in outwitting a pair of villains in a court of law!

'And then,' Counsellor Rose prompted again, 'he went into the stables with his comrade.'

'Yes, sir.'

Mr Rose smiled at his client. The defence was proved. 'No further questions my lord.'

Mr Bowen seemed disgruntled as he rose to sum up. He confined himself to praising the good offices of the military in general, 'here to protect us in our hour of need' and of Privates Scolfield and Cock in particular, 'fine men who are rightly concerned when seditious sentiments are uttered in their presence and have brought this charge to ensure that such sentiments are never uttered again.' 'I call upon you,' he said addressing the jury directly, 'to do your patriotic duty and to find this seditious person guilty as charged.'

Counsellor Rose, on the other hand was gently persuasive, and sounded frail after the rumbustious tone of his opponent, pausing from time to time to cough into his white handkerchief. 'Here then, gentlemen,' he said, 'is a charge attended with circumstances of the most extraordinary nature. A man, we have been told, comes out of his house for the purpose of addressing a malignant and unintelligible discourse to those who are most likely to injure him for it. For it has been said under oath that he came out into the garden and, without any provocation, without one word being spoken on either side, began to utter the seditious expressions with which he is being charged. This, if you believe the evidence given by the two troopers, is what you must also believe. On the other hand, if you believe the evidence of Mr Blake's neighbours, you will believe that not one word on the charge was actually said. Scolfield confines himself to the words in the garden, the other says they were uttered before the public house. If they were spoken in the garden, the ostler must have heard them – but he has said on oath that he did not – if they were uttered before

358

the public house, the other witnesses must have heard them – and they swear on oath that they did not. In short, the testimony of these soldiers...'

But at that point he was overcome by such a violent coughing fit that he had to sit down and was quite unable to speak. Blake was most concerned and so, as the coughing went on, was the duke. He conferred briefly with his fellow judges, as Blake bent to ask his champion if there was anything he could do for him and the courtroom buzzed and fidgeted with concern, then he sent the usher out for water and brandy, rose and made an announcement.

'My fellow judges and I,' he said, 'are of the opinion that there is no need to prolong this trial by an adjournment. All the necessary evidence has been adequately given, the closing speeches have been made to all intents and purposes. In the light of the indisposition of our colleague, and if both counsellors are agreeable, we suggest that the jury should now consider its verdict.'

They were remarkably quick. By the time the usher had returned with the brandy and Counsellor Rose had taken a few sips and had begun to recover his breath, the foreman was on his feet, signalling that he was ready to give their decision.

It was short and to the point. They found the defendant not guilty and that was the verdict of them all.

There was an uproar, as people cheered and threw their hats in the air and declared what a splendid verdict it was. Blake's friends and neighbours ran from their uncomfortable benches to shake their hero by the hand and thump him between the shoulder blades and tell him how glad they were to see him set free, 'which is no more than you deserve an' we thanks God for it,' as he smiled and smiled and grew rosy with triumph and relief. After such a long anxious wait he felt like a bird released from its cage, rising on a current of pure clear air and dizzy with the delight of freedom.

The soldiers were gone in a second and in high dudgeon, but everybody else stayed where they were to celebrate. Mr Hayley wept for joy, Mr Rose, still pale but no longer coughing, was praised and cheered until he said they were making his head spin, and Mrs Haynes and Johnnie were the heroes of the hour, thumped and patted and congratulated until their arms were sore. Finally, Mr Hayley dried his eyes and strode to the dais to congratulate his old enemy on a job well done.

'I congratulate Your Grace,' he said, 'that after having been wearied for so long with the condemnation of sorry vagrants, you have at last had the gratification of seeing an honest man honourably delivered from an infamous persecution. Mr Blake is a pacific, industrious and deserving artist.'

The duke accepted his dubious congratulations in the spirit in which they had been offered. 'I know nothing of him,' he said coldly. 'Clear the court.'

Chapter Nineteen

It was a riotous journey home. Although there was a sharp rain falling and it was as dark as pitch, they talked and laughed and told one another what a triumph it had been all the way from the Guildhall to Felpham village, and halfway there they broke into a rousing chorus of 'Rule Britannia' led by Mrs Taylor who said she'd never seen such a trial – as if she'd been frequenting courthouses all her life – and wouldn't have missed a second of it, even though she hadn't been called. Even Mr Cosens' little mare, which was normally a very sober animal, caught the mood and ventured a canter.

Betsy was the first person to be dropped off and was kissed goodnight by the entire company, Johnnie included. ''Tis a feather in your cap,' Mr Grinder told her, as she climbed out of the cart. 'You and young Johnnie here.' And that was the opinion around the supper table at Turret House, where the tale was told at great length and with every detail embellished.

By the time he got to bed, after an evening in The Fox where he was admired and petted and treated to more porter than he'd ever drunk in his life, Johnnie was beginning to feel like the hero they all said he was. He lay awake in the inky darkness, feeling so pleased with himself his chest felt as if it was about to explode. Despite it all, they'd stood together and given their evidence in exactly the right way and refused to be bullied and now Mr Blake was a free man because of what they'd done. And Betsy had smiled at him all the time he was in the witness box, which was the best thing of all. Oh, they'd be back together now. He was sure of it.

The next morning Mrs Beke warned them all to be quiet about their work because Mr Hayley had come home very late and was still in bed and asleep. Not an easy thing, Johnnie thought, when his first job was to fill all the coal buckets and carry them up to the rooms where they were needed. But chores were nothing to him that morning and he worked easily, his head full of happy dreams.

Halfway through the morning, Bob the boot boy came up to the library to tell him that his mother had arrived and was waiting outside the back door to see him.

It didn't surprise him. News of his triumph was sure to spread and Father would have told her about it last night, when he got home from The Fox. 'Come to hear how I got on,' he said, as he wiped his hands on his apron, and went down at once to tell her. He was so full of himself he'd rushed into a description of the trial before he noticed how drawn and anxious she looked. 'You should ha' been there, Ma,' he said. 'You'd ha' been proud of us.'

'Yes,' she said and her voice was so weary it shocked him. 'I heard. Your Father told me.'

'What is it?' he asked her. 'Is something the matter?'

'Can we walk somewhere away from the house?' she asked. 'Would they let you?'

'I'll get my jacket,' he said and went, feeling horribly anxious. Someone must be ill. It couldn't be Father. He'd been fine in The Fox last night. So it had to be young Harry. They walked in silence along the winding street, past The Fox and Blake's empty cottage, heading for the grey sea and the debris on the beaches, as the wind buffeted their faces and whipped his mother's heavy skirts about her legs. When they reached the shore, he couldn't wait to hear what it was any longer and begged her to tell him.

'Is it Harry?' he asked. 'Has he took a

fever? Is he ill? Is that it?'

'No, son,' his mother said, sadly. "Taren't your brother. 'Tis you. Oh, Johnnie, I don't know how to tell 'ee. We've had the bailiffs round.'

Now, with a shrinking of his heart, he knew what it was, could feel the threat under her sadness. But he needed to hear it spoken and to know the worst. 'What did they want?' he asked.

'They didn't say exactly,' she told him, grey eyes brimming tears. 'Just how they thought 'twould be better if you was to go away. They said they was considerin' all the tied cottages and – what was it they said? – how to use 'em to best advantage. Yes. That was it. To best advantage. An' then they said they'd got a ticket for you on the stagecoach to London an' how 'twould be best all round if you was to take it. Oh, Johnnie, what are we to do? If you don't go they'll have us out sure as eggs is eggs.'

It was the retribution they'd all feared. It was what they'd all said would happen in the weeks when he and Betsy had been pushing and persuading.

'Did they go to anyone else?' he asked.

'No,' she said. 'Not so far as I knows. 'Tis just us, seemingly. Just you. Oh, Johnnie, what are we to do if they turns us out? Your father's in such a state you wouldn't believe.'

He took charge of the situation. He'd caused it, so it was only right and proper he should answer for it. 'Don't 'ee fret,' he said to her, speaking gently and comforting her, as if she were the child and he the parent. 'I won't let them turn you out.'

'But what will you do?'

'Go to London if needs must,' he said. 'But first I shall visit all the others in case they been threatened, too. Go and tell Pa not to worry. Everythin' will be all right. I'll come an' see you soon as I know what's going on, an' tell you what's what. I promise. Don't 'ee fret. I won't let them turn you out.' Inwardly he was shaking with anger that punishment should have been meted out so swiftly and in such an underhand way but outwardly he stayed calm. It was the risk they'd all taken. He couldn't pretend he hadn't known it was likely. Now he had to face it. I'll visit Mrs Haynes first, he thought, as he kissed his mother a temporary goodbye. She was the other one who'd fought them in that court and if they're after me, they could be after her, too.

To his relief, Mrs Haynes was still happily enjoying her triumph. 'No,' she said, when he'd told her his news. 'No one's been here. I'd've given 'em a piece a' my mind if they had. What a thing to do to put pressure on your poor Ma.'

'What about Betsy?' he asked. 'Has she

been to The Fox yet this morning?'

'Been an' gone,' her mother said. 'An' no, no one's after her, I'm glad to say. Except that ol' Miss Pearce. She was on at her for stayin' out so late. She told me this mornin'.'

So far so good. 'I can't stop,' he said to Mrs Haynes. 'I want to see all the others.' He felt more and more responsible for them the more time he had to think. And more and more resigned to the fact that he would have to do as the bailiffs suggested.

She wished him luck, 'whatever you decides to do. Come back an' let me know.'

Mr and Mrs Grinder were busy in the taproom, dispensing porter. They were angry to hear what had happened to his mother 'but not surprised'. And no, they hadn't been approached by anyone and neither had William.

'But then,' as Mr Grinder explained, 'they'd be hard put to it to come after me, being I'm my own landlord.'

'If you ask me, they're pickin' you out for a scapegoat,' Mrs Grinder said, 'on account of you give the best evidence.'

On to old Mrs Taylor, who was incensed to hear what was being suggested, but hadn't had any visitors at all that morning. 'Not that they're like to pick on me. I never said nothin'.' Down to the mill to see Mr

Cosens, who'd been hard at work since dawn and hadn't seen anybody either. Then back to the house to ask Mr Hosier, who, since it was past midday, was sitting in the kitchen with the others waiting to be served a portion of one of Mrs Beke's meat pies.

'We'd given you up for lost,' Mrs Beke said in her acid way. 'Where have you been, if I may make so bold as to ask?'

He told her briefly and without any emotion, for by now the news hung about his heart like the heaviest of Mr Cosens' millstones. And like all the other people he'd talked to that morning, they wanted to know what he was going to do. The answer was engraved on the millstone. 'I shall go to London,' he said. 'I can't have my family turned out on my account, an' Heaven knows there's little to keep me here. I shall go to London and make my fortune.'

'Good luck to 'ee, then,' Mr Hosier said. 'Tha's what I says. When d'you have to go?'

It was the one thing Johnnie hadn't thought to ask, and the first thing he *did* ask when he saw his mother that afternoon. Her answer came as a shock that stopped his breath.

'Tomorrow mornin',' she said. 'They give me the ticket. See. Here 'tis. Tomorrow mornin' on the first stage.'

So soon, he thought, taking the ticket. So quick. There was barely time to digest what

367

had happened or to think what he would do when he arrived. But his mind was made up to it, quick or not. He'd been the one who'd urged revolution and organised that meeting and pressed his neighbours to stand up for the right. He'd felt like a god standing there in that courtroom, fighting back and answering up, and now there was a price to pay for it.

'If you go I shall never see you again,' his mother wept. 'We can't let you do this, Johnnie.'

'I'll come an' see you whenever I can,' he promised. 'It could be the makin' a' me. Think a' that. Off to London. I could make my fortune there.'

But she wept and wouldn't be comforted and in the end he had to leave her red-eyed and head back to Turret House to tell Mrs Beke he would be leaving his job at first light the next morning.

The announcement caused a stir, for like him they hadn't imagined he would have to go so soon, but they wished him luck and hoped he would find a good job and Mrs Beke told him she wouldn't go into details when she told Mr Hayley in case he wanted to argue about it, 'which would make matters worse for your poor mother, would it not? You know how he goes on when he means to do good. Like a bull in a china shop. I shall tell him you've a good job

368

offered and that I've urged you to take it, so I hope you'll prove me right. You must write to us and tell us how you get on.'

Then there was nothing more to be done except tell his mother, finish his work and wrap his few belongings in a piece of sailcloth that Mr Hosier found for him. Not that there was much to wrap. Gardeners don't run to many possessions.

His mother wept all over again and said he was a dear good boy, the best a mother could wish for. While she was crying his father came home and was told the news too and he went off to his bedroom and returned with a small leather pouch.

'Oi been keepin' this for a weddin' present,' he said, 'but tha's gone by the board now Oi s'ppose.'

'That went by the board a long time since,' Johnnie admitted, surprised by how calmly he was speaking. 'We 'aven't been walkin' out for months.' And now they never would again. But he was calm about that, too.

'In that case,' his father said, 'you'd best have this now. 'Twill buy you lodgin's an' vittles an' such until you gets settled.' He put the pouch into his son's hands.

It contained two silver sixpences and a gold sovereign and the sight of them moved Johnnie so much he couldn't trust himself to speak. To have saved such a sum when he was so poorly paid was miraculous – and more generous than he deserved. 'Oh Pa!' he said.

Hiram was gruff with unshed tears too. 'Don't thank me,' he said. 'Tha's little enough in all conscience. Oi wish Oi could do more for 'ee.'

At which Johnnie threw his arms round his father's neck and wept for quite a while.

When they were both recovered, they made plans for the next morning. 'We'll walk with 'ee part way,' Hiram said. 'See you off loike.' Which they did.

It was very cold out there in the fields and very dark for the sun was only just beginning to rise and apart from a few pale green streaks in the east, the earth and the sky were black. The family trudged along in silence with Annie clinging to her son's arm and Harry rubbing the sleep from his eyes when he thought his father wasn't looking. And if Johnnie shivered from time to time, that was only to be expected on such a raw morning.

When they'd been walking for a mile or so, they reached a bend in the lane and Hiram stopped. 'This is as far as we goes,' he said to Johnnie. 'You got enough light now.' Which wasn't quite true for, although the sky was laced with spreading colour, the downs were still as black as ink and the distant spire of the cathedral was little more than a ghostly shadow. 'You'll write to us. Oi knows we can't read much but Oi daresay we shall make out, an' Mr Grinder will read what we can't manage.'

Johnnie was shivering in earnest now. He promised to write, kissed them all, over and over again, and let his mother cling about his neck for as long as she wanted, but the parting had to be made for all that. It was like being wrenched apart with hot irons and the pain of it was so acute it was an agony to walk away. He turned to wave again and again until he had rounded the bend and they were out of sight. And then he was miserably on his own in the darkness.

Hiram took Harry's hand and held it firm. 'Don't 'ee ever forget,' he said angrily, 'that this is what comes a' speaking out against a landlord. When you're a grow'd man with a wife an' family to support, you just remember it. There's onny one defence against the rich an' tha's to keep your mouth tight shut an' never say nothin' to annoy 'em. Never, ever forget.'

Harry was shivering now. 'No, Father,' he said, solemnly.

'You promise?'

'Yes, Father. I promise.'

'Well tha's all roight then,' Hiram said. 'Now we'd best be gettin' back.'

As Johnnie walked on, the sun rose slowly and the ploughed earth began to steam. The dawn chorus began, with a single blackbird piping alone and plaintive in the darkness. And gradually the countryside was unveiled and the mists rolled away and after a while he could see the huddled shapes of a flock of sheep, gathered together under the bare branches of a spreading oak tree, folded into breathing bundles and still half asleep and he watched as they knelt to stand, one after the other, and began to graze. The sky lightened with every step he took, the grass grew green, and the anguish of walking through this familiar landscape for the last time made his chest ache. This is my home, he thought. This is where I belong and where I ought to stay. But the sun was a red disc in a pale green sky and Chichester was waiting on the horizon and every step took him nearer to the new life he'd been pretending to accept and the fortune-making adventure he didn't want.

When he finally reached Lavant, he'd made such poor time that the London coach was already waiting in the courtyard and many of the passengers were on board. There were two women climbing into the coach as he approached, one very fat and the other very thin and both carrying enormous baskets covered in cloths and tied about with string; and four men settling themselves in the outside seats with a great deal of fuss and laughter and their brandy flasks at the ready;

and an old countrywoman wearing a brown blanket like a shawl over her head and shoulders and sitting very still in one corner. Poor old thing.

He climbed aloft and took the last remaining seat, which was next to the old woman, packed his bundle neatly underneath the slats and wished he'd brought a flask to sustain him on the journey. And then the chocks were being removed, the horn was sounding and they were off. And the old woman turned her head towards him and she was Betsy Haynes.

The shock of seeing her there beside him was so profound he could barely breathe. 'Betsy?' he said. 'What are you doin' here?'

She smiled at him and slipped her hand from underneath that blanket shawl so that she could hold his arm. 'You surely don't imagine I'd let 'ee go all the way to London on your own,' she said. 'What next? I'm a-comin' with 'ee.'

He was so happy he wanted to jump up and down. She was coming with him. His own dear darling Betsy was coming with him.

She gave him the benefit of her blue eyes, sitting there in that icy morning, smiling and happy. 'You'll have to marry me, though.'

'Oh yes, yes, a' course,' he said, and he bent his head to kiss her, to the delight of their fellow passengers who chirruped and whistled and asked him if that was the way he always went on and said he was a dog 'damn their eyes if he wasn't.' But he didn't care about being teased. He didn't care about anything. He could kiss her whenever he wanted to. 'Oh, my dear darling Betsy,' he said. 'I never thought to see you again an' here you are. How did you know I'd be on this coach? An' why aren't you wearin' your cardinal?'

'I sold it to buy my ticket,' she said, 'an' don't make that face. I got a good price for it, an' Ma give me this to keep me warm. I shan't feel the lack.'

She was feeling the lack already for her hand was icy cold. He took it in both his and chafed it to warm it. 'I'll buy you another one the first thing I do,' he promised.

'I brought us a pie for the journey,' she told him. 'I made it for ol' Miss Pearce but she can go without, an' serve her right, nasty spiteful ol' thing. 'Tis in the basket. An' there's a bottle a' porter an' some brandy an' water to keep us warm. We shall do very well.'

Oh, yes, Johnnie thought, as they sped along the London road. They would do very well.

Chapter Twenty

Saturday April 24th 1852

Farmer Harry Boniface was in a very good humour that Saturday morning. It was his father's ninetieth birthday and although the old man was frail and deaf and toothless the family meant to celebrate it in style. The birthday feast was prepared, the table set and now it only wanted the guests for the festivities to begin. He was just climbing into the farm cart to go and fetch them, when the potboy trotted into the yard, breathless and urgent with a message from the publican to ask if he would be so kind as to take Mr Gilchrist into Chichester with him, if it wasn't too much trouble. He agreed cheerfully. That lawyer feller had been poking around the village quite long enough. High time he was off. Although, being a practical man, he did ask what had happened to the carriage.

'The wheel come off,' the potboy explained. 'What'll take all day to fix. An' Oi reckon this ol' pony's gone lame on me. Oi been kickin' loike billy-oh an' he won't go more'n a trot.'

'Don't look lame to me,' Harry said. 'Bit disagreeable moind, but tha's hardly a surpoise if you been a-kickin' of him. Talk to him gentle an' he'll go loike the wind. Roight then, young feller-me-lad, you cut back an' tell Mr Gilchrist to be ready an' waitin' in twenty minutes an' he shall roide in with me.'

Mr Gilchrist was ready and waiting within two minutes of the potboy's return, and climbed up gratefully into the cart, with his carpetbag in one hand and a rolled umbrella in the other. 'This is very civil of you, Mr Boniface,' he said.

'We aims to please,' Harry said, amused to see how the lawyer's long hair was being blown by the wind and how pink in the face he was. For a second he felt quite sympathetic towards him. He was such a dreamy looking, moon-faced young man and couldn't have been more than twenty or so. 'You had a good day yesterday, I'm told,' he said, and clucked to his horse to walk on.

'I did indeed,' Mr Gilchrist said, as they headed off towards the church.

'And found the answers to all your questions, Oi don't doubt,' Harry said, looking at him out of the corner of his eye. Now that the young man was leaving it suddenly seemed important to find out how much he knew. If he really was a writer and meant to make his findings public there could be trouble.

Mr Gilchrist was guarded. 'To many of them, yes. The accounts of the trial were most interesting.'

'Now there's a thing,' Harry said. 'Oi never knew there was an account of it. Although Oi s'ppose, givin' thought to it, there must've been.'

'Several,' Mr Gilchrist said. 'None as full as I would have liked but sufficient to give me some sense of what happened.'

'He was found not guilty,' Harry said stoutly. 'Tha's what happened an' a good thing too, to moi way a' thinking.'

'I gather that was the opinion in the village at the time,' Mr Gilchrist said.

There was no harm in admitting it. 'Aye, so it was. He was a good man.'

'I also gather,' Mr Gilchrist went on, 'that giving evidence on his behalf was a somewhat risky thing to do, given the preponderance of tied cottages hereabouts.'

'Well as to that,' Harry said sternly, 'I couldn't say.'

'Nor will you,' Mr Gilchrist said, 'and the more honour to you.'

'You'll be glad to get back to Lunnon, Oi daresay,' Harry said.

'Indeed, yes.'

'We're in good toime for the coach.'

'I hope I'm not taking you out of your way,' Mr Gilchrist said.

'No, sir, you aren't,' Harry said happily.

'Oi got business in Lavant moiself. Oi'd ha' come in anyway.'

The coach down from London arrived with horns blaring and harness jingling ten minutes after Mr Gilchrist's coach had trundled away. It was full of people, most of them in holiday mood, and eleven of them were Bonifaces, Johnnie and Betsy and their son Frederick and his wife and their two daughters, and their pretty daughter Hannah and her husband and their three children. Johnnie was the first to jump down, looking very smart and prosperous in a new green jacket and twill trousers and a fine pair of leather boots, his grey hair bushy under the broad brim of his green top hat. He waved at Harry but then busied himself helping Frederick's wife and her two little girls to climb down. And there was Betsy climbing down after them her wide skirts swinging like a bell, wearing a little blue jacket the colour of her eyes and the prettiest poke bonnet framing her grey hair and her plump face, rosy and smiling and calling out to him. It was a homecoming, as it always was when they came a-visiting.

'Your Billy's grow'd so's Oi wouldn't ha' know'd him,' Harry said as he handed Betsy into the cart. 'Quite the young gentleman.'

'He starts apprentice in a week or so,' she said, beaming at her grandson as he settled alongside her.

Harry was impressed to hear it. 'So soon?'

'He *is* fifteen,' his grandmother said. 'Time he learnt the trade, eh, Billy? How's Lizbeth?'

'She got a foine ol' feast ready for 'ee,' Harry told her happily. And a fine old feast it was, with the entire family gathered round his kitchen table with porter and small beer aplenty and more food than they could possibly eat. Johnnie's daughter Hannah sat between Lizbeth's two daughters, chatting nineteen to the dozen, for they were great gossips, and gentleman Billy sat beside his cousin John, who was ten years younger than he was and a very messy eater, and was told what a kind young man he was by the messy eater's mother, and didn't admit that his altruism was actually because he enjoyed being hero-worshipped, and Lizbeth and Betsy had so much news to exchange they had to be reminded to pause from their talk to eat. The brothers carved meats at the sideboard and filled plates to capacity and talked to their father who sat at the head of the table, looking stooped and very wrinkled, as well he might on his ninetieth birthday, but enjoying the occasion despite his frailty. In short it was just what a family gathering ought to be.

When the meats had been cleared to Lizbeth's satisfaction and the fruit pies had been brought to the table, the talk turned to the work they were doing. Harry told his brother what a fine herd he'd got that year, Betsy said her dame school was thriving, 'I took four new pupils this term', and Johnnie spoke at some length of the improvements he was making to his printing firm. 'There are more newspapers comin' out than ever,' he said, 'and our print works is renowned for reliability, though I says it who shouldn't.'

'Oi allus knew my boys 'ud do well,' Hiram said. 'An' if your Ma could ha' been here to see you, she'd ha' said the same.'

The brothers sent quick eye-signals to one another. The subject had to be changed and quickly or he would be in tears. It was nearly twenty years since their mother had died but he still felt it keenly.

'We've had a bit of a stir down this way recently,' Harry offered. ''Aven't we Father?'

Hiram cupped his ear with his hand. 'What? What's 'at?'

'A stir, Pa,' Harry shouted. 'Oi was tellin' Johnnie we've had a bit of a stir hereabouts.'

'Not so's Oi've noticed,' Hiram said. 'What stir?'

'Some lawyer feller's been stayin' in The Fox askin' after William Blake,' Harry said, explaining to them both. 'Wanted to know about his trial seemingly. Who gave evidence an' so forth. I got the feelin' he thought there was more to it than met the eye. Things what should ha' come out an' was kept hid. What do 'ee think to that?'

'Well I never,' Betsy said, much surprised. 'Fancy that, Johnnie. After all this time. Did he find anythin' out?'

'Not from us,' Harry said happily. 'We sent him off with a flea in his ear.'

Betsy enjoyed that. 'You would.'

'Not that there's many people left for him to ask now,' Johnnie said, eating his pie. Apart from Pa here – and Will Smith, I s'ppose. Is he still around?'

'An' me, don't forget,' Harry teased. 'He come up to the farm to see me.'

'He had time to waste then,' Johnnie teased.

'Oh, Oi never told him nothin', if tha's what you means.'

Johnnie was still teasing. 'On account of you don't know nothin'.'

Harry gave his brother a wicked grin. 'Now that,' he said, enjoying his moment, 'dear brother John, is where you're wrong. If Oi'd had a moind to Oi could ha' told him a great deal. On account of Oi heard every word.'

Betsy was intrigued 'What do 'ee mean, every word? Every word a' what?'

'Every word a' what went on in the garden,' Harry said.

'You never did!'

'Oh, Oi heard roight enough. 'Twas a hot day if you remembers an' Oi'd took toime off for a breather. Father'll tell you, won't you Father. An' Oi was sitting leanin' against ol' Blake's garden wall an' Oi heard him come out into the garden. Furious he was. "Oi don't allow soldiers in moi garden," he says. "Be off out of it." An' the soldier says, "Oi'm a member a' the 1st Royal Dragoons," he says, "an' Oi can go where Oi please, so you can put that in your poipe an' smoke it."'

'Good lord,' Johnnie said, round eyed at such a revelation. 'You really did hear it. I thought you were too young to know anything about it.'

'Oi was twelve,' Harry said. 'Nearly as old as your William here. Oi knew about it roight enough.'

'So go on,' Betsy urged. 'What did he say next? I bet you don't remember *that*.'

'Ah well,' Harry said. 'Now that would be tellin'.'

The publishers hope that this book has given you enjoyable reading. Large Print Books are especially designed to be as easy to see and hold as possible. If you wish a complete list of our books please ask at your local library or write directly to:

Magna Large Print Books
Magna House, Long Preston,
Skipton, North Yorkshire.
BD23 4ND